Grady gla——————t think it's a——————to be alone u

"How long is this cozy little arrangement supposed to last?" Sabrina's assessing stare pinned him.

"Until we nail whoever is after you. Then you go back to your life, and I—"

"Take off again? Thanks for the gallant sacrifice, but no thanks."

"What the hell does that mean?"

"Clueless much, O'Rourke?" The sparks in her eyes had him backing up. "You can't keep showing up and making me crazy, then retreat. It's not like you haven't done it before."

Grady reeled under the one-two punch. She was right. He *had* run out on her.

And God help him, he'd done it *twice*.

Dear Reader,

I've come to deeply love my O'Rourkes, and writing Grady's story was bittersweet. Like you, I couldn't wait to find out what the daredevil O'Rourke brother would do next!

Grady didn't disappoint. During his journey to find himself, he learned that a life empty of family isn't a life worth living. And life can be much shorter than we realize. Whether your family is one you were born into or one you chose, take time today to say "I love you" to the people who matter most.

I shed copious tears saying goodbye to Aidan and Zoe, Con and Bailey, Liam and Kate, and Grady and Sabrina. Yet I'm looking forward to falling in love with new characters who will take me on new, exciting adventures. I hope you'll come along for the ride.

Sláinte!

Diana Duncan

LETHAL ATTRACTION

Diana Duncan

Silhouette
Romantic
SUSPENSE

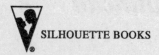

SILHOUETTE BOOKS

ISBN-13: 978-0-373-27580-9
ISBN-10:   0-373-27580-3

LETHAL ATTRACTION

Visit Silhouette Books at www.eHarlequin.com

Printed in U.S.A.

DIANA DUNCAN

Diana Duncan's fascination with books started long before she could walk, when her librarian grandma toted her to work. Diana crafted her first tale at age four, a riveting account of Perky the Kitten, printed in orange crayon. The discovery—at age fourteen—of her mom's Harlequin romance novels sparked a lifelong affection for intelligent heroines and complex heroes. She loves writing about men and women with the courage to dive into the biggest adventure of all—falling in love.

When not writing stories brimming with heart, humor and sizzling passion, Diana spends her time with her husband and children and their two cats and very spoiled puppy in their Portland, Oregon, home. Diana loves to hear from readers. She can be reached via e-mail at writedianaduncan@msn.com.

For my fabulous, talented editor, Susan Litman,
who, when presented with a wild and crazy idea for a
24 hour series said, "Go for it."

Thanks so much for your hard work, patience, wisdom,
advice, encouragement and unfailing sense of humor.
You are truly one in a million.

Prologue

Classified Covert Biological Research Laboratory
Oregon Desert
Thursday, May 22 1:00 p.m.

Viper caressed the pistol at his hip as he clocked in after lunch. He'd worked here seven long months. Today he would not be clocking out.

Neither would anyone else.

He waited until the scientists suited up before he drew the gun and attached the suppressor. The other guard dropped before he realized he'd been hit. The scientists' limited visibility made them soft targets, and one round to the head instantly neutralized Dr. Vega. Dr. Reeves and Dr. Hopkins didn't reach the intercom before he rendered them unconscious.

It wasn't their turn to die…yet.

Viper donned a biohazard suit. Releasing the lab's air locks with Dr. Vega's palm print took seconds. The retinal scan was more complicated, but the laser required an open eye…not a living one.

His hacked code accessed the vault, and he extracted two vials.

He dragged the doctors inside, peeled off their hoods, then dropped liquid onto their skin. As he resealed the vial and eased it into a padded canister, his glance flicked to his scarlet-stained glove.

An eye for an eye.

He walked out and smashed the keypad, sealing the men inside with the monster they'd created.

Justice.

He decontaminated himself and removed the suit. Isopropy alcohol dumped into a trash can with a lit match torched the file A computer disc wiped the system of everything…including h existence.

Shooting as he went, he left behind a string of blood-soake bodies, and he timed the breach alarm to sound in forty-eig hours.

When he started his SUV, Viper expected a surge of triumph But he felt nothing. Betrayal had killed his compassion. Pain ha burned away his humanity.

His glance flicked to the canister as he drove into the barre central Oregon desert. The beginning of the ultimate end. Memorial Day weekend nobody would forget.

Judgment Day.

Chapter 1

Riverside, Oregon
Saturday, May 24 11:00 a.m.

Sabrina Matthews shuddered in the warm air as an eerily intent gaze crawled up the back of her neck. *Again.*

She sent a wary glance behind her, and smiled tightly. *Twit.* Of course she was being watched. Two hundred people were assembled on the grass beside the hospital. The administrator introduced her, and applause crested. She resisted wiping damp palms on her red silk sheath. *Don't screw up.* Her stomach jittered as she walked toward the podium. *Don't barf.* She ascended the stairs. *Don't fall on your butt and give your coworkers more ammo for blonde jokes.*

Public speaking...argh. About as much fun as her annual pelvic exam.

"G-good morning." Staring at reporters, news cameras, the sea of faces, she stumbled over the greeting. Then her attention focused on her father, sitting in the front row. Sabrina locked wobbly knees. She'd macarena through the hospital naked before she'd fail in front of the iron-willed trauma surgeon. "I'm Sabrina Matthews, head child life specialist here at Mercy Hospital." She cleared her throat. "On behalf of my late grandfather, Senator William 'Filibuster Bill' Vaughn, thank you for attending the ground-breaking for our new pediatric wing." Her voice evened, and Dr. Wade Matthews nodded approval.

Sabrina's glance swept over friends, neighbors and coworkers, then lingered on the empty chair in front. The now-ragged Reserved card fluttered forlornly in the breeze.

Did you really think Grady would come?

Her heart fisted. But she'd also thought he'd be there when she'd stood shivering in the bitter March wind beside her granddad's coffin. Not her first, or even her second, mistake where he was concerned. And because the word *surrender* wasn't in her vocabulary, also not her last.

But today wasn't about what *she* wanted…at least in her private life. She was here for Granddad and needy children. She gripped the podium. "I was a very…strong-willed child." She glanced at her father, his head tipped in rueful acknowledgment. "*Nothing* frightened me. My adventures scared off four nannies and caused my share of childhood injuries. I broke my wrist when I was eight. At ten, I had to have an appendectomy. There was no time to prepare, and the fear was overwhelming. I've always wanted to work with children, but didn't want to make life-or-death decisions as a physician. And I didn't want to be an evil needle-wielding nurse." That earned hearty chuckles from her coworkers and a hard stare from her father. Yeah, as a kick-ass trauma surgeon, he considered empathy a weakness. But it was her greatest strength.

"Which is why I became a child life specialist. Many of you may wonder what a CLS does. We're certified professionals trained to ease children's anxiety during medical situations." Sabrina adjusted the microphone. "A child's illness disrupts the family structure. Our programs alleviate that stress and help everyone cope."

Warmed to her crusade, she smiled at the rapt crowd. "We're go-betweens for overwhelmed parents who don't know the right questions to ask and busy medical staff who sometimes forget to speak 'civilian.'" She arched a brow at her father, and received his stern "doctor face." He still attempted to intimidate her into obedience the way he did his staff. *As if.*

The audience chuckled again. Whew! "We also initiate therapeutic activities to help relieve a child's suffering. When the time comes for treatment or surgery we've prepared both the child and the family. Easing a child's terror makes their treatments not only more bearable but more medically effective."

Her work meant everything to her, and her department's funding depended on her pitch. "My grandfather, Senator Vaughn, devoted his life to children's causes, and his estate was bequeathed to build the new pediatric wing. I urge each of you to consider a personal donation. A pledge to Child Life Services supports children and their families during traumatic times."

Sabrina concluded with a video of her kids engaged in program activities and updates on their progress. Then she introduced families who offered heartwarming testimonies.

By the time the first symbolic shovel was thrust into the ground and cake and punch were served, she was giddy at the stream of envelopes being dropped into well-guarded strongboxes.

A wide smile—her emotional cloaking device—held steady. But she couldn't help searching for the one face she knew she wouldn't see. The bitter awareness of being utterly alone in the crowd hollowed her insides. She shook it off. *Stop being a wuss!* She'd learned long ago to bury the pain, to throw her all into her job and ignore the inner restlessness, the yearning ache.

Sabrina said her goodbyes and strode into the depths of the parking garage to fetch her silver Miata convertible. Surreptitious footsteps whispered behind her and she spun, seeing nothing but cars. "Hello? Who's there?"

Enveloped in uneasy silence, she was again assaulted by the skin-crawling sensation of being closely observed. Her stare probed dark corners as she scrambled inside the car and hit the lock. She'd experienced heebie-jeebies since her granddad had died two months ago. And recently someone had searched her apartment and office. She had no proof, other than the perception that her things weren't positioned as she'd left them. Nothing the police could investigate. Only a creepy sense of violation.

Sabrina didn't see anyone as she drove outside, but kept the convertible top up. Launching a new wing was a huge undertaking. Her father was right…her reaction had to be stress or anxiety. Maybe lingering grief. Though sorrow over losing her vibrant grandfather had dulled, perhaps his passing had magnified other emotions.

She maneuvered through traffic, brows scrunched in contemplation. The cerulean skyline in her rearview mirror would eventually be graced by a twelve-story pediatric complex. Her grand-father had left a tremendous legacy.

What was *her* legacy?

Her mischievous youth had been blamed for her father's pre-mature gray. But every challenge had molded her into the woman she'd become. She sighed. Perhaps she'd been too headstrong.

Maybe her heart was stubbornly clinging to the one man she couldn't have…and she would never be truly happy.

Memories of Grady O'Rourke haunted her, from when they were kindergarteners to their agonizing confrontation nine years ago…before he'd abruptly left for the Army.

After he'd mustered out and returned home, they'd spoken at neighborhood gatherings and run into each other via their jobs. But each meeting had been painfully casual. Don't ask, don't tell.

He'd dropped off the face of the earth seven months ago, right after the long-delayed trial of the man who'd murdered his father. Where was he? Was he all right?

Her fingers tightened on the steering wheel. Regrets? She had a cartload. She was professionally successful but lost and lonely. Like a tree trapped in shade, yearning for sunlight. No blossoms. No fruit. Never fulfilling her true purpose.

Sabrina checked her mirrors again and scowled. Had that black sedan been tailing her since the hospital? She stomped on the gas, changed lanes and swung right.

She watched all the way home. Nobody followed when she finally pulled into her apartment complex. Paranoid much?

Fatigue weighed her limbs as she unlocked the sunny sanctu-ary of her apartment. She hadn't taken a day off in…wow…several months. Sabrina dropped her purse and kicked off her heels inside the door. Past time for a mental-health day. She would bake her favorite apple crisp, brew a pot of Earl Grey and curl up with a romance novel.

She unzipped the restricting dress. Silk was a pain to iron, and she wanted to hang it up ASAP. In red satin bra and panties, she meandered through her jungle of potted plants. Cool leaves brushed her body, and she inhaled the earthy scent that carried her back to her childhood. After the nanny fiasco, Letty Jacobson, the Matthewses' neighbor who'd wrangled five kids of her own, had offered to babysit. Wild child Sabrina had found a soul mate in the feisty senior, and they'd shared wonderful times in Letty's garden.

Lost in anticipation of her stolen afternoon, Sabrina strolled into her bedroom. She froze inside the doorway, the dress dangling from numb fingers.

Two strange men stood at the end of her bed, staring at her.

With neat haircuts, tailored black suits and conservative ties, they could be any average businessmen.

Except for the guns pointed at her.

Choking fear clawed in her throat, and she gasped. The tall, sandy-haired man motioned with his gun. "Don't scream. You'll die before anyone hears."

Clutching the dress like a shield, she swallowed terror. She'd never shown fear to her enemies and now didn't seem like a good time to start. "I'm not the screaming type." She inhaled a quivering breath. "Who are you and what are you doing in my apartment?"

The stocky blond man laughed, but it wasn't reassuring. "She has nerve. She inherited more from the old soldier than those sharp brown eyes."

Sabrina started. They meant *Granddad.* She stared at the silencers attached to the pistols. Her grandfather had been in politics for three decades. She'd heard his stories. Knew the reality behind the rhetoric. Granddad was a straight shooter, but arrows in other quivers were bent. The crisp suits and sharp haircuts suddenly made sense. Who had Granddad crossed? "Are you FBI…CIA… NSA? What's going on?"

"Smart," the sandy-haired one said. The men exchanged a glance that made her stomach lurch. *Too smart.* "Cooperate, and nobody has to get hurt."

These guys weren't street criminals. Soulless eyes and steady hands with silenced guns. Professionals—who made people disappear.

Cooperation be damned—they were here to execute her.

The certainty she was about to die froze her blood. *Granddad, what did you do?*

"Give us what the old man sent you."

"Who?" she asked, stalling.

"Too late to play dumb," the blond said. "Senator Vaughn mailed you something. What was it?"

If she lied, they'd kill her. If she told the truth, they'd *still* kill her. The dress crumpled beneath her shaking fingers. They could toss her apartment and stage the murder as a burglary. Nobody would question it. "I don't know what you're talking about."

His lips thinned. "Don't play games. You won't like the way we keep score."

Breathe. "Granddad didn't send me *anything.* You can't tell me your information is a hundred percent reliable. I know better." Delaying the inevitable was her only tactic. Twenty minutes ago she'd worried about an unhappy future.

Now, she had *no* future.

The sandy-haired man pinned her with an icy stare. "If you don't have what we need, you're useless."

She bit the inside of her cheek. Tasted blood. Should she tell them she had a package in another place? If she could get outside, she could relay an SOS…or escape.

"And don't try a bait and switch. One of us will stay with you, while the other checks. If you're lying…" He sliced his finger across his throat.

Her instincts screamed *run!* Sabrina shifted, and both men tensed. Their impassive eyes narrowed, and her heartbeat pounded in her ears. She'd be dead before she turned around. "I don't know anything."

"I'm beginning to believe you. We've searched everywhere. If you had it, you'd have used it by now." The blond pointed his gun at her head. "I'm out of patience."

Sabrina stared into the black barrel. She had nowhere to run. Nothing would save her. She swallowed. If she had to die, her final defiance would be thwarting them. "I have nothing to say."

The blond smiled coldly. "Then say goodbye."

She braced herself. Who would miss her? Her mom had died when she was four. Dad was married to his work. She and Letty were close but had their own lives.

His finger tensed on the trigger, and her eyes slammed shut. Her life coalesced. A face rose in her mind.

Her last thought was for the man who'd captured her heart. The man whose rejection had *broken* her heart. Would he grieve for the girl who'd been his friend? For the woman he'd refused to know?

She'd never see him again.

She'd die, without ever knowing what might have been.

That hurt worse than anything her assailants could do.

A boom shattered the silence. Sabrina flinched as brilliant heat seared her closed lids. Then the bullet slammed into her head— and everything went black.

"Sabrina."

She surfaced to consciousness. A man was calling her name.

"Can you hear me?"

Was she hallucinating? Or dead?

"Sabrina, *wake up.*"

"Di-did…" Her mouth wouldn't work right. "Did I die?"

"No, sweetheart. You're very much alive."

She jerked. She recognized that low, husky voice. She forced heavy eyelids open, and her heart kicked. She knew those sooty-lashed mossy eyes. Knew that square jaw and stubborn chin. Knew the full, sensual curve of that gorgeous mouth.

She blinked at the hovering man in camouflage fatigues. *"Grady?"*

Grady O'Rourke's concerned gray-green gaze tangled with hers. Grim emotion flickered in those expressive eyes before he shuttered his expression. "You're gonna be fine."

"Now I *know* I'm not dead. Because you're no angel."

"Not even close." Relief warmed some of the anxiety from his handsome face. "The halo doesn't fit over the horns."

Gunpowder stung her nostrils, mixed with the metallic tang of blood. Sensation returned, flooding her with pain. Her head pounded with each heartbeat. "Ow." She frowned. His hand was applying aching pressure to her right temple. Was he shaking? Or was she? "Some suit shot me. Call 911."

"Honey, I *am* 911." The SWAT cop/paramedic smiled crookedly. "Nobody shot you. I had to take you down from behind to get you out of the line of fire. You cracked your head on the doorjamb."

Grady was here. Her coconspirator. Her confidant. Her child-hood hero. He cupped her cheek with his other hand. He *was* trembling. What was that? *Nothing* rattled her Irish daredevil. She'd never seen him fazed by anything, except… Terror hurtled back. "Two men! Guns!" She struggled to sit up.

"Stay still." His big body filled her field of vision. "The threat has been neutralized."

The former Army medevac chopper pilot's capability was no surprise. The loud boom she'd heard must have been his gunfire. "You mean dead."

His features hardened from caring friend to lethal soldier. "It was them or you. I picked you." His dual nature never failed to fascinate her. A Gemini, Grady managed to meld two disparate instincts often at war with each other—healer and warrior.

"Those men tried to murder you, Sabrina. Would have, if I hadn't arrived when I did. Too bad I wasn't able to interrogate the bastards first. I overheard the confrontation while I did recon. You have no idea what this is about?"

"Zero." Someone had sicced pros…maybe government pros…on her. They'd send more. Grady had saved her life; she had to save her strength. Not only was she down, injured and under attack, but being with him again would require shoring up all her defenses.

She needed to keep what wits she had functioning. "Did you call the station?"

"Perps aren't going anywhere. I'll call it in when I'm sure you're okay."

"I didn't hear you break into the apartment."

A dark, glossy brow arched. "You weren't supposed to."

"What if more goons show up?"

"Then I'll handle it."

Her glance drifted to the Glock holstered on his thig**h**, then back to the glittering resolve in his eyes. His expression might be hard, but his heart was not. "Thank you," she said softly.

His pale face was somber. "Just doing my job."

She frantically inventoried his muscular torso. "You weren't hit?"

"I dodge bullets for a living." His warm fingers pressed against her jugular. "You were only out a few minutes and your vitals are strong. Relax and let me fix you up."

That's what he'd done his entire life. Fixed wounded animals

nd found them new owners. Fixed broken people and sent them
ome. "Am I bleeding?"

"All head wounds bleed profusely." He gently caught her hand
nd pressed it to the cloth-covered injury. "Hold this. I'm going
o lift you."

Her fingers tangled in the fabric, and she groaned. "Please tell
me my new silk dress isn't a field dressing."

His lips twitched. "I didn't exactly have time to be choosy."

"Sorry." She groaned again. "Of course not."

He yanked the comforter from her bed. "Hey, you just got
locked. You're not thinking clearly."

She probed her injury through the silk. "*Youch.* How bad is it?"

"Stop that, and keep the pressure on." He covered her hand with
is. He wasn't shaking anymore, but was still far too intense. What
vas wrong with him? "It's not critical. How do you feel?"

"Like I was trampled by a 190-pound SWAT cop."

"*There's* my girl." His smile warmed into a grin.

And *there* was the Irish daredevil she knew and loved. Those
iller twin dimples *so* did it for her. And she *so* didn't want them
o. "Did you at least call an ambulance?"

"No need." He wrapped her in the comforter and scooped her
p. "Average ambulance ETA to this neighborhood is eighteen
ninutes. I'll have you patched and into Mercy before they can even
rocess the request."

"No doubt." He was the best—at everything. With one infuri-
ting exception. Cooking a microwave dinner took longer than
vhat passed for Officer I-Live-for-Excitement's "relationships."

He carried her out the bedroom door. When she tried to look
ack, he blocked the view. "Don't, Sabrina."

She pressed her cheek to his broad chest and inhaled his
amiliar essence of fresh citrus and warm man. The reassuring thud
f his heartbeat was rapid. He probably had a major adrenaline
ush going, which would account for his earlier shakiness.

His stride was easy, as if she weighed nothing. "I left my
nedical bag in the Jeep. Do you have a first-aid kit?"

"Bathroom cabinet."

He laid her on the sofa. "Be right back." He returned within
econds and sat beside her. He found gauze, and then tugged a

Swiss Army knife from his cammo pants pocket to slice tape. She still remembered his proud grin when his dad had bestowed the traditional O'Rourke thirteenth-birthday gift.

"Grady?" Reality clouds rolled in, and the initial luster of seeing him again dimmed. "Nobody has heard from you for seven months." Two weeks after he'd gone missing, Sabrina had learned from his sister-in-law Zoe that he'd taken a leave of absence from his Riverside SWAT paramedic job. But nothing more. His disappearance shouldn't have shocked her. When the climate turned stormy, Grady was a pro at fast takeoffs.

"I've been…busy." His enigmatic gaze flickered. Busy with another woman? She had no ties to him. No right to ask. He'd just evade questions.

But the flash of a bullet fired at her head had illuminated her perspective. Nearly dying had snapped her priorities into clear focus. She *would* settle things with Grady O'Rourke, once and for all.

Even if neither of them liked the answers.

She touched his hand, now strong and steady at her temple, and taut awareness hummed between them. "Where have you been? And how did you get here just in time to save me?"

Chapter 2

Grady had known the ground-breaking ceremony was today. He might have been out of touch, but Sabrina was never far from his thoughts.

He stared into her smoky amber eyes. Her confusion had dissipated, and she was asking lucid questions. Tough questions. "I've been working for an independent covert high-risk extraction squad."

"You're a *mercenary* now?" She studied his camouflage gear and frowned. "Interesting development."

So, she'd caught the lack of insignia on his fatigues. "Something like that." He had to give her props. In spite of being terrorized and injured, her bravado was firmly intact. She was maintaining almost *too* well. Usually, victims fell apart when they were rescued.

This time, *he'd* freaked.

He'd picked up his new assignment hyped by the chance to save another civilian from execution in a third-world hellhole. Until he'd read Sabrina's name on the dossier. A greasy ball of fear had churned in his gut as he'd pushed his chopper through the endless night.

"Care to explain, Dimples?"

"Not really." Grady smoothed back her silky blond hair and

applied a gauze pad. He'd trained hard not to let emotion dictat
his actions. It had paid off when he'd done recon on her apartmer
and seen her facing down two armed men. He'd been forced t
form and execute an instant tactical plan. Before they could exe
cute *her.*

Then he'd spun around after the firefight and found he
crumpled on the floor, pale and bloody. He thought he'd been to
late. Thought she'd been shot. The impact had rendered him daze
and shaky and sick to his stomach. And too damned slow.

Corporal Cool had lost his friggin' mojo in the middle of a missio

He swore under his breath. That's why he didn't let himself ge
attached. When feelings cluttered his radar, he couldn't hel
anyone. Couldn't save anyone. A gut-wrenching lesson learne
when he was seventeen.

"No discussion. Gee, what a surprise." Her full pink lips pursec
making his body tighten. "How did you know I needed help? Ho
did you get here just in time?"

"Twelve hours ago, I received orders, intel and payment lik
always, in a secure satellite transmission. Someone shocked th
hell out of me by claiming you might be in danger and paying m
to guard you. As for my arrival on the razor's edge—"

He almost hadn't.

His helicopter's radio and half the electronics had blippe
offline during a mission, and he had returned to HQ early. He'd see
the new orders bearing Sabrina's name and immediately grabbe
another bird. It was luck. Chance. If his chopper systems hadn
failed, the assignment would have sat until morning. Sabrina wou
have died.

Taking his heart with her to the grave.

Grady clenched his jaw. His prized detachment had been blow
to hell. "Your guardian angel must be working overtime."

"*Who* hired you?"

"No idea." But he would damn well find out.

"You flew off without knowing who hired you or why?"

"That's how the company operates. Our clients prefer anc
nymity." But this time, whoever had hired him was aware c
the plan to kill Sabrina. And Grady had a few questions for th
bastards.

"Okay…" Her eyes sparked, and he steeled himself. *Incom-g.* "The reason you came is because someone *paid* you?"

Ouch. The hero-worship phase of the rescue was obviously over. don't give a flying Finnegan about money, and you know it."

"What *do* you care about?"

You. More than I want to. More than is safe for either of us. This isn't the time, Sabrina."

She scowled. "It's never the time."

Dammit. Neither the Army nor the police academy had trained m for heart-to-heart combat. He stood to pick her up. "Time to to the hospital."

"Wait! I am *not* going to work in my underwear."

"You're not going there to work. You're a *patient*." He gestured. You have a blanket."

"Not good enough."

"It's a hospital, not a burger joint, sweetheart. You don't get to ve it your way. They'll just take them off." He frowned. "CSI goes llistic when the first responders muck up the scene. One stray hair n affect a case, and I've already compromised by covering you ith the blanket. Do you have clothes anywhere else?"

"No. What will I wear home?"

He scrubbed a hand over his stubbled chin. Damned stubborn oman. "I've extracted special-ops units from a firefight and taken ss flak," he muttered. "Too bad I left the tranquilizers in the Jeep." e yanked his fatigue shirt from his waistband and unbuttoned it, vealing the black T-shirt beneath.

Eyes wide, Sabrina sat up. "Ow!" She winced. "What are you ing?"

Literally giving her the shirt off his back. "You wanted clothes." quelching his own desires where she was concerned was tough ough. He'd always found it nearly impossible to deny *her* ything—may God have mercy on his soul. His only option was force himself to stay away from her. The attraction that sizzled tween them was deadlier than bullets.

A muscle ticced in his jaw as he draped the garment around her. t'll cover you. Take it or leave it."

"Thank you again. This time for saving my pride." She rested r hand on his chest, and his heart leaped. "As a blond woman

and the head trauma surgeon's daughter, I have to fight for cre
ibility. You know the razzing I'd take if my coworkers saw me i
nothing but scraps of scarlet satin."

Yeah, he knew. And Sabrina strove not to show vulnerabili
to anyone…except him. "Which is the only reason I didn't sho
you up with happy juice and pack you outta here…sexy red undie
be damned." The red lingerie *did* leave an enticing expanse
creamy skin exposed.

She's simply another patient.

Yeah. And he was the Dalai Lama.

He guided Sabrina's arms through the sleeves and rolled th
cuffs. As he rebuttoned the placket, his knuckles brushed the warn
soft swell of her breast. She inhaled, and heat blasted through hir
Chill out, boyo. That's all he needed to make this cluster bon
complete. Total loss of objectivity.

He drew his Glock, and she raised her hands in mock su
render. "Stand down, Officer O'Rourke. I wasn't going to tal
your pants."

His lips twitched into a grin. Most of the time he wanted
toss her down and make love to her until she lost the power
speech. The rest of the time she tempted him to throttle he
He'd die before doing either. "I'm gonna sweep our escaj
route. Do *not* move."

The outside was clear, and he holstered his weapon and returne
to Sabrina's apartment. The stench of gunpowder and death hur
in the air. Yeah, the unavoidable killing bugged him. The day l
didn't feel a twisting ache in his chest when he shot someone w
the day he'd surrender his shield.

But the scumbags weren't the *real* opponents. Death was h
personal enemy. An evil fought on two fronts, as a cop and as
medic. Didn't matter if the Grim Reaper rode in on a bullet
drunk behind the wheel of a speeding car…dead was dead.

His mission to save lives didn't leave much personal time.

"All clear. Let's blow this pop stand." He gathered Sabrina u
Gun hand at the ready, he strode across the living room.

"I'm perfectly capable of walking."

"Don't bother. Not going to happen."

She frowned. "At least grab my shoes and purse from besi

e door." He scooped up the items, and she clutched them to her
est. "Aren't you going to call the police?"

"Yeah, on the way to the hospital."

"You're going to earn a reprimand for not following procedure."

Rules were a safe place to hide when you didn't have imagina-
on, and the stones to see it through. "If I call from here, dispatch
ill order me to put you in an ambulance and stay at the crime
ene. I'd be snarled in red tape for hours." He scanned the perime-
r before stepping away from the building. "I'm on leave from the
iverside PD. I still have my badge, but don't officially have to
iswer to anyone at the moment."

"Convenient. Just the way you like it."

"The PD doesn't have a spare officer to ride shotgun, and I'm
ot about to let whoever ordered the hit take another whack at you.
crew that."

"You never were good at coloring inside the lines, O'Rourke."

He snorted. "If the good die young, then why be good?"

Grady carried her to his Jeep and settled her into the passenger
at. "Keep a low profile until I get the top up." He adjusted the
at to a reclining position. "On second thought, just stay down."

She touched his arm as he buckled her seat belt. "Why didn't
u call one of your brothers to check on me? Or another officer?"

"I tried. At the time I had no idea the scenario was critical.
ut Riverside PD is short-handed because something big is
ing down in Eastern Oregon, and central has loaned out most
our officers." He went cold again thinking about how close
e'd been to death. He cupped her cheek. "I won't let anyone
irt you, Sabrina."

Her smile was wobbly. "I trust you to keep me safe," she whis-
red.

"You couldn't be in better hands in combat." As he sprinted
ound the front of the vehicle and jumped into the driver's seat,
s heart stumbled painfully in his chest.

If only he deserved her trust everywhere else.

Grady started the engine and raised and locked the ragtop. He'd
istomized the top himself. It worked like a convertible, except
e locks and lift activated from inside the car. That way, he never
d to screw around when the sky was pouring buckets or he was

in a rush to load bulky sporting equipment. A canvas roof would
thwart a bullet, but it was hard to hit what they couldn't see. H
wheeled into traffic and sped down the street.

After the third signal light abruptly went green at their approac
she turned a puzzled face toward him. "What are you doing?"

He tossed her an innocent look. "Driving to the hospital."

Her brows scrunched. "That hydraulic top lift isn't the only gadg
you rigged in this Jeep. You're changing the traffic lights somehow

"I'm blowing on them." He pursed his lips, another light flash
from red to green and they sailed through the intersection.

"Give it up, Dimples. I haven't believed that trick except for
few gullible weeks when we were in first grade."

He grinned. He'd never been able to snow her for long. "It's
MIRT…a mobile infrared transmitter hidden in the grill. A lot
emergency vehicles have them. It's faster."

"And you're all about fast." Her frown deepened. "This isn't
emergency vehicle."

"It is on occasion. Relax, sweetheart." He switched on his iP
and handed it to her. He didn't own any tunes that came close
being soothing. Next best option was her favorite when they we
teenagers, Guns N' Roses. Her peaked face warmed at the famili
strains of "Sweet Child O' Mine."

While she listened to music, he used his secured handheld u
to phone Riverside PD, then Mercy Hospital. He also track
down his brother Liam's friend at the FBI. He wanted a gover
ment agent he trusted on the case.

He finished his calls and tapped her on the shoulder. Sabri
tugged off the earphones, and he visually examined her bandag
No signs of bleed-through. "Why do the bad guys think yo
grandfather sent you something?"

"Because he did. But if I'd given it to them, they would ha
killed me anyway."

"I know." He had a big hairy, bone to pick with whoever w
in charge of that effort. "What did Bill send?"

"I wasn't home when it arrived. After Granddad died, I w
busy with funeral arrangements, upset and distracted. I forg
Dalton put it in his storage compartment."

"Dalton?"

"My neighbor. He's a fireman—a total sweetheart. Always glad to lend a helping hand."

I'll bet. He shot a death glare at the speedometer. He was pushing fifty in a thirty-five.

Sabrina giggled. "Don't spontaneously combust. The only fire he doused was on my kitchen stove."

Apparently, his poker face had been flushed down the crapper with his detachment. He shook his head to clear the enraged buzz. He'd relinquished all rights and any say. So why did the idea of another man's hands on her send him into a tailspin? *Pull out of it, fly boy.* "So, you have no idea what the package contains?"

"No. But a few days ago I got an anonymous phone call from a woman, reminding me about it. The visit from the goon squad afterward is hardly a coincidence."

He scowled. "Your phone must be tapped."

"There's more weirdness." She hesitated. "Ever since Granddad died, I've had the feeling someone is watching me. I've seen strange cars parked outside my apartment and office at odd hours. They never stay long, and they're different vehicles, but it feels *wrong.* And I'm positive my apartment and office were searched."

His fingers strangled the gear shift. While he'd wheeled around the globe rescuing strangers, Sabrina's life had been at risk. "Why didn't you call Aidan, Con or Liam? My brothers would have helped you in a nanosecond."

"I told my father everything. But I had nothing tangible. He thought it was stress. Or grief."

"Damn it, Sabrina. We've known each other since we were five years old…we're practically family. My brothers would have believed you." Guilt swamped him. *He* should have been there to help her.

"What could they have done? Anyway, we're not five anymore." Her voice went soft. "And we're *not* family."

No, they weren't. He had no hold on her. "My mom loves you like her own, and my brothers consider you their little sister."

"And what about you?"

He hesitated. "I…I've never thought of you as a sister."

Her somber glance snared his. "How *do* you think of me?"

"You've always been my friend." Before and after it got complicated. He steered the discussion out of hazardous territory. "For now, I don't think you should mention Bill's package to anyone. Not even the investigators."

Her jaw dropped. "Grady Stephen O'Rourke, did you just tell me to lie to the cops?"

"I advised you to censor sensitive intel." She shot him a wry look and he rolled his eyes. "Okay…lie through your teeth if necessary." He held up a hand. "If the men who ambushed you *were* government spooks, we don't know who else is involved. Until we know who they worked for and what's in the package, trusting the wrong person could get us killed."

"All right, it stays between us. For now."

During the short remainder of the drive, he grilled her about the past few months' events.

Grady slid into the ER's only open parking slot—for physicians only. Ignoring Sabrina's objections, he carried her to the entrance, where he commandeered a wheelchair. He bypassed admitting and the resulting paperwork and pushed Sabrina's chair into a cubicle. Brenda, the dark-haired head trauma nurse, skewered him with her gaze. "Winging in patients on your off time now, cowboy? I don't suppose you have vital signs."

"Sure I do. Otherwise, I'd be dead." Sabrina snickered and Brenda glowered at him. If the woman had ever possessed a sense of humor, she'd had it surgically removed in nursing school. At least he'd coaxed a chuckle from Sabrina. "Twenty-eight-year-old female, pulse 120, pupils normal and reactive. Laceration and hematoma from a blow to the right front skull quadrant at approximately thirteen hundred hours."

They coaxed Sabrina onto the bed and covered her with blankets. Two more nurses entered, and Grady turned to walk to the foot of the bed.

Sabrina grabbed his arm. "Don't leave me."

His independent girl's uncharacteristic plea wrenched his heart. She wasn't as steady as she claimed, physically or mentally. "I'm not going anywhere for a while."

Dr. Wade Matthews strode inside. "Sabrina! Are you all right?" He didn't wait for her answer. "I want current vitals," he barked at the nurses. "Order a blood panel, neurological work-up and CAT scan."

"Dad, I'm okay."

"Get Michaels in here from plastics to examine her scalp laceration, and Franklin from neurology to read the films."

"Dad!" Sabrina sat up. "Call off the trauma team. I *bumped my head.*"

Wade's brows slammed together. "I was told gunshots were fired."

Grady lowered Sabrina back to the bed. "Yeah, but most of them were mine and they hit the bad guys." Normally, Sabrina went toe-to-toe with her dad, but damned if she'd have to while he was around. "Everybody take a breath and gear down. Sabrina's injury isn't serious."

"I'll ascertain what's serious." Wade slapped Sabrina's chart on the countertop. "You fly back into town for—what—an hour? And already she's been injured in a gun battle."

Grady gripped the bed's metal railing. He'd held the top slot on Dr. Matthews's hit list from day one. He *had* teased Sabrina into a few scrapes over the years. Not that it required much enticement, since Ms. Competitive had always been game. "If you'd taken her concerns about being followed *seriously* instead of blowing them off as stress, she might not have been shot at today."

"So instead, you would have cooked up one of your schemes… and she'd be in the morgue."

"Hello!" Sabrina sat up again. "I'm right here, faculties intact." She pointed at her father. "What happened today had nothing to do with Grady. As for *you,*" she turned an accusing stare on Grady. "I'm responsible for myself." Her glare fried them both. "I don't appreciate being snarled over like Dobermans with their favorite chew toy. Chill out."

"Hell." Wade ran an unsteady hand through his salt-and-pepper mane. He awkwardly patted Sabrina's shoulder. "When the call came in, I thought you were—" His mouth trembled, and he turned aside.

Grady braked his temper. He'd been sucker punched when he'd seen Sabrina unconscious on the floor in a pool of blood. How much more traumatic would it be for her father to hear she'd been shot at and fear the worst?

"Sabrina hit her head on the doorjamb." He attempted to penetrate the father's terror and reach the medical professional. "She was out less than five minutes. She's lucid and her vitals are stable. Her only injury is a minor laceration on her right temple."

Wade fired a steely look at Grady. "I'll take care of her. Then I want a word with you, outside."

"*There's* a news flash." He and Matthews continually butted heads over procedure. Though Grady was an advanced paramedic, regulations still required him to get a doctor's permission to administer anything but emergency care. However, a savvy physician wasn't always available. Or the medical protocol sucked. Grady wasn't above improvisation to save lives. Dr. I-Invented-the-Rules Matthews had sent more than one resident fleeing the OR in tears. And not only women. Rumor was he'd actually made a first-year intern piss himself. "I'll be in the hall."

Sabrina scowled. "You can talk right here."

Ironically, Matthews's tactics had never worked on his own daughter. Grady glanced at Sabrina's set mouth. The last thing she needed was additional conflict. "It's better for you if I go."

Hurt flashed in her eyes, then was quickly extinguished. "So you always claim."

Grady slipped into a corridor to avoid the packed waiting room. He leaned against the wall and shut his eyes against the fluorescent glare. But he should have known better. When he stopped moving and started thinking, his demons came out to taunt him.

The day's events ambushed him and delayed reaction pounded his control, threatened to overwhelm him.

Sabrina's bright light had come within moments of being snuffed out forever.

He went rigid. Men didn't surrender to pain. They didn't fall apart. He would *not* lose it. *Never again.* He forced himself to take slow breaths, and focused on Sabrina. Now there was some serious moxie. He snorted. And Gran used to call *him* trouble on legs.

They'd both been five years old when Sabrina had moved in next door. His first impression had been a tangle of sun-gilded curls, a generous mouth with a stubborn bent and golden-brown eyes glowing with a mixture of sweetness and fierce mischief.

The following day he'd rescued a stray puppy being tormented by a gang of older boys at the end of the block. They'd retaliated by beating the crap out of him. Sabrina had roller-skated past the melee. Next thing he knew, she'd fearlessly charged into the fray, swinging her skates by the laces. She'd smacked down two bullies before they'd realized what hit them. She and Grady had fought back-to-back and sent the rest into sniveling retreat.

She'd helped him carry the puppy home, and insisted on pasting an entire box of Band-Aids on Grady's boo-boos. He'd nursed the tiny bulldog to health and then found him a new mom—their neighbor, Letty. Sabrina had told her father that her black eye was the result of a fall from skating over a rock. Like a lame-assed fib would fool the sharp trauma surgeon.

Grady smiled. So began a combat-bonded alliance that had spanned their entire lives.

He heard footsteps and opened his eyes to see Sabrina's father. Caught unawares and awash in tender memories, Grady snapped upright.

As their neighbor, Wade had seen worse behavior from him. *Way* worse. He'd seen him on his knees, broken and sobbing. He'd witnessed the most horrible moment of Grady's life. Stinging shame crawled up his throat, and he swallowed. "How's Sabrina?"

"She's on her way back from radiology. She told me what happened. She nearly died today." Matthews dismissed him with a wave. "You can leave. I'll hire professional bodyguards."

"You know someone more qualified than a SWAT cop? More equipped to handle a medical emergency than a paramedic?" Matthews didn't believe him worthy of his daughter's affections, but Grady *could* protect her. He crossed his arms. "Someone better trained for battle than a soldier?"

"Sabrina said you're renting yourself out as a mercenary." Wade's steely blue eyes were as penetrating as an X-ray diode. "What's your going rate?"

"Dammit, I didn't ask for *payment!*" He'd earned a bundle the past seven months. He'd sent some to his mom, created college funds for future nieces and nephews and anonymously donated to the new pediatric project. He didn't need material anchors weighing him down. "I don't shake down my friends. Or profit from others' pain."

"Your typical course of action *is* to make an end run around the rules."

"Don't crawl up my butt about my 'wild-card methods.' My patients have the highest survival rate of any paramedic in the tristate area." His jaw felt almost too tight to speak. "Because I didn't follow the rules, I was here to put myself between Sabrina and a bullet."

"Pure chance." Wade frowned. "Where my daughter is concerned, I don't take chances."

Grady wrestled his temper for the second time in an hour. An outburst would reinforce Wade's doubts. "Fate brought me here at the right moment. *Skill* got the job done. Whoever is after her doesn't follow the rules, either, which makes me the best man for the job. Only a wild card can beat another."

Wade's frown morphed into a scowl. "This isn't a game, O'Rourke."

"I was the one eating gunfire, remember?" His hands fisted. "I care about her, too. Enough to bet my life. Besides you and me, how many men are willing to die for her?"

"You'd die for her. But you don't have to watch her cry for weeks every time—" Wade swore softly.

Grady took the verbal punch without flinching. "We both know why I can't stick around permanently."

"I would never operate on a member of my own family. As a surgeon, I have to maintain a certain coldness, a distance from my patients in order to perform a life-or-death job." His measuring stare bored into Grady. "Soldiers need to do the same. You're too close to the situation."

Simply another variation of the "touch-my-daughter-and-die" warning Wade had spouted since Grady hit puberty. Matthews didn't want him around Sabrina. Never had, never would. Grady got that. Past history accounted for Wade's lack of faith in him. He got that, too. In spades. "I learn from my mistakes. I don't repeat them."

Dr. Matthews studied him the way he might examine a sutured incision. Would he hold under duress? Or rupture and bleed out?

Grady's gaze didn't waver. He knew what he had to do. He had to kill his emotions in order to keep Sabrina alive.

The nurse stuck her head into the hallway. "Dr. Matthews, Sabrina's films are ready."

Wade gave her a curt nod. "Thirty seconds." Wade stabbed a

finger at Grady. "You're my only viable option at the moment. Until we sew this up, do not let Sabrina out of your sight."

"I'm your man." Grady couldn't suppress a smirk. "No charge."

"You'd better be as good as you think you are, kid. If anything happens to my daughter, I'll have your ass in a sling. And you'd damn well better protect her heart." Matthews turned and slammed back into the ER.

Grady's knees went weak and he leaned against the wall. Lord, what had he done? Sabrina Matthews was the one woman in the world who could get under his skin. The only woman who threatened his hard-won control.

No enemy conjured up by heaven *or* hell scared him more than the prospect of enforced confinement with her.

Spinning in the backwash, he swallowed bile. How could he avoid a crash and burn if he was shoved into nonstop togetherness with her?

But he couldn't abandon her. He would not let her pay for his sins, even if *he* paid the ultimate sacrifice.

Even if it cost him his soul.

He was jammed between the proverbial rock and one helluva scary hard place.

Grady gritted his teeth. *So what?* If you were meant to auger in, nothing could save you. This time, he might not walk away intact.

So be it.

If he was destined to auger down in flames, he might as well make it a spectacular crash.

Chapter 3

4:00 p.m.

"Grady?" a deep male voice inquired.

He whirled and found FBI Special Agent Alejandro Cortez standing behind him. The tall, long-haired man in the immaculate suit and tie frowned. "Are you all right?"

"Never better." *Dammit.* Ambushed twice in less than twenty minutes with his emotional pants down. If Alex had been one of the bad guys, Grady would be dead. So would Sabrina. "I don't know if the Bureau can get involved, but you're the only Fed I trust right now. Thanks for coming quickly."

"Your family has always been kind to me. There's nothing I wouldn't do...officially or otherwise."

"I appreciate it." Grady set his jaw and steadied his emotions. He could handle this assignment for the short term. Protect Sabrina and help her regain her balance—from a safe distance. He would not get involved. Wouldn't let it turn personal.

God willing, they'd both live to fight another battle...another day.

He briefed Alex without mentioning Senator Vaughn's mystery package. He could disclose that later, or not. Depending on who the guys he had shot were, he might need an FBI agent on his team.

If you looked up integrity, Alejandro Cortez's picture popped up, but leaks happened. And the Feds were hamstrung by pesky regulations. Grady was taking zero chances with Sabrina's life.

As Grady led Alex into the cubicle, Wade moved to the head of Sabrina's bed. She sat on the gurney dressed in blue scrub pants and his cammo shirt, having her blood pressure taken by a nurse. Her face had regained color and was shielded in tough-girl attitude. Her expression and tone were a shade too jaunty. "I see you're still around."

Okay, maybe he actively avoided the commitment trap, but that didn't make him a total bastard. "I don't go back on my word."

Her bare feet swung nonchalantly, but she hugged his shirt tightly around her. "In Dimples Standard Time, 'I'll stay awhile' can mean an hour."

Her false bravado reminded him so much of her little-girl you-can't-break-me bluster, it brought a lump to his throat. He battled the desire to hold her. "How are you doing? What did the tests show?"

"I'm fine. No concussion, no internal bleeding, no stitches." She gave him a strained smile. "And they have photographic evidence I actually possess a brain."

"Good to know." He returned her smile. *Hang in there, honey.* He'd bet she had a hell of a headache, and her body language was scared and vulnerable. But she was playing it cool for her father and coworkers. Tactics he recognized, having often employed them himself. Her strong, stubborn spirit manifested in more than competitiveness. Maybe because her mom had died when Sabrina was so young, or because her dad had mile-high expectations, Never-Surrender-Sabrina gritted it out to the max. She had always refused to cry in front of anyone, although she had let go with him a few times. And she resolutely kept her pain to herself. Another thing they had in common.

Her wary glance flicked to Alex. "Hello. And you would be?"

Grady inclined his head. "Remember Alex Cortez? He used to hang with Liam in high school. He's FBI now."

"Alex?" She blinked. "I didn't recognize you."

Alex smiled. "Yes, skinny, geeky Alejandro Cortez finally grew up."

"I always thought you were cute. And sweet."

"Like you noticed me. You only had eyes for—" He cleared his throat. "Maybe a bit of the geek is still in evidence, eh?"

"Pretty wild coincidence, you showing up here."

"Not at all. Gr—"

Grady's violent coughing spell interrupted Alex. Sabrina didn't need to know he'd called in a favor on her behalf. Much safer to keep a buffer between them. He didn't want her jumping to the wrong conclusions about his involvement in her life. It wouldn't be the first time—and the fallout wasn't pretty.

Sabrina slanted a sideways glance at Grady. "Somebody get that boy a ventilator."

"Water would be fine." He eyed Alex.

Alex took the hint and pulled up a chair, then withdrew a notebook from his jacket. "Sabrina, tell me everything that's happened."

Grady stalked the perimeter of the small room and gulped water from a plastic cup as Sabrina spoke. When she reached the part about knowing she would die and hearing the gunfire, her voice caught and her words stumbled.

Grady crushed the empty cup, his feelings rioting between the need to comfort her and the urge to slam his fist through the wall. Just give him five minutes alone with the bastard who'd put that tremble in her lip.

Alex finally rose, ending the torture. "I have all I need for now. I'll be in touch."

Wade's stern face creased in a smile at his daughter. "I'll get your pain medication and discharge papers." He strode out, leaving Grady and Sabrina alone.

Grady glanced around. "Where are your shoes? You can't navigate the dock to my houseboat in bare feet."

"Under the bed— Your *houseboat?*" Sabrina's brows scrunched. "As in, you and me…together?"

He bent and scooped up a paper bag containing her purse and shoes. "Your father agrees that I should—" *Watch over you* would instantly have her claws out. She was slightly sensitive on the topic of babysitters. "We don't think it's a good idea for you to be alone until this is settled."

"You and Dad agreed that *you* should protect me?" She rubbed her arms. "I think hell just froze over." Her assessing stare pinned him. "How long is this cozy little arrangement supposed to last?"

"Until we nail whoever is after you. Then you go back to your life, and I—"

"Take off again?" She hopped down from the bed, and he shot out a hand to steady her. She shoved him away. "Thanks for the gallant sacrifice but no thanks."

"What the hell does that mean?"

"Clueless much, O'Rourke?" The sparks in her eyes had him backing up. And moving the equipment tray out of her reach.

Why was she suddenly upset with *him?* He set her shoes beside her. "I won't get in your way. I'll leave as soon as—"

She planted her fists on her hips and glared up at him. "And they claim women send mixed messages."

He flung his hands in the air. "I need a navigational chart to follow your train of thought."

"One minute you're all smiles and dimples and 'I'm here to save you,' and the next you can't bear to be in the same hemisphere. We did this same dance seven months ago."

Yeah, and he'd wounded her by furiously declining her offer of pity sex. He did *not* want to tango that number again. "Let's get you home, fed and rested. Then we'll hash out details."

She shook her head. "You can't keep showing up when I've managed to find an even rhythm and make me crazy, then retreat. One time too many, because I—" She inhaled shakily and turned her back to him. "Just go."

"What was I supposed to do? Not come? Be cold and impersonal…after what you'd been through? I treated you the same as any other trauma victim." *Sort of.*

"Why, because I'm just another *job?*"

The Army should use women's logic to transmit encrypted data. No man alive could decipher it. "Wait a damned minute—"

"And when the babysitting gets boring, you'll tear outta here at Mach 5 with your hair on fire."

That got his Irish up. "Now that's insulting."

"It's not like you haven't done it before." Her lips wobbled, then her mouth firmed. "I'll save you the trouble of sneaking away."

Grady reeled under the one-two punch of guilt and grief. *He'd* put that tremble in her lip. She was right—he was a clueless moron. She had reason to doubt his dependability. Though he'd acted in her best interests, from her perspective he *had* run out on her.

Twice.

Dammit, he knew how agonizing it was to be left behind. "Sabrina...I never meant to hurt you."

Her mouth trembled again. "Leave now, while I can watch you go."

"I've spent my entire life trying *not* to hurt you. Apparently, I've managed to do the exact opposite. I'm sorry." Grady wanted to kick his own ass. He scrubbed an unsteady hand over his face. "Don't let me make you cry. I'm not worth your tears, sweetheart."

"*Oh, Grady,*" she whispered. Then she squared her shoulders. "I am *not* crying. You are who you are. I need to get smart and stop—" She pressed her fingertips to her temples and closed her eyes. "Thank you for saving my life. Now say goodbye, okay?"

"Not okay." She resisted as he tugged her into his embrace. He rubbed her rigid back muscles. "I'm sticking around. This time, I'm here for you."

"Fool me once, shame on you. Fool me twice, shame on me. Three times makes me a complete imbecile, Dimples."

Gut check time. He stepped back and inhaled air that stung his lungs like diesel fuel. Sweat pooled in the small of his back. This was more terrifying than his first chopper landing during combat. But it was the least he could do for her. He'd screwed up...he'd fix it. "I swear on Pop's grave. I..." Grady swallowed with a throat gone bone-dry. "I'll stay."

"For a week? Two weeks?"

He forced the promise out. "Until you tell me to go. And mean it."

She gasped. "What did my father say to you?"

"Forget him. This is about you and me."

"Look at how fan-freaking-tastic that always turns out."

Yeah. A smoking hole in scorched earth. Love...his kryptonite. His saving grace was that he *knew* it. As long as you were aware landmines existed, you could avoid them, right? *Good luck dodging the shrapnel this time, O'Rourke.*

"There's no reason for you to stay. I'll hire a bodyguard."

"I've had this discussion with your father."

She shook her head. "No matter what 'Daddy' says, I don't need another sitter. I don't need *you*."

He recognized her defensive tactics. He'd once shouted those words to his father...and lived to regret them forever.

I don't need you.

Hindsight whammied him. Like two planets that orbited the same solar system for years but were set on a collision course, his and Sabrina's impact had been preordained since the moment they'd met. He'd outmaneuvered the crash for two decades, but Destiny was a persistent bitch.

He refused to be Sabrina's big regret. He'd rather earn her rage.

"Too bad, because you've got me." He narrowed his eyes. "You coming, or do I have to sling you over my shoulder and pack you outta here?"

"You can try."

His fierce laugh held no humor. "You know better than anybody those are fighting words, sweetheart." Her eyes fired a warning, and he shook his head. "Don't test me."

She snatched up her shoes and jammed her feet into them. "I'll go with you, because, *drat,* it *is* sensible. My physical safety is in your hands. But I'm done letting you make my emotional decisions." She stabbed her finger into his sternum. *"I'll* choose how I feel, not *you.* Then *I'll* live with the repercussions. Got it?"

He rubbed his chest. The curvy blonde in front of him vibrating with fury, her cheeks flushed, her eyes smoldering. She'd *always* made her own choices. But a smart man knew when to keep his mouth shut.

He extended a peace offering from her favorite movie. "As you wish." Stomach jittering, he followed her into the hallway.

Wade handed Sabrina a prescription bottle. "Check in with me tomorrow for a follow-up exam." He kissed her cheek, then watched her stomp down the corridor. Matthews turned to Grady. "Don't disappoint me, O'Rourke." Wade inclined his head at Sabrina, tapping her foot in front of the elevator. "Most important, don't disappoint my daughter."

Perhaps disappointing Sabrina was his destiny. But he'd give his life in order not to *fail* her. Bitter experience had taught him the price of failure. "I won't."

Alex waited for them downstairs. "I received a disturbing message. The police found nothing amiss at Sabrina's residence."

Sabrina started. *"What?"*

The FBI agent glanced at them. "No bodies, no blood, no bullet casings."

Grady swore. Who the hell had hired him, and what mess had he and Sabrina been shoved into? "I want to see for myself. And Sabrina needs her stuff."

Alex followed them to Sabrina's apartment. The polished oak floors gleamed, and previously blood-spattered walls were immaculate. The first-aid supplies had been returned to the bathroom. Even the doorjamb, grazed by the bullet that had nearly hit Sabrina, had been impeccably repaired.

She gasped. "This is impossible!"

Grady checked his watch. "PD response is delayed because of the manpower shortage. We were at the hospital almost three hours." He exchanged a wordless glance with Alex. "It's possible...for a professional cleaning crew."

Alex nodded. "Sabrina, are you sure you have no idea what those men wanted?"

"I..." She faltered, and Grady shot her a silent warning. "Yes."

Grady stayed in the bedroom and Alex strode to the front door wordlessly creating a two-point-entry defense. Alex's deep voice carried in the taut silence. "We might still find traces of blood spatter, depending on what cleaning chemicals were used. But they won't provide any information other than the fact that there was blood on the premises."

Blood spatter was useless without DNA samples to compare. The men he'd killed wouldn't be listed in any database. Grady rested his palm on the Glock holstered at his thigh while a subdued Sabrina packed a suitcase and her laptop. Whoever was after her had money, manpower and connections.

As they prepared to leave, Grady inclined his head at Alex. "I've been gone for months. I don't have any fresh food on hand and need to make a stop on the way home. I wouldn't turn down backup."

"Of course." Alex smiled graciously at Sabrina.

Alex followed them in his car and then guarded Sabrina while Grady made a rapid sweep through the grocery store. Grady appreciated the additional eyes watching for a tail—and the extra firepower—during the drive to the solitary river bend where his double-decker houseboat rode low in the water.

Juggling grocery bags, Grady unlocked the security gate protecting the private dock. Alex departed, and aside from gulls squawking over the choppy water, Grady and Sabrina were alone.

He punched in the alarm code for the front door. The property was fortified by a chain-link fence around the woods and the river on three sides. Nobody would touch her. Even if someone managed to penetrate the woods or brave the river, they wouldn't get through *him*.

Goose bumps prickled over Grady's skin as he escorted her inside. He never brought women to his home.

Sabrina had been here once, for three hours. They'd talked in front of a crackling fire. Sipped wine. Cuddled. Nearly kissed. He'd yearned to finally surrender to temptation. Ached to unleash his feelings after years of restraint. Then he'd summoned every iota of self-control to push her away. And she'd bolted in tears.

Suck it up, O'Rourke. Nothing would happen. He'd make sure of it.

Grady dumped bags on the kitchen counter. "Coffee, tea or Guinness?"

"Let me see what kind of pain meds Dad prescribed." She pulled the pill bottle from her purse. "Vicodin. I could stand a couple of these about now."

"You can have *one*." He took the bottle and set it on the counter. "But not on an empty stomach, and nix the alcohol. What sounds good to eat?"

"I don't care. Chef's choice." Her shoulders slumped. "I should call Dalton—"

Grady held up his hand. He slid the new R.E.M. CD into the player. "Cover noise to thwart long-range listening devices," he murmured to Sabrina. "Besides, you enjoy their music." He passed her his handheld unit.

She stared at the high-tech device. It was the size and shape of a slim cell phone and had a color LED screen, but the similarities ended there. "Um…I'd hate to hit the wrong button and accidentally put Moscow on red alert."

He chuckled. "The most dangerous function it performs is sensing body heat through walls. That's how I knew exactly how many people were in your apartment and their positions."

"Whoa. They don't sell these babies at Wal-Mart."

"The official term is high-tech infrared tactical communication unit, TCU for short." He showed her how to make a call, and didn't miss—or like—the fact that she knew the fireman's phone number by heart.

After several minutes she disconnected. "He's not answering at home or on his cell. He must be out on a fire."

Or if whatever was going down in Eastern Oregon was as critical as it sounded, the fire department could be there. Grady pocketed his TCU. "The package is safely hidden for now. We'll retrieve it tomorrow, when you're feeling better."

She dragged her suitcase through the open great room that comprised the bottom floor. "I *really* need a shower."

Sabrina trudged into the bathroom, and Grady decided to cook a quick-and-easy ham-and-veggie omelet. But first things first. He loped upstairs and made his king-size bed with fresh linens... while fighting erotic mental images of Sabrina sliding naked between his sheets.

He opened the bank of windows in the sunny kitchen to coax in the river breeze. As he stowed groceries, he reached for a Guinness, then checked. He needed all pistons firing. He sipped a frosty root beer instead as he chopped tomatoes, green peppers and onions.

Screeching gulls wheeled overhead, and waves kissed the houseboat in a gentle rocking motion. A rare moment of peace. It was good to be home. Nice to stop running. Grady looked out at the gilded water, knife poised over the cutting board.

As long as the lull didn't last too long.

Muted daylight filtered through the bathroom shutters, and Sabrina didn't bother to switch on the light. She didn't have the nerve to examine herself in the mirror, and brightness would sharpen her pain. She had "censored sensitive intel" when she'd told Grady she was fine. The inside of her skull throbbed like the amplifiers at a Metallica concert, and her body ached in a thousand places.

When steam billowed from the shower, she stripped off her shoes and scrub pants. She slowly removed Grady's shirt and then hugged it to herself. She breathed in his familiar, comforting scent for several long moments. Finally she resolutely dropped it to the floor, stripped off her undergarments and stepped under the hot water.

It would be easy to lean against the wall and blubber, but crying would waste her ebbing energy. Besides, her nose got bright pink when she cried, and Grady would know. She'd already behaved like an idiot in front of him today. Had almost blurted out the one thing that would send him running from her forever.

She picked up the body wash and shampoo she'd brought. The nurse had said she could shower if she didn't drench her wound, sealed with butterfly bandages. After scrubbing her blood-matted hair and sore body with fragrant honeysuckle lather, she finally felt clean.

With her long hair dried, and wearing her favorite pink cotton capri pjs, she padded barefoot to the kitchen. Grady stood at the stove with his back to her.

"Just in time. Food's almost done."

Sabrina cocked her head. He hadn't seen or heard her, but he knew she was there. From the moment they'd met, an almost supernatural awareness had hummed between them.

She studied him, mouth watering. But not at the scrumptious smells wafting from the skillet. Grady's shoulders stretched his black T-shirt, his agile movements making toned muscles ripple beneath the fabric. His strong neck and big biceps were deeply tanned. Cammo pants covered long, lean legs and cupped a primo male butt that was as gorgeous and hard-muscled as the rest of him. Growing up, she'd spent more time at his house than her own, had overheard enough teasing from his brothers to know his secrets. The pants fit just snugly enough to reveal that he'd followed his usual habit of going commando.

Skillet in hand, he turned and smiled, flashing killer twin dimples. "Hungry?"

Her stomach pitched. *You bet that luscious butt.* She blinked. Thank goodness he couldn't read her mind. "Um...starving." Why couldn't she control her reaction to him? She had no problem not jumping the rest of the male population.

She followed him to the table beside the windows, admiring his self-assured, lithe stride. The man was a walking lethal weapon, all smooth grace and dangerous competence. He put her plate on the table, seated her and went to the counter for toast and juice. She stared out at the river and attempted to squelch the glittering attraction.

She couldn't afford to fall under his charismatic spell again. Twelve years ago, a few weeks after his father's murder, Grady had shattered her heart by leaving, unannounced, to join the Army the day he'd turned eighteen. The day after she'd thrown herself at him and declared her love. He'd turned his back and walked away. She'd cried into her pillow every night for weeks. Eventually she'd pulled herself together, and tried to be enthusiastic about starting college.

He'd arrived home on leave three months later, with bulked-up muscles and new confidence, tall and straight in his uniform, no longer the boy she'd known. He was a man…with new distance in his eyes. An invisible wall around his heart she couldn't breach. They'd engaged in awkward conversation and cautiously avoided the emotional time bomb ticking between them. She'd agreed to his stipulation they remain "just friends" only because if she pushed it, she'd have ended up with nothing. He'd departed for his first assignment shortly afterward. And started the disconcerting cycle that continued to this day.

He returned, and they began to eat. Grady wasn't playing games. He was always careful to maintain neutral status. She had no idea why he insisted on keeping the wall between them. But he'd rebuffed all overtures, and she hadn't dared attempt to scale it after having her heart ripped to shreds.

Then, seven months ago, the man who'd murdered Grady's father all those years before had been found and finally brought to justice. The trial had visibly torn Grady apart. She had come to his houseboat to comfort him. Things had escalated, they'd nearly kissed and he'd rejected her, again. The next day he was gone. Her heart wounded, again.

His family hadn't even known where he was this time—only that he'd taken indefinite leave from his SWAT position. Grady O'Rourke's actions had proven he didn't want an intimate relationship with her.

Yet…he was highly aware of her as a woman, undeniably attracted to her. And it wasn't merely sexual. In unguarded moments, she'd seen him looking at her with sadness and longing in his beautiful eyes.

Like right now. She glanced across the table and caught him staring. Silently devouring her. Their glances locked, and heat ricocheted between them. Grady shifted in his chair and his glance shot to his plate.

Sabrina pressed her palm to her cartwheeling stomach. What was she supposed to think? How was she supposed to contain the feelings that rioted inside her? She ached as though she were missing a limb, missing part of herself that only Grady could complete.

And in spite of his bungee-jumping, skydiving, globetrotting adventures, he didn't seem happy, either.

She'd attempted to move on, had tried dating other men. But nobody else made her heart race, her palms sweat. Nobody else had the daring, the drive…the dimples. She craved Grady O'Rourke with every cell of her being, and no other man would satisfy.

She'd settled for friendship because she'd rather have him marginally in her life than not at all. But after nearly being killed today, she wasn't sure she was willing to settle for lukewarm anymore. She slammed down her juice glass. Life was too short. She wanted more, dammit.

She wanted blazing hot…with Grady O'Rourke.

Was she better off with tepid friendship than enduring the icy coldness of being utterly alone? Like Grady, she'd never spurned a dare. But was a bold move on the man she'd loved her entire life worth the risk of losing him forever?

A heavy sigh whispered out. She was damned either way.

"Earth to Sabrina." He waved. "Something wrong with the food?"

She started, her fork suspended in midair. "It's great."

His grin seemed forced. "Better than 'can-do casserole.'"

Maureen O'Rourke had made sure her boys wouldn't rely on women to cook, clean or do laundry. Grady's cooking reflected his personality, fearless and imaginative. He'd invented recipes— more like biohazards than food. One had even exploded in the microwave. Out of the kitchen, he'd also blown up Liam's bicycle, attempting to add "turboboosters." Grady had caused more than a few explosions.

Sabrina's chuckle was equally strained. "Anything is better than those wild experiments you used to refer to as 'cooking.'"

She finished her meal, needing a break from the high-voltage tension. Maybe because she was tired, vulnerable, hyperaware of life's fragility, the attraction seemed stronger than ever before. Grady dispensed a white pill and then escorted her upstairs.

"Wow!" She paused just inside the doorway. She'd never seen his bedroom. Floor-to-ceiling glass panels offered a 360-degree panorama of the river and woods. An arched open doorway revealed an ensuite bathroom with a decadent glass shower enclosure, fitted with multiple jets and a rainhead.

Grady flipped a switch and one glass wall opened to reveal the top deck, complete with whirlpool tub and high-powered telescope for star gazing. Grady and his father had shared a love of astronomy. Many nights, she'd seen them in their backyard, their dark heads bent together over the telescope. Grady flipped another switch and a huge skylight in the roof opened.

"This is incredible!"

"Liam and I rebuilt it. We planned to sell, but I liked it so much I bought him out."

"Why am I not surprised?" Grady had always been inventive…and good with his hands. A houseboat was the perfect retreat for someone who avoided putting down roots. He could haul up anchor and move on a whim.

"It's even better at night, when you're surrounded by stars."

Beneath a star-washed midnight sky would be an amazingly romantic place to make love with him. A wave of yearning washed over her and she swayed. He stepped close behind her, supporting her with his big body. Comforting heat radiated from him, and she reveled in the intimate contact.

"You're fading." His low, smoky voice vibrated in her ear, and his breath feathered her neck. "Into bed with you."

She shivered under the erotic onslaught. His bed faced the river, beckoned her in.

If only you were climbing into bed with me.

The room blurred, and she blinked. Omigosh, had she said that out loud? The medication made everything muted and dreamy. She half turned, looked up at him. Grady's tender gaze met hers, his sensual mouth a whisper away. He didn't bolt for the door, so she must have only thought it.

Grady steered her to the bed, then tucked her in. "Sleep sweet, Sabrina."

A jolt of panic ambushed her. She grabbed his arm. "Don't leave me alone up here!"

His large, capable hand cupped her cheek. "You're safe. I'll be close by."

Physically. Emotionally, he stayed beyond her reach.

Sadness weighted her chest as she tumbled into oblivion.

Sabrina was naked and cold. So cold. Evil hands grabbed her, hurt her, yanked her toward the black pit. She fought with all her strength, battled to her feet.

"Help me!" She was frozen in an icy coffin with the monsters. Fear roiled inside her. "Let me out!" Vicious fingers clawed her naked flesh, tried to jerk her back into the darkness as she beat on the wall of ice with her fists.

Suddenly Grady appeared on the other side. He put his finger to his lips, then turned and walked down a long, fog-cloaked corridor. Walked serenely toward Death.

"Stop!" she screamed. "Grady!" The skin on her fists split open, bled down the ice in crimson ribbons. Sabrina tried to wipe off the blood, smearing the ice as the man she loved walked away from her forever.

"No!" Helpless, terrified, she watched through a red haze of pain as each step took him farther away. "Grady, please!" she sobbed.

"Sabrina!" Grady's husky voice pulled her out of the cold horror. "You're safe, sweetheart."

"No, don't go. Grady, come back!"

"Sabrina, *wake up.*" He gave her a gentle shake and chased away the monsters. His calm voice dissolved the confusing haze. His warm embrace shattered the ice, and she struggled awake.

She forced her eyes open. Darkness surrounded her, broken by jagged beams of moonlight. Her glance flew to Grady. He was dressed only in faded, snug jeans. Water droplets glittered on his wide bare chest and his ebony hair was damp. Concern edged his eyes.

She flung her arms around his neck. "Grady!" She sobbed. "Don't leave me. I don't want you to die!"

"Shh. We're safe. You're all right." He rubbed her back. "I left your side for a three-minute shower, but I was within seeing and hearing range. You're having a nightmare."

Tears streamed down her face. "I've had nightmares, but that was…something else." Unlike anything she'd ever experienced. Her hands and her heart still thrummed with pain. "I was bleeding and we were d-dying."

"Not on my watch." He stroked her hair, his tone soothing. "You're experiencing post-traumatic stress to the blood and violence, probably combined with a bad reaction to the pain meds."

"It wasn't a replay," she whispered. "It was a preview." Why couldn't he feel the oppressive cloud of doom? "I *have* to die, but you don't."

"No, Sabrina." His voice grew fierce. "You aren't going to die."

"You don't understand." She choked on a terrifying surge of certainty. "You can't stop it."

He cradled her face in his hands, and his thumbs wiped away her tears. "I damn well *will*." His gray-green eyes flared. "No matter what it takes."

Then he crushed her to him and kissed her.

Chapter 4

1:00 a.m.

Grady's kiss was fast and hot. A marauder's kiss, a possessive invasion of warm, silky tongue. Sabrina knew his scent, but not the intoxicating rush of his heady taste. Knew the shape and breadth of his shoulders, but not the sleek feel of heated skin and honed muscles beneath her fingertips. Knew Grady's friendship and protection, but not his erotic command.

Until now.

Years of suppressed passion exploded between them. His hands thrust into her hair, urged her impossibly closer. His mouth claimed hers in urgent demand, and the world tilted.

Sabrina smothered her internal warning voice and tangled her fingers in the short damp strands of Grady's hair. Through her cotton pajama top, the primal drumming of his heartbeat called to hers.

Grady. She'd longed to touch him. Yearned to be his. Her heart belonged to him. It always had.

She moaned into his mouth. Embracing her, he tumbled her backward onto the bed and covered her with the welcome weight of his big body. His teeth nipped her lower lip. The soft love bite fueled her desire, and her nipples tightened. Strong fingers kneaded the nape of her neck as he deepened the kiss. His tongue advanced, retreated, each satin stroke making her tremble.

Grady O'Rourke was the best thing that had ever happened to her—and the scariest—and she wanted him so badly she ached. He was the man she'd waited for all this time.

She wrapped her arms around his neck and clung to him. He was shaking, violently aroused, his breathing rapid. Heat poured off his skin, scorched her, branded her. His hands glided down her body, inciting her emotions, rocketing her desire. Since adolescence, he'd always been so reserved, so careful not to touch her. He cupped her bottom, lifted her to press against the hard ridge of his arousal, and she jolted in surprise. Clearly, his restraint had fractured.

The warning voice shouted at her. *Why?*

Passion evaporated in the icy grip of reason, and she went cold. Why, suddenly, had he lost control? The harder she'd tried to cling to him in the past, the faster and farther he'd run. He hadn't admitted any feelings for her. Nothing had changed.

Trembling, she reluctantly released him. No way could she let him inside her body and still hide what was in her heart. Unless she concealed her emotions from him, he would tune right into her. If they made love, he'd know she craved much more from him than friendship.

Grady voiced a low, throaty sound of protest and broke the kiss, proving her right. His beautiful gray-green eyes glowed with desire. "What's wrong? Did I hurt you?"

Tears threatened. The truth would make him bolt again. He'd reject her completely. *Permanently.* She'd get no more chances. Their uneasy truce, and her bruised heart, would be shattered. She wasn't willing to risk that. Not yet.

"Grady. What are we doing?"

He blinked. "We—" He looked down at their entwined bodies, bewildered as if he'd never seen her before. "We're, ah—"

She'd believed that if given the chance to be with him, she'd go for it and damn the consequences. But now she knew differently. She wasn't willing to settle for scraps anymore. Her stomach twisted. When it was over this time, she would either have everything from him...or nothing. "Did you suddenly decide you want to be friends with benefits?"

"No!" He swore. "I guess I got carried away."

"Why here? Why now?"

"We're under stress. Forced into close proximity." One broad shoulder jerked in an attempt at a shrug. "It happens."

Yet he'd made sure it had never happened before. Sabrina swallowed the tears. She needed to tread carefully. Protect them both. She wanted to make love to Grady more than her next breath, but not on a whim. Not swept up in the heat of the moment and ruined afterward by awkward excuses and fumbled apologies. He had to choose to be with her.

She wanted him not just for now, but forever.

Or not at all.

"Are you trying to prove something? Did the argument with my father throw you off balance? You know he's overprotective of me. He doesn't dislike you personally—"

"Like hell. If looks could kill, he'd have sliced me in half years ago." His voice dropped so low she didn't think he meant her to hear the rest. "This isn't about your father," he murmured. "It's about mine."

"I don't understand." She kept her voice quiet, her tone gentle. *Get him to consider his motives without spooking him into retreat.* "What's changed from when I tried to comfort you after DiMarco's trial, and you accused me of offering you a mercy—"

"I was an ass. Then *and* now." Fury flashed in his eyes, and red streaks mottled his cheeks. He shoved himself off her. "Misplaced passion can be a reaction to a near-death experience. You majored in psychology—you know the theory."

"Biological imperative to preserve the species." She might buy that flimsy bit of rationalizing. Except her near-death experience had happened to her, not him. *Hours* ago. "Once the initial adrenaline rush subsided, you seemed okay."

"Today was the worst— I heard the gunfire, saw you crumpled on the floor, bleeding, and I thought—"

Sabrina watched him pace the floor as emotions warred on his face. Watched as his confusion and anger morphed into stark fear. She frowned. Grady, *afraid?*

She'd never seen him show fear. *Ever.* Grady bungee jumped as easily as most people crossed the street. Whitewater rafted down rapids that made experts queasy. Leaped out of airplanes miles above the earth with nothing to slow his plummet except ribbons of flimsy nylon. He challenged danger, laughed at risk.

The memory of his pale face and shaking hands this morning blazed into her mind. She caught his troubled glance, and he quickly looked away.

Her breath hitched. Was it possible…? Grady had mentioned his father. Brian O'Rourke had been accused of being a dirty cop the year before he'd died, but was murdered before he could prove the half million missing from an armored-car robbery was a setup. Brian's demotion to desk duty and subsequent murder had devastated seventeen-year-old Grady. Perhaps Grady had never fully recovered. Had the trauma of his father's betrayal and brutal death made him mistrustful? Scared to form attachments?

There could be only one reason why the man who feared *nothing* stood terrified and trembling in front of her.

Grady possessed feelings for her.

Emotions that went deep enough to scare him.

How could she have missed it? All this time she'd thought he felt suffocated by her desire to be close. Sorrow and self-doubt had blinded her. And Grady had hidden his vulnerability behind a devil-may-care shield. Realization sent her reeling. His behavior finally made sense. He'd sought adventure so he'd be too busy to think. Threw himself into action rather than deal with his emotions.

Grady had run from her all these years—had fled the first time she'd told him she loved him at seventeen and the last time they'd nearly gotten physical seven months ago—not because he *didn't* care enough.

But because he cared too much.

He wasn't afraid to gamble his life. Grady didn't hold *anything* back…except his heart.

He must feel so lost. So alone. It was her turn to look away as the tears she'd battled spilled over. The only thing that scared Grady was love.

And her love was the only thing that might save him.

Grady stalked out to the deck. It was as far as he could escape this time. His promise held him to Sabrina as firmly as ankle shackles. Damn him, he'd brought her to tears. *Again.*

He'd fought to numb his need for her, but it always returned stronger than before. He'd stayed away with good reason. Only Sabrina's common sense had aborted disaster tonight. His worst-case scenario had become reality. He'd lost his tenuous grip on control and royally screwed up.

So what else was new?

He slammed his fist into the railing, hoping the pain would clear his head. *Man up, O'Rourke, and fix your mess.* He forced himself to turn and walk into his bedroom. To approach the bed. To look at Sabrina's tear-streaked cheeks.

He'd caused the grief on her face, the pain in her eyes. *This* was what happened when he steered with his emotions. He let people down. They got hurt. They *died*.

And don't you forget it, boyo.

He forced his fists to unclench. "I lost control. I apologize."

"It's all right." She surreptitiously wiped her face. As if he wouldn't notice he'd made her cry. "Like you said, stuff happens."

"It won't happen again."

"Relax. I'm not going to freak out."

He should be relieved. Instead, sexual frustration and anger ate at him. "You're just letting me off the hook?"

"Who said you were off the hook?" Sabrina stared at him for a few heartbeats. "I put on the brakes because we were moving way too fast." Her lips curved in a sweetly determined smile that made the hair on his neck prickle. "Not because I don't want you. After that kiss, you should have no doubts."

No, no doubts. About her wants or his. He backed away. "I never should have touched you." The heady rush of Sabrina's sweet taste, her welcoming warmth had spun him into a free fall. The punch of adrenaline had scrambled his senses, left him wheeling and dizzy like the giddiness of high-altitude oxygen deprivation.

"Lose the hair shirt. I'm not mad, and I'm not sorry, either." Her smile widened. "What did you tell me when Rob Masters dumped me in the middle of prom and took off with that slut Maggie Leonard when I informed him I wasn't putting out?"

"That we should insert a tactical surveillance camera under their hotel room door and rig it to broadcast the show on every TV in the place—including the one in the lobby—and then phone Maggie's father, the longshoreman, to say she needed an emergency ride home."

"My hero." Sabrina laughed. "I'll never forget the way Rob squealed like a girl when Maggie's dad kicked down the door." She sobered. "But I meant before that. When you noticed I was missing and came to find me sobbing in the bathroom. You said any guy who only wanted sex didn't care which woman scratched his itch and that I deserved better. Deserved someone who wanted *me*. The entire package." She brushed a finger over her bottom lip, plump and moist from his kisses, and his throat constricted. "When you kissed me just now, was it only to satisfy a physical urge? Or something more?"

Hell. Sabrina wasn't afraid to shoot from the hip, a trait he admired. Until she aimed at him. His focus lingered on her mouth. "I...followed a spur-of-the-moment impulse." He swallowed hard. "I don't know why," he lied.

Grady paced to the other side of the room. Now that he'd touched her, tasted her, need was eating him alive. The craving *wasn't* merely physical; he could have handled that. Lust had never shaken him to the core. Passion had never left him raw and adrift and hurting.

Lost in Sabrina's kiss, he had felt no fear. No pain. His demons had been silenced. For the first time in over a decade he'd known peace.

He'd finally found his refuge. And he could never go back.

The truth lodged hot and jagged in his chest. The only way to protect Sabrina was to seal off his perimeter and barricade her out.

The one place where he'd finally found absolution was the one place he couldn't stay.

He turned away so he wouldn't have to look into those discerning brown eyes. "It was just a kiss. Don't read more into it." The forced nonchalance cost him more than she'd ever know. "From one day to the next is as far into the future as I go."

Yet in her arms, he'd had a glimpse of what his future could be. A future he could never have. And it ripped his heart out. *Give me the strength.* "I'm not like my brothers, I'll never settle down. I'm missing the commitment gene."

"You really believe that?" The soft words stung like bullets. "Or s it what you say to the guy in the mirror so you can live with him?" She rose and walked toward him, her face etched with sorrow. "Don't you get tired? Lonely? How long can you keep lying to yourself, Grady? Until you're too burned-out to make the effort anymore? What happens when you finally decide you want more…and it's too late? When you've realized you wasted your entire life?"

The ammo hit perilously close to the target. Terror roiled inside him. He couldn't be living a lie…or his father had died for nothing. "My life is protecting people. Saving them. I put my ass on the line every day. And once you're safe—"

"I'm not an abandoned kitten that you can coddle and protect and then give away." Her mouth firmed in a stubborn line. "I *won't* be another of your 'fix and release' projects."

When she touched his cheek, survival instinct made him recoil. "You *do* deserve better, Sabrina." Nearly losing her had been a shock. A rock smacking his windshield, chipping his composure. The damage had seemed contained. Then the cracks had started spreading, snaking along invisible fault lines.

Grady caught her hand, held it aside. He would not crack apart. Refused to crumble. "You deserve someone who can give you stability. Security. I'm not that man."

"Usually when a person runs, it's because something is chasing them."

His throat was raw. "You have no idea."

"Oh, I might. Remember, I was barely five when mom drowned. I was furious at the entire world, at myself. But even as young as you were, you somehow understood exactly what I needed over the years. You were my ally." Her delicate blond brows tipped into a thoughtful frown. "Grady, if you don't face your monsters, you don't get to live the life you were meant to have. They win by default."

This was exactly why he'd kept her at arm's length. She was so perceptive it was terrifying. "Some monsters are—" He abruptly shut his trap. What the hell was he blabbing? She didn't need to hear him snivel about his personal boogeyman.

"Too big? Too scary?" She squeezed his fingers. "Not if we stick together. Fight them side by side, like we used to."

He wanted to let her wrap her arms around him and hold him.
Let her kiss away the pain. But his selfish needs didn't matter.
Involvement with him would cost her too much. He had to try twice
before he could speak. "I'm not playing kiddie games, Sabrina. My
fight isn't your fight, and I won't put you in harm's way."

"But you can risk everything for *me?*" Her eyes flared to molten
gold. "I pick my own battles. Always have, always will. Nothing
you say or do can stop me."

Grady knew that firsthand. Had been the recipient of her determination and loyalty.

He needed time, distance. He couldn't think straight with her
crowding him. "It's the middle of the night, and we've had enough
drama for one day. You're beat, and you need sleep to heal."

"You, too." She sighed. "All right, we'll table the discussion—for now."

He had a flashbang for her. This discussion was DOA. "You
should go back to bed."

"I doubt either of us can sleep right away. I could use that
Guinness about now. Care to join me?"

A beer? Hell, he needed a fifth of Jameson Gold. He glanced
at the digital clock beside his bed to ensure enough time had
elapsed since her pain meds. "Go ahead. I'll be right there."

Sabrina padded downstairs. The houseboat was locked, security
engaged. She'd be fine for a few minutes.

Grady splashed cold water on his face and reassembled his scat-
tered wits. He had to engage his brain and think like a soldier, not
a hormonal, stupid schoolboy.

He leaned on the sink and stared at the guy in the mirror. One
truth he could never escape. If anything happened to Sabrina, his
world would be as cold and dark as if the sun had fallen from orbit.

Failing her would destroy him.

Grady tugged on a T-shirt and jogged down to the kitchen. He
would find out who'd hired him, and who was behind the attempt
on Sabrina's life. He would keep her safe.

Even if it was the last thing he did.

When dawn etched a neon strip of light on the horizon, Grady
sat upright, instantly awake. He and Sabrina had sipped Guinness

and eaten popcorn at the kitchen table, keeping the conversation light. After tucking her back into bed, he'd strummed his guitar to help her relax.

When she'd finally drifted off, he'd sat alone in the dark and counted every soft exhalation. Listened to the silken rustle of her limbs beneath his sheets. Breathed in her heady fragrance—her favorite honeysuckle, like the vines she and Letty had planted to ramble up to her second-story bedroom window, directly across from his old room.

Too many sultry summer nights he'd lain awake, teased by the sweet fragrance drifting on the breeze, tormented by longings he didn't dare express. At first they'd been too young. Later it had become impossible.

He flexed his shoulders. He'd spent the past hours in the easy chair beside the bed, his subconscious primed to leap to alertness. Even with his eyes closed and body motionless, he'd remained aware. The fact that his muscles had stayed taut with arousal was actually a bonus. No danger of relaxing into oblivion.

He glanced at Sabrina's sleeping face. He'd often imagined her in his bed, but the reality staggered him. He stifled a groan. God help him, she was tempting. A waterfall of hair bright as spring sunshine tumbled over his pillows. Dusky lashes curved in golden crescents against her creamy skin. Her complexion was rosy with slumber, her lush pink lips parted, inviting a kiss. His hands fisted against the urge to scoop her into his embrace and wake her with that kiss. To watch her intoxicating eyes fire with passion.

He jerked his focus out the window to the river. He'd promised her he'd hear any attempted break-ins while resting. Combat naps were a learned survival skill. So was staying in close proximity to Sabrina.

Seagulls diving for breakfast mocked him with hoarse cries. In less than twenty-four hours, personal lines he'd sworn never to cross had tangled into knots around his heart.

He forced himself to rise and turn his back on her. She felt safe enough with him to lose herself in the vulnerability of slumber. He wouldn't betray her trust.

He would protect Sabrina…even from himself.

Grady stumbled downstairs and into the kitchen. He knew her

habits as well as his own. Both high-energy, they operated on less
sleep than the average person. They'd always been morning
people, the first ones stirring in the old neighborhood and waving
to each other from bedroom windows. Being the only two awake
in a still-sleeping world was like membership in a secret club.

A Dropkick Murphys CD was his choice of music as cover noise
this morning. His TCU vibrated with an incoming call. "Yo, Alex."

"*Buenos días, mi amigo.* One vehicle approached your perimeter at oh-three-hundred, but drove on past."

Grady frowned "You didn't have to stay all night."

"Your brothers are busy."

Still? The operation must be complicated. "Are they safe?"

"As far as I know. I cannot divulge details at the moment."

Guilt sank into him. He should be with them. The last thing he
wanted was to leave his family hanging again. "Thanks for the
above-and-beyond, Alex. Now head home and hit the sack."

"Doesn't Sabrina have to return to the city for a medical exam?
I will follow you."

Grady rubbed his chin. He couldn't have a Fed on his tail when
he retrieved the package. "Go home. I can handle it."

"I'm sure you can. But I will stay."

"You're so damn mule-headed, you should be Irish." At Alex's
crack of laughter, Grady disconnected. He hated to do it, but he'd
have to lose the FBI agent once they reached the city.

He dumped organic, roasted beans into the grinder and pressed
the button. The fragrance of brewing coffee was Sabrina's favorite
wake-up call.

Before the carafe was half-full, she strolled into the kitchen. "I
use the timer on my machine at home, but this is much nicer. The
coffee smells yummy." She stretched like a lazy kitten, pulling the
fabric of her pajama top tight against her generous breasts. Then
she rested her head on his shoulder. "So do you."

A blast of desire racked him, and Grady pulled away. Swearing
under his breath, he stuck his head in the refrigerator. If he had a
say, coffee would fast become her second-favorite way to wake up.

He emerged with some grapefruits to see her combing graceful
fingers through her wild mane. She shook her head, tossing her hair—
and his hormones—into a glimmering riot. "Were you able to rest?"

His eyes narrowed. Was she seducing him on *purpose?*

He couldn't confront her. If she wasn't, he'd look like the village idiot. If she was, she'd know it was working. Grady dumped the fruit onto the countertop and slammed open the juicer. "Yeah."

She scooped her hair to one side, leaned over the coffeemaker and inhaled a slow breath, baring her slender neck. "Mmm. Hurry up."

Apparently, last night was only the beginning of his descent into hell. He wanted to start at the tender spot just beneath her ear and lick and nibble every inch, down to her bare toes and ripe-peach-painted toenails.

He grabbed coffee mugs off the wooden rack, clumsily clanged them together and broke one. He barked out a word reserved for engine failures and enemy gunfire.

Her golden brows arched. "Someone woke up on the wrong side of the bed."

No, he'd awakened watching her. Wanting her. "You woke up in my bed," he growled. "I woke up in a chair."

She studied him with eyes far wiser than her years. As if she knew why he was edgy and off balance. Knew exactly how much their connection had messed with his head. Sweat slicked his spine. Relieved for an excuse to avoid her gaze, he wet a paper towel and scooped broken shards into the garbage.

That stupid, impulsive kiss was the elephant in the room. And the elephant was kicking his ass.

"We'd better get moving. You can use the shower off my bedroom." The security system was armed and Alex was on duty outside. Grady resorted to the only coping method that had ever worked with Sabrina.

He ran.

Chapter 5

5:00 a.m.

Inside the shower, Grady cranked the "hot" lever open. He propped his hands on the wall, letting the pulsing stream hit his knotted muscles. Water-pressure fluctuation told him Sabrina had turned on the upstairs shower. A forbidden picture shimmered into his mind. Sabrina, naked and beautiful, stepping into the steamy enclosure...with him. He would lean her against the hot tiles and nibble water droplets from her creamy neck and shoulders. Skim his soapy palms over her warm, damp skin. Trace the curves of her bottom, tease her rosy nipples until they were hard with desire. Her softness would cradle him, their wet, soap-slicked bodies creating sweet, aching friction as he slid into her welcoming heat.

Grady groaned and banged his head on the tile. What was wrong with him? He had to get his libido under control, which left him two choices.

Bracing himself, he wrenched the temperature to pure cold, gasping as icy needles stung his skin. He was in deep trouble when a cold shower was his best recourse. Tortured by the same frustration at sixteen—would he ever learn to stop wanting Sabrina?—he'd been driven to the DIY option.

His Glock was within easy reach, Alex was guard-dogging the property and his top-of-the-line security system would alert if anyone attempted a breach. But he had no desire to dawdle in ice

rady toweled off, then yanked on jeans, a sage-green
socks and his combat boots. Unable to postpone the
e flung open the door and strode back into the kitchen.
red half a dozen toasted whole wheat muffins with
rape jelly, a gift from Letty. He was gulping a glass
queezed juice when Sabrina strolled into the kitchen, en-
ng him in a fragrant cloud of honeysuckle. Her hair was
athered into a high ponytail, and she was wearing slim khakis and
white sneakers topped by a sleeveless blouse the color of ripe, juicy
watermelon. Another mental image he could have done without.

"Your fancy shower rocks! With that many massage jets, who
needs a man?"

Grady choked on his juice. "Well, I sure as hell don't." He
needed a woman. One special woman. He barely resisted the urge
to smash his glass in the sink. So much for regaining control. Why
was Sabrina the only female in the world who nuked his self-
discipline? He tugged his TCU from his pants pocket. "Call your
smoke eater and arrange to retrieve the package."

She dialed. "Still grumpy, I see. That's not like you."

The freezing shower had chilled his desire to a dull ache, but
hadn't done much to improve his mood. So he wasn't at his best
under torture. He picked up his gun from where he'd laid it on the
kitchen counter and shoved it into his back waistband.

She disconnected. "Dalton's still not answering."

Shake it off, O'Rourke. It wasn't Sabrina's fault he was as randy
as Riley's bull around her. He summoned a smile and repocketed
the device. "Grab some chow and let's head to the hospital. Then
we'll try him again."

"Good idea. I hope you don't mind, I had to borrow a pair of
socks. I forgot to bring mine." Before he could reply, her cell
phone burst into a hit pop ballad.

"Remember, it's not a secured line," he warned.

After a short conversation, she hung up. "Weird. My answering service says there's a patient waiting in my office. But I don't
have anyone right now who would present an emergency case."

"Could be bait." He yanked open a cupboard and accessed the
hidden combination lock that released a concealed latch. The entire
cabinet swung ajar to reveal a wall safe bristling with weapons.

Sabrina's eyes went huge at the sight of guns, knive
ing stars and the odd incendiary device. "Geez, I thou
paranoid."

He buckled on an ankle rig holding a smaller G
risks, but I'm not reckless." His grin was genuine th
to be prepared."

"For *what?* Armageddon?"

Grady strapped a sheath of throwing stars to his forearm. *"Bás
ná an bua."*

"Victory Or Death." She considered the platter of muffins as
gravely as if her life depended on the right choice. "Yeah, I finally
get the All Or Nothing motto."

"If I go down, it'll be fighting."

"There's a bombshell." She picked up a muffin and flashed the
smile he'd seen the night before. The secret feminine smile that
had him breaking out in uneasy goose bumps. "Before this is over,
my big, bad Gaelic warrior, you might wish you'd chosen death."

The subtext thrumming beneath her words chilled him colder
than the shower. He shrugged into his bomber jacket. Although the
battered brown leather didn't thaw his insides, it camouflaged the
fact that he was armed to the teeth. "Wait here while I conduct a
perimeter sweep and inspect the Jeep."

Grady trusted Alex's capability, but he wanted an eyes-on
assessment. He disarmed the security system, palmed his Glock
and stalked outside. As he reached the porch, a frustrated sigh
exploded from his throat.

For about the thousandth time, he'd been routed by the girl next
door.

When he returned five minutes later, Sabrina had donned a
white hoodie and had her purse slung over her shoulder. She shot
him an anxious look. "Is everything all right?"

"We're cleared for takeoff."

She glanced up as he bundled her into the Jeep. "I'd love to fly
with you sometime."

Not gonna happen. The wild blue yonder was his sacred space.
The only place where he flew utterly solo and in complete
control. Him and the stars—where nothing could intrude. If he
allowed Sabrina in, the memories would stick and he'd never be

alone up there again. "Stay low." He jogged around the vehicle, jumped into the driver's seat, then shoved a Nickelback CD into the stereo.

He concentrated on driving and imminent threat assessment, and Sabrina kept quiet. Too quiet. She was thinking—more trouble for him.

Grady geared down to enter the city limits, and she snickered. "Remember when you tried to teach me to drive a stick?"

"How could I forget? You burned out the clutch in my GTO and I had to take the rap." He gave her a wry smile. "To this day, my brothers still think *I* was the culprit...and occasionally razz me about it."

"Like Liam has room to be righteous. He taught you to drive a year before you were legal."

"Next time he rags on my driving skills, I'll mention that." He and Liam had shared a room and lead-singer duties in their garage band. Liam was his closest brother agewise and his partner in crime—game for anything.

"If your father had known you guys used to climb out your window in the dead of night and cruise—"

"Holy crap, talk about Armageddon. Pop wasn't big on rule breaking." Nausea flooded his system. Maybe that's why Pop had thought Grady was the only O'Rourke in four generations unworthy of being a cop. Why he'd been furious when Grady had proudly announced his intention to join his brothers in law enforcement.

He'd proven his father wrong. But Pop hadn't lived to see it. One mess he could never fix. The mistake that would haunt him forever.

"Hey." Sabrina rubbed his knee. "I'm sorry. I didn't mean to upset you by talking about your dad."

"No problem." He jerked his glance from the sympathy in her eyes to the rearview mirror. Alex was a pro, but Grady spotted his sedan several cars back. He checked both side mirrors. No other tails. "It was a long time ago." Yet some days, the horrific event that had changed his life haunted him as if it had happened yesterday.

"You know, you never thanked me for the payback," she teased.

She'd reimbursed him for driving lessons by teaching him a skill he'd desperately needed—how to dance with a girl. He looked over at her the same instant she looked at him, and then they spontaneously broke into a campy rendition of "When a Man Loves a Woman."

He grimaced. "If I'd had to hear Michael Bolton whine those lyrics once more…"

"It was *romantic*." Chuckling, she squeezed his knee. "Seeing you stroll into a room nowadays, nobody would ever guess you used to klutz around the tree house like a charging rhino."

He stared at her hand resting possessively on his knee…and for the first time since he was seventeen, didn't want to retreat. Conversing easily with her again after a decade of strained small talk felt good. Felt right. He'd missed their spirited camaraderie. Missed Sabrina's humor and smarts and staunch integrity. "You can't knock my enthusiasm. But I did trample your poor feet."

He and Sabrina had also snuck out in the middle of the night…for clandestine dancing lessons in Castle O'Rourke, the boys' childhood tree house. Heaven forbid Grady's brothers or Sabrina's father had caught them in an awkward embrace, swaying to sappy love songs turned low on a portable boombox. Luckily she hadn't realized his clumsiness was because he'd been so painfully aroused he could barely function.

"You got better with time and practice."

"At dancing." He winked to disguise the bleakness. Nothing had changed. Twelve years later he still secretly longed for her.

She laughed. "I'm glad you came home, Grady. It's been too quiet around here without you."

All his best memories included Sabrina. What would have happened if he'd stayed back then, toughed it out? He wheeled around a corner, checked his tail again. No point in looking backward. No use torturing himself with what-ifs. Life didn't offer do-overs. If he had the power to rewrite history, Pop would be alive.

Grady had to live with his decisions. So other people didn't die because of them.

He knew exactly what would have happened if he'd stuck around. Sabrina would have gotten hurt. Grady stomped the clutch and wrenched the stick into Second with unnecessary force. He'd assured Wade he had learned from his mistakes. How much misery did it take to ram home the lesson?

Focusing on the road, he carefully lifted Sabrina's hand from his knee and placed it on the console. "Quiet isn't necessarily bad. Besides, you know I can't hang around."

"Can't?" From the corner of his eye he saw her turn to stare out the window. Her low voice was even. "Or won't?"

Did it matter? The reasons…and the result were the same.

He nabbed a parking spot close to the ER entrance and escorted Sabrina inside. As they entered the doors, he saw Alex drive by, still watching their backs.

When they walked into Sabrina's office, he cased the empty waiting area. Nothing appeared amiss, but his intuition flared.

Sabrina tapped her blank appointment calendar. "I don't get it."

Despite the balmy weather, the atmosphere felt supercharged. *Something* was brewing. "The drive would have been the perfect time for an ambush. No pro assassin would attempt a hit in a crowded hospital."

"Well, that's reassuring."

"I won't let *anyone* hurt you, Sabrina."

She studied him for long, silent moments. "Which, I believe, might be the issue."

He was *not* getting trapped into that confab. "You should report in to your father."

Grady escorted Sabrina up to Wade's office, then waited outside. He didn't want another run-in with Dr. Frankenstein. Arms folded, he leaned against the wall. His Irish blood never quailed at a dust-up, but for Sabrina's sake he'd keep the peace.

His next-to-oldest brother sauntered down the corridor. Dressed in battle gear, sans body armor, Connall had to have recently arrived from the incident site.

His brother stared him down. "I see the prodigal son finally returned."

"Con." Smiling, Grady straightened. "How a—"

Con's arm whipped back and his fist smashed into Grady's jaw. The impact knocked Grady to the floor.

He worked his throbbing jaw. Not broken. Barely. He blinked up at Con through stinging shock. "What the—"

"That's for Mom, since she loves you too much to do it herself." Con shook the pain from his hand. "Why didn't you call her?"

"I sent word home."

"A postcard from Uganda. Four scribbled lines from the Middle East at Christmas. Hope all that chatty correspondence wasn't too much trouble."

Grady gingerly rubbed his sore face. "I needed space."

"No return address. No phone number." Con scowled. "No way to contact you."

"I figured nothing would crop up that you, Aidan and Liam couldn't handle." Grady hadn't seen Con lose his fierce temper for years. "Is something wrong with Mom? Is she okay?"

"You might've considered that before disappearing for months." Con's palm slapped the wall above his head. "You pulled this same crap when you were a kid."

Sabrina strode out of Wade's office. "Done! We—" She halted and looked down at Grady. "*What's* going on? Are you okay?"

"I slipped."

She snorted and her eyes narrowed at Con before perusing Grady again. "You slipped and ran into Con's fist?"

Con squared his shoulders. "Baby brother wasn't watching his step."

"Connall Patrick." Sabrina drilled her index finger into Con's sternum, and his brother winced. "As I counsel my little patients, use your words instead of fists. You're not ten anymore."

"Tell *him* that." Con gestured at Grady. "Grow up, bro. Act like a man." His brother pivoted and stalked away.

When Con reached the end of the hallway, his wife, Bailey, emerged from a nearby restroom. She patted her distended abdomen and smiled up at Con, who tucked her arm in his and led her into an elevator. He must have met her for a prenatal check. Barely into her first trimester when Grady had left Riverside, Bailey looked like she could deliver any minute. He mentally counted. Yeah, she could. Maybe the stress of impending fatherhood had wound Con too tight. But it didn't explain his dig about their mom.

Sabrina gave Grady a hand up. "What got his shorts in a bunch?"

"Sabrina, is my mom all right?"

"As far as I know, why?"

"Con's tailspin was over her."

"That's odd." She dusted off the back of his jeans, making his belly clench. "She had a flu bug around Christmas, but after a rough six weeks, she bounced back."

"I need to call her." Breaking contact, he turned to dial his TCU. "She's not picking up her home or cell phone." He speed-dialed his brothers, then their wives. "Aidan and Liam aren't answering, either. Or Kate." Anxiety rode him as he shoved the device into his pocket. "Zoe's phone went straight to voice mail."

"Back in my apartment, you mentioned a situation in Eastern Oregon tying up Riverside PD. Ace reporter Zoe is probably neck-deep in the crisis." Sabrina consulted her watch. "And this is the one day a month Kate volunteers with the preschool community center art project." She tucked her hand beneath his arm. "After we get the package, we can run by Maureen's house."

With Sabrina under attack by unknown assailants, Grady didn't want to lead trouble to his mom's doorstep. "Let's case the ER and see if she's scheduled for a shift."

"I have to hand it to your mom. I don't know how she manages all her civic and community projects along with nursing *and* captaining her women's rowing team." Sabrina patted his forearm as she stepped into the elevator. "Not to mention raising four hellions."

After Brian's murder, Grady had withdrawn from everyone. He and Sabrina hadn't discussed personal stuff for years. Their most meaningful conversations lately had been about the weather. Smiling, Grady hit the down button. "The red hair should clue you in. Mom's always been a ball of fire."

"And your anchor," Sabrina said softly. "After the initial slam, she really pulled herself together for you boys."

"She did." And Brian O'Rourke's sons had stepped up to the plate. Aidan shouldered the lion's share of responsibility and became the surrogate father. Con offered emotional support. Middle brother Liam pitched in wherever needed and kept everyone laughing.

"The maddest I ever saw her was when you refused your soccer scholarship senior year to work construction. I heard her yelling over at my house."

"She has no qualms about expressing herself." Grady's mouth slanted. "An affliction you share." He watched the numbers tick downward. During the first dark weeks after Pop's murder, he'd let his mom fuss over him because he could barely breathe in and out. And doling out TLC seemed to lift her spirits. Then he'd summoned the fortitude to force his leaden body and numbed mind to face a world that was too loud, too bright.

Too empty.

When he'd blown off the full-ride to Georgetown University that included a prestigious soccer camp, he'd insisted on giving his furious mom every penny he'd earned. Funerals weren't cheap.

Neither was redemption.

In spite of his mother's objections, he'd toiled on construction sites until he'd turned eighteen and signed on the dotted line to "be all that he could be." As a medevac pilot, the Army had trained him to heal. And to kill. Then he'd come home and joined his brothers on Riverside SWAT.

The doors slid open, and he automatically scanned the area as he and Sabrina traversed the long hallway. Grady stopped at the desk, and Christina, the charge nurse, offered him a jaunty grin. "Hey, flyboy. I didn't know you were back."

"Just got in. Is Mom on today?"

"Let me check. She'll be glad to see you." The nurse briskly tapped her keyboard. "Con breezed through a minute ago."

"Yeah, he caught me." Grady rubbed his jaw. After his four-year hitch, his brothers had readily accepted him as one of the SWAT team. And he pulled his weight with the family by taking charge of the fixer-upper projects around the house. Even though he was the youngest, his brothers had no problem with him being crew boss to install a new roof or rebuild the back deck. Yet to this day, he burned to prove his worth. As a son, a sibling and a SWAT officer.

Christina consulted her computer screen. "Sorry, Grady. Maureen isn't on till Wednesday."

Where the hell was she? Maybe Con had a point. Maybe it *was* past time to settle down, be a man. His gaze tangled with Sabrina's, and the impact jarred him to his toes. Men like his brothers devoted their best to their wives and children.

Grady's best was nowhere close to par.

He and Sabrina headed toward the exit. She could try contacting Dalton again when they reached the privacy of the Jeep. The overhead PA system paged Wade to the ER, code yellow. The big double doors slid open.

And the bodies started rolling in.

Over two dozen bodies shrouded in body bags, pushed on gurneys by somber, silent firefighters, paramedics and cops.

Grady recognized most of the paramedics, as would Sabrina. He'd worked alongside them, and they'd all hung out at the local pub. He grabbed Ronnie Nguyen's arm. "What in the *hell* went down out there?"

The wiry medic was pale, his hands unsteady. "Mass casualties, GSWs. Looks like the work of one shooter."

Grady scowled. "Did SWAT nail the bastard?"

"Perp could be here, self-inflicted. Won't know until the coroner sorts 'em out."

"Any vics not DOA?"

"Yeah." Ronnie inclined his head. "But the dead are the lucky ones."

Two firefighters accompanied by Ronnie's EMT partner, Kim Swanson, wheeled in another pair of gurneys. The EMS workers wore the stunned expressions he'd seen on combat soldiers pushed beyond human endurance. Clear plastic isolation tents blanketed the victims. A firefighter with a portable ventilator hose snaked through the tent was doing the breathing for the first vic.

The second victim was screaming.

Grady had fought in combat, both sanctioned and unofficial. Had tried to save men and women whose flesh had been mutilated by fire, knives, bullets, bombs and other human beings. But the high-pitched, animal shrieks curdled his insides. As did the victim's appearance.

The man's blistered skin appeared to have peeled off in sheets, as if his entire body had been scalded. Bloody lymphatic fluid wept from raw, exposed tissues, and blood streamed from his nose, mouth, eyes and ears.

"Oh my God," Sabrina whispered. Her hand went to her throat, and she staggered. "I've seen this before."

Chapter 6

6:00 a.m.

"Easy, sweetheart." Grady slid an arm around Sabrina's shoulders as she swayed. "Let's take a walk." He led her away from the carnage into a vacant exam room.

Pale and shaking, eyes blank with shock, she buried her face in his chest and shuddered.

"It's all right." He wrapped his arms around her. Her silence worried him. "Sabrina, talk to me."

Her fingers fisted in his T-shirt, and hot, silent tears soaked through to his skin.

"Okay." He stroked her hair. "It's okay." He'd never seen his intrepid girl this rattled. Hell, yesterday she'd unflinchingly confronted two hit men and imminent execution.

"Here, sit down." Grady tried to guide her to a chair in the corner, but she was too unsteady to walk. He scooped her up and carried her, then sat cradling her in his lap.

Trembling, she clung to him.

"I've got you, sweetheart." He rubbed her back. The trauma victims were afflicted with a condition he'd never run across. Yet Sabrina had recognized it. The false patient call this morning had specifically summoned her here, now. Uneasiness wormed in Grady's gut. Was it possible someone had staged the horror show in the ER? Engineered it for Sabrina's "benefit"?

How? The wild hypothesis made no sense, but he couldn't shake his dread. Why over a dozen gunshot fatalities and two vics with... What had caused them to be skinned alive? Would someone commit mass murder to send Sabrina a warning?

His arms tightened around her quaking body. Whatever hornets' nest her grandfather had disturbed was lethal. And Grady would do whatever was necessary to ensure she didn't get stung.

He briskly rubbed her back. "I'm here." He rocked her. "You can talk to me, about anything."

She inhaled a quivering breath. Hesitated.

"Tell me, Sabrina."

"Wh-what's killing those men is a rare condition called toxic epidermal necrolysis. TEN."

Grady frowned. "You're sure they're going to die?"

"TEN has a sixty percent mortality rate when diagnosed *early.*" She gulped. "They're in the advanced stage."

A clutch of fear gripped him. He'd thought the medics had encased the men in isolation tents to prevent infection of raw subcutaneous tissue. She'd been standing right next to the screaming victim. "Is it communicable?" At her negative response, he relaxed a fraction. "What's the etiology and how does it manifest?"

"It's caused by hypersensitivity to medication. Like an allergic reaction, only magnified. The progression is *awful.* The patient develops a high fever and rash, and the skin blisters as if their entire body was scalded. Their skin peels off in sheets, exposing tissues and muscles...and causing unbearable pain." She inhaled another choppy breath. "All the mucus membranes, including those inside the mouth, nose and esophagus, disintegrate. Multiorgan failure follows, and the patient bleeds out."

He swore softly. "And you encountered this *where?*"

"It was...slightly over a year ago. I'd been accompanying a young patient named Isaiah to chemo for seven months." Her lips wobbled, and she pressed them together. "His treatment was progressing well, but I tried not to grow too attached. You know how it rips your heart out."

"Yeah. I've seen veteran cops and medics fall apart on an incident site with kids involved." He'd lost it on several gutwrenching calls. He tried not to think about them often, but they

were still branded into his psyche. He didn't know how Sabrina
handled working with terminally ill children. And in spite of he
efforts not to become personally involved, she cared deeply fo
each one. "Your job requires unique dedication and fortitude."

"Isaiah sailed right past my defenses. He was smart and funny
and compassionate. For being only six, he was incredibly wise. A
amazing little person." Tears welled, spilled over. "Grady—h
was no more than a baby!"

Horror assaulted him. He'd assumed she'd seen the TEN i
another chemo patient. "Are you telling me a six-year-old suffere
through what's making those men…scream in agony?"

"Y-yes. Isaiah had a reaction to one of his cancer drugs. He wa
so sweet. So brave. The doctors loaded him with pain meds, bu
it wasn't enough." Stark desolation stole the light from her eyes
"It took three days for him to die."

"*Damn,* Sabrina." His palm stroked slow, soothing circles ove
her quivering back. "I'm so sorry."

"Right…right at the end, he rallied for a few minutes. I'd starte
to cry. I couldn't help it."

"Of course not. Nobody could."

"I'll never forget…Isaiah looked up and saw me crying. H
slowly reached out to me…and touched my hand." She clutche
Grady's arm, and her nails bit into his skin. "That little boy wa
bleeding, suffering, *dying*…. H-he couldn't speak because…
because, oh God, his throat was gone. And he was breathin
through a ventilator tube. But his final act was a selfless gestur
of comfort. For me."

Grady locked his jaw against the pressure behind his eyelids. H
was supposed to be consoling her. He had to swallow the lump i
his throat before he could speak. "It wrecked you. And no wonder.

"I couldn't stop crying for *days.*"

"Why didn't you come to me? Let me help you?"

"You were…in the middle of Tony DiMarco's trial. You ha
enough on your mind."

She'd stood staunchly beside him during the trial of the ma
who had beaten Brian O'Rourke to death in his own study. Ha
been in court daily. Reliving the trauma had tangled him up s
badly he hadn't questioned her when she'd disappeared for a fe

days. One more failure to support his own. One more nail in his emotional coffin. "I'm sorry, Sabrina."

She firmed her chin. "I was able to make Isaiah's last months better for him. Losing patients is a reality of my profession. If I can't deal, I should be working elsewhere."

They both threw themselves into the line of fire for others. Both took risks for a living. A bolt of insight seared him. While he put his body on the line, Sabrina invested her heart, mind and soul. She was stronger than he was. Braver. She risked parts of herself he wasn't willing to.

Respect and admiration winged through Grady. Hell, he was in *awe* of her. "You have unbelievable courage and strength."

She leaned into him, and holding her felt irrefutably natural. "Blarney. I found them."

"Found what?"

"This morning when I was hunting for socks, I found your drawer stuffed with medals. Bronze stars. Silver stars. Distinguished service. Meritorious service. *Three* distinguished flying crosses."

He shrugged. "Uncle Sammy handed them to me for doing my job."

She smiled at him, her eyes like burnished topaz, gilded lashes sparkling with teardrops. "You are an uncommon individual, Dimples."

Her steady regard told Grady she valued him. Cherished him. Once more, elusive, undeniable peace stole over him. His thumb brushed the dampness from her lashes, caressed her cheek, and then glided of its own accord to stroke the moist silk of her lower lip.

Sabrina's mouth parted on a sigh. Drawn beyond will, he leaned down. He craved a morsel of hope. A sweet sip of forgiveness.

Just one taste.

Sabrina's gaze embraced his. Her shallow breath feathered fast and warm over his mouth. Her own special essence enveloped him, a heady elixir of summer flowers and Sabrina. Their lips touched in a soft whisper, a promise of shimmering heat.

Someone in the room coughed. Loudly.

Grady jerked back. Mere hours ago, he'd vowed never to touch her again. He'd blanked on everything, including where they were. How crazy and stupid could he get?

Angry at the interruption, angrier at himself, Grady yanked his gaze up to see the firefighter who'd been bagging the first TEN victim.

Sabrina scrambled off Grady's lap. "Dalton! I didn't see you before. What are you doing here?"

The muscular firefighter had changed into blue surgical scrubs and his dark wavy hair was wet. His disapproving glance scoured Grady. "Apparently, playing third wheel."

Grady took the guy's measure and didn't like the numbers. The tall fireman was ripped, and his sinuous movements said he had martial arts training. Worse, Grady recognized the possessive glint in the other man's eyes. The fireman was hot for Sabrina. Barbs of unfamiliar emotion bristled inside Grady. He rose and stepped forward in silent, deliberate challenge.

Color flooded Sabrina's face. She clasped Dalton's right hand between both of hers, and Grady saw the fireman's body tense in response. "What happened to those men? Are you okay?"

"We haven't been debriefed yet, but your father ordered decontamination protocol." Lasered by Grady's intent stare, Dalton jerked his head in Grady's direction. "I assume you're the elusive chopper jockey."

"Oh! Right. You guys haven't met." Sabrina's flush deepened. Because she and Grady had been caught kissing, or because she had feelings for the fireman? "Dalton, this is Grady O'Rourke. Grady, Dalton James."

The sight of Dalton's fingers cozily entwined with Sabrina's was like a garrote around Grady's throat. He thrust out his hand. "James."

The fireman released Sabrina to grasp Grady's hand. "O'Rourke." Both squeezed too hard. Neither wanted to be the first to let go.

Sabrina rolled her eyes. "You two have a lot in common."

More than she obviously realized. Dalton finally relinquished his grip, and Grady smirked. "You don't say."

"Yes, you both have a penchant for rescuing people."

Dalton shot him a dark look. "But apparently only one of us has staying power," he muttered.

Grady's upper lip curled in a snarl. "You calling me out, Backdraft?"

"I call 'em as I see 'em. If you can't take the heat—"

Sabrina elbowed Grady aside and scowled up at the other man. "What is wrong with you? *Totally* out of line, pal."

"Sorry, rough shift." Dalton glared at Grady, then scrubbed a weary hand over his face. "Why the urgent voice mails, Sabrina?"

"Remember the package you accepted for me and locked in storage for safekeeping? I need it."

"You bet." He extracted a ring of keys from his pocket, disengaged two and handed them to her. "I'm stuck here until the paperwork is done, but help yourself." The fireman tossed Sabrina a cocky smile. "To anything you want. And if you need me, just call. Day or night."

Grady clenched his teeth, struggling not to punch the guy's ticket. "I'm watching her back."

"You'd better be." Dalton pivoted and stalked from the room.

"What got into him?" Sabrina ruefully shook her head. "He's usually not so intense. The TEN victims must really have thrown him off balance."

"Your friend seemed to have a problem with me. You talk to him about…" *Us?* "ah…personal stuff?"

"*No.*" She gnawed her lower lip. "I mean, I mentioned you from time to time. And Dalton knew I was—I was hurt when you didn't make Granddad's funeral."

"I was headed back. Then some brilliant ex-CIA suit decided to conduct an archaeological dig on the Kuwaiti-Iranian border and got his retired ass kidnapped. Along with his wife."

Sabrina gasped. "I saw them interviewed on CNN. They said the only reason everyone didn't die was because the pilot kept his cool and did some crazy flying. Over a thousand rounds were fired on the rescue chopper. That was *you?*"

"The op wasn't as dire as the media made it sound."

"But you saved them." She nodded. "Granddad would have approved. He really liked you, you know. He always hoped—" Her gaze dropped to the keys in her hand. "We should go."

Interesting that she didn't see Dalton was carrying a torch for her. Grady cased the parking lot as they hurried to the Jeep. Well, he sure wasn't clueing her in to the competition.

He stabbed the key in the ignition and revved the engine, choosing to ignore his faulty reasoning. *How could Dalton be his competition if Grady wasn't even in the race?*

A fragrant breeze poured in through the scant inch he'd cracked the windows, pumping renewed energy through his veins. Summer was his favorite season. Long, hot months with plenty of daylight to expend in the great outdoors.

Grady zigzagged through traffic, making decent time. The fireman seemed capable, intelligent and clearly cared about Sabrina. He'd know the toll of losing people he'd attempted to save and would understand the stresses of Sabrina's job.

They were perfect for each other.

He viciously stomped the gas and swerved around a truck. He wanted Sabrina to forget the past, forget *him,* and move on. Marry, have kids. Grady had to step out of the picture and let her live the life she deserved. His stomach cramped. The thought of Sabrina as another man's lover seared him with a red-hot poker through the guts.

And the thought of a future without her left him hollow and aching.

He parked at her apartment complex. If he were a selfish bastard, he'd just sleep with her. Purge her from his system. After the kiss back at his houseboat, he had no doubts she could be seduced into his bed.

Unfortunately, making love to Sabrina once wouldn't do the job. When he gave her a hand out of the Jeep, her lips parted in a smile that arrowed into his soul, and his heart stuttered. Damn, a *hundred* times wouldn't do it. Besides, he would never hurt her, in any way.

He did a fast visual sweep of the area. Under the pretext of brushing a kiss on her temple, he whispered in her ear. "Your mystery assailants might be surveilling your apartment complex and have satellite audio devices in the area. Keep it casual."

She shivered and moved closer to him, and he winked at her. "Nice weather we're having."

Her smile bounced back. "Perfect for a driving lesson."

Inside Dalton's storage unit, boxes and bags were stacked in neat rows beside well-used luggage and a primo set of golf clubs.

Sabrina indicated a skydiving rig. "Another thing you guys have in common. Dalton lives to smoke jump during forest fire season."

Grady bit his tongue on a retort about who Dalton really wanted to jump. Dammit, he wasn't in junior high. "Where's the package?" he whispered in her ear. His breath stirred the baby-fine tendrils at her nape, and she shivered again.

"He locked it inside his fireproof safe," she whispered in reply. "He's careful that way."

Grady's tongue was gonna be hamburger at this rate. He watched as she unlocked the safe and extracted a large Tyvek mailing envelope.

She started to tear it open and he stopped her. "Not here," he murmured. He eyed the golf equipment. Smiled. *Driving lesson.* "Glad Backdraft doesn't mind if we borrow his clubs," he said aloud to mask the sound of unzipping the bag, tucking the envelope inside and rezipping. Much better camouflage than stuffing the package inside his jacket. "Been years since I hit a hole in one."

"Aww, too bad." Sabrina blinked in mock concern. "Defective wood?"

Grinning, he shouldered the bag. "Nah, I get more loft with my nine iron."

Her lips quirked, and then her expression inexplicably sobered. "Just so you know—" she looked up at him, her face earnest "—I believe everyone is entitled to one mulligan."

She was offering him another shot. A second chance to fix his mistakes. Warmth wreathed his heart, followed by an icy punch of pain. He had to live with the consequences of his actions, but Sabrina didn't deserve to pay for them. Would he ever reconcile how he felt with his obligation to her? Honor was a bitch...wielding a double-edged sword. Sabrina was right. He couldn't keep doing this to her—or himself. When the case was wrapped, he had to go.

Forever.

Grady turned and walked to the door. He flicked off the light, leaving the room, and his heart, shrouded in darkness.

Sabrina stood alone in the murky storage compartment and released a frustrated sigh. In a heartbeat, Grady had morphed from laughing, teasing companion to closed-off warrior.

Damn him, he'd withdrawn again.

He'd only gone as far as the hallway, but may as well have put a continent between them. She fought the urge to pound the wall and scream. She'd been making progress until the threat of real intimacy had slammed his blast doors shut.

He stuck his head in the doorway. "We have to keep moving, Sabrina. It's not safe to linger."

His life philosophy. Sabrina stomped out, yanked the compartment closed and locked it. Sometimes, she just wanted to *slug* him. Did that make her a terrible person? Sure, he was fearful, but so was she. *Everybody* was freaked at first. Relationships—of all types—were scary. *So what?*

What they could have together was worth any risk.

She marched out to the Jeep beside him, almost wishing her pursuers *would* show. She was so in the mood to kick butts and take names.

Grady hefted the golf bag into the backseat while she buckled her seat belt. When he pulled into traffic, Sabrina plugged in a Celtic Woman CD without consulting him. They'd been consistently using music to camouflage conversation, and this time, she was getting *her* choice. The CD whirred, and the ethereal beauty of "The Prayer" floated into the air, soothing her temper. The poignant lyrics reminded her what was truly important. That everyone deserved some grace. "Bailey plays this song to close every meeting of the police officers' wives support group she started."

Grady's expression turned thoughtful. "Ah. That's why she gave it to all of us guys. A prayer for our safety."

Actually Sabrina had asked Bailey to give one to Grady, but that intel was on a need-to-know basis. "She's really come to grips with being a cop's wife. Police wives have to be so strong. Heck, all first-responders' spouses do."

"Including firefighters' wives." Grady's tone was oh, so casual, but whoo, baby, the glare he fired out the windshield should have blistered the paint. "Sounds like you've thought about it."

Surprise stole her voice. Grady was *jealous*. Of Dalton! *That* was the reason for the testosterone spill back at the hospital! Okay, she'd looked at Dalton; she wasn't eighty, or blind. They'd done some casual dates, shared a lot of laughs and a few kisses. She'd *wanted* to feel more for the appealing fireman, wanted to get over Grady and find the peace that eluded her. But she couldn't banish Grady from her thoughts…or her heart. Dalton had conceded to her decision not to jeopardize their relationship as friends and neighbors.

Both men were tall, dark and delicious, but the comparison

ended there. Dalton didn't possess her daredevil's penetrating gray-green eyes and smoky voice. Dalton's presence didn't steal all the oxygen from the room. His kisses didn't turn the universe upside down and inside out.

She studied Grady's strong profile, his narrowed eyes and set mouth. The attraction wasn't merely physical. She and Grady had been best friends since they were five. They *got* each other...like nobody else. They stuck up for each other. Worried about each other. Had shared hopes and fears, secrets and dreams.

Their feelings ran deep...on both sides.

Heck, despite the absence of sex and the current tension between them, she and Grady had a better relationship than most couples. For over two decades. Which made his terror totally bewildering.

She started to reassure Grady that nobody compared to him, and then stopped. He was a thrill seeker, and there was nothing men loved better than the thrill of the hunt. Maybe letting him think he had a rival would inspire him to examine his true feelings. Hey, every weapon was fair in love and war. And the battle between them was definitely both.

Grady stopped the Jeep for a red light, pulled out his James Bond TCU contraption and redialed. Dialed again. Clearly disconcerted, he disconnected and stuffed it into his pocket. The light changed, and he hit the gas. "Still nothing from Mom. And neither of the brothers I assume are still speaking to me answered."

"Con's probably home by now. Do you want me to call him?"

"He'd know you were on a fishing expedition." His fingers drummed the steering wheel. "Anyway, it's not your problem."

"Your problems *are* my problems, Grady." *In more ways than one.*

"No," he declared hotly. "They aren't. That's exactly what I'm trying to avoid."

There was no question in Sabrina's mind that he wanted her sexually. Needed her emotionally. Seriously cared for her. But he was too leery to move forward. She could understand his fears, empathize with his pain. Losing her mom at such a young age had taught her that life *was* scary. But also unpredictable and way too short.

What on earth had happened to make him erroneously believe that braving an unknown future alone was better than being with someone you loved and trusted?

She watched him assess dwindling traffic as they drove out of town, and she checked her side mirror. "Nobody seems to be following."

"Or—" He shook his head.

"They're too good to be seen. Or waiting to ambush us."

"I knew trying to blow sunshine up your skirt was futile." He smiled wryly.

He turned down the deserted gravel road to his houseboat. No, she wasn't anyone's little merry sunshine. And eventually she'd figure out what was messing with his head.

Grady shut off the Jeep. She climbed out and stared at his sleek black helicopter he'd parked in the grassy field in front of the dock. "Is that lethal-looking machine yours?"

"The guy who runs the outfit I work for owed me a favor. He'll get the chopper back."

When Grady left. The unspoken words resonated in the air. Sabrina squared her shoulders. Circumstances had forced her hand. Things had gone too far…there was no turning back. If he hopped in that chopper and flew away after this was over, he was gone for good.

She marched inside. But for now she had the opportunity to help him desensitize his fears. She just prayed he stuck around long enough.

She wanted him more than anything, but she wasn't a martyr. One mulligan…and then she was done offering her heart for him to stomp on.

Grady entered the kitchen behind her and swung the golf bag to the floor with a graceful shrug. Sabrina crushed her longing, steeled herself against the pain. She had to prepare for the eventuality that he might leave her again.

She would have to find the strength to plan the rest of her life without Grady.

"You ready for this?"

Sabrina started. He was holding out the envelope.

Swallowing hard, she took it. Her reply rang with double meaning. "Ready as I'll ever be."

Chapter 7

An ordinary package. A Tyvek envelope found in post offices everywhere.

Sabrina's hands shook as she stared at her name and address scribbled in black ink. The same bold script had winged encouragement and surprises to her as long as she could remember. Except the letters were wobbly and unevenly spaced, as if Granddad had been unsteady. Or hurried.

Memories of her irascible, witty grandfather swirled like sparkling motes in a sunbeam. Her chest tight and aching, she traced the letters of her name. One remaining link. Once she opened it, Granddad's death was final, his absence from her life absolute.

This was the last gift she would ever receive from her grandfather.

Grady slid an arm around her, drew her close. His warm, solid strength offered comfort. "Do you want me to do it?"

"No. He sent it to me." He passed her a knife, and she slit open the flap. The contents were padded with crumpled industrial-type paper towels. She emptied the envelope onto the counter.

They stared at the items, then each other.

Sabrina bit her lip. "This makes zero sense."

Grady lifted the rosary, and the delicate gold chain and carved white roses spilled over his masculine hands. "I've never seen anything like this. It's two rosaries joined into one."

"Granddad wasn't Catholic. Or even particularly religious." She frowned. "Is it an artifact? Something valuable?"

"It appears to be carved ivory, but I don't think so. The beads are worn on the edges. It's been well used and the workmanship is modern."

She picked up the other item, a homemade paper card. The cross graphic and simple font were typical choices included with a basic computer print program. Granddad had probably created it on his laptop. She read aloud:

"Ask and it will be given to you; seek and you will find; knock and the door will be opened to you. For everyone who asks, receives; he who seeks finds; and to him who asks, the door will be opened."

She laid it back on the countertop. "Why would Granddad send me a rosary and prayer card?"

Grady read the envelope. "No return address. Postmarked February twenty-first. Sacramento, California."

Sabrina gasped. "That's the day he died! When Granddad had his heart attack, he was checked into a Sacramento motel. He must have put it in the mail right before—" Her voice faltered. "Maybe he got confused. Maybe if he'd called for medical help instead of assembling this package, he'd still be alive."

"Not Filibuster Bill. He was too sharp. I'm sure he knew exactly what he was doing."

She glanced at the shaky handwriting again and swallowed hard. "Sending this was the last thing he did."

"Then it has to be important. Bill expected you to figure it out."

"Grady, there's something you don't know." She leaned against him. "We managed to keep it from the media, but there were…concerns about Granddad's mental state. Two months before he died, his housekeeper found him wandering outside in his pajamas at 4:00 a.m. And he had rambled several times during Senate meetings. Medical tests didn't reveal anything, but his doctor couldn't rule out the onset of dementia."

"No way. Not buying it." Grady's arm tightened around her, and his palm stroked her spine. "Hell, maybe he went to fetch the newspaper and got locked out. And if rambling in congress indicated insanity, three-quarters of our elected officials would be wearing white jackets with sleeves that tie in the back."

A smile sneaked out. "Good point. There has to be a reason why the suits were willing to kill for this."

"You said you received a phone call a few days ago. Tell me everything you remember."

"It was a woman's voice, low and rapid, like she was nervous, or in a hurry. She asked, 'Did you get the envelope?' She sounded older than me, but not elderly...probably in her forties or fifties. Oh, and she had an accent, Hispanic, I think."

"Did she know your name, and was the call on your home or cell phone?"

"She asked for Sabrina Matthews, and it came to my cell. Could she be the person who hired you to rescue me?"

"Possibly. Either way, I have questions for our mystery woman. Did you dump the number from your received calls yet?"

"No!"

"Now we're getting somewhere." Twin dimples flashed, and her heart skipped. He retrieved the number from her phone and dialed his TCU. "No answer."

"I tried calling back yesterday, and nobody answered then, either."

He used his TCU for an Internet reverse-number search. "Nothing. I'll call Riverside PD and request a trace." He completed the call and shoved the unit into his pocket. "They'll call back with any info." He picked up the card and leaned his elbows on the counter. "Now, to break the encryption."

"'Seek and you will find.' If this *is* a message, Granddad was telling me to look for something."

Grady straightened. "I know these verses. New Testament." He pulled out his TCU again and typed the phrases into an internet Bible search engine. "Ha! The book of Matthew, chapter seven, verses seven and eight."

"All those years of giving the sisters fits in Sunday school paid off." She smiled, enjoying watching his quick mind work the problem. Sharp intellect lurked behind his gorgeous face. "Perhaps the numbers correspond with something important."

"Too few for a phone number. Not specific enough for an

address. Navigational coordinates?" He opened another search and keyed in numerical combinations for longitude and latitude. "Sri Lanka. Nigeria." He snorted. "The middle of the Arctic Ocean."

"'Knock, and the door will be opened.' Are we making it too hard? What if the numbers open the combination to a locker or a safe?"

"Did your grandfather own a safe, or rent a locker?"

"I'm not sure about a safe. His golf club has lockers, but that hardly seems secure."

"As savvy as Bill was, he'd know the bad guys would search everywhere."

"Hmm. 'Seek and knock.' You said it's from the book of Matthew. Could it be a play on my last name, Matthews?"

"But why send a rosary?" Grady took the card from her, studied it. "Matthew...Matthews. *St. Matthew's!*"

"The church?"

"No place your secrets are safer than with a priest. Confessional confidentiality is protected by secular *and* spiritual laws."

"I suppose Granddad *might* have left something for me in the church, but how do we know we're not haring off on a faulty assumption?"

Grinning, he waved the card. "Because that's a Celtic cross. And I happen to be an Irish boy who grew up in St. Matthew's parish, which is seven blocks from Mom's house. On Seventy-eighth Street." He keyed in a command that erased his searches and repocketed the device. "Let's rock!"

Twenty minutes later Sabrina walked up the stone steps of St. Matthew's hand in hand with Grady.

Entering the huge church always made her feel as if she should tiptoe inside. As a kid, she'd occasionally attended Sunday school with Grady and his family. She'd been beside him when he was ashen and silent during his father's memorial service. Watched him proudly stand up for his brothers at their weddings.

The familiar fragrance of incense, polished wood and reverence drew her in. The hushed interior was resplendent with burnished woodwork and gleaming marble. Stained-glass windows sparkled like jewels. Rows of votive candles glimmered in red glass jars, each bright flame a petitioner's prayer.

Grady dipped his fingertips in the holy water and crossed himself. As they walked along the carpet, she tried to read his solemn expression. She'd dreamed of gliding down this long aisle in a beautiful white gown, with their friends and family on either side, and Grady awaiting her at the altar.

What did he dream of in secret? What was he thinking with his expression somber, his beautiful eyes wistful? Did he wonder about his future? Wonder if they could have a future together?

Sabrina sighed. Probably not, because he didn't turn and bolt. If kissing her sent Grady into a tailspin, the idea of marrying her would wig him out.

The priest bustled in from a side door. The gray-haired man saw them and smiled. "Well, I'll be. Trouble on legs just strolled into my church." Warm blue eyes twinkled, and he clasped a hand over his heart. "Here for confession, are you, Grady? And with only three hours till next Mass."

Grady chuckled as they crossed the room to greet the priest. "Lucky for you, I don't have time today to do the penance. Father, you remember Sabrina Matthews?"

"Indeed. It's a pleasure to see you again."

"Nice to see you, as well, Father Niall."

"I was sorry to hear of your grandfather's passing. He was brilliant, that one."

"So you *did* know him?"

"We met at a young parishioner's funeral. Hit it right off. Spent a fair amount of time together toward the last."

"Granddad never said a word about it."

Grady withdrew the rosary from his jacket pocket. "Do you recognize this, Father?"

The priest took the rosary from him and examined it. "It's a lazzo, a Hispanic wedding rosary. What would you be wanting with that?"

"I...ah—"

Both amused and touched, Sabrina saw dismay flicker across Grady's face as his instincts to protect Father Niall from danger warred with the idea of fibbing to his priest.

"The rosary was a gift," Sabrina said, then forged ahead. "Did Granddad leave a message or something here for me?"

"That he did." The priest inclined his head at Grady. "And William's note instructed me to give it to you only if you came here asking with this scamp."

Sabrina frowned. She hadn't been able to keep her feelings for Grady a secret from her discerning grandfather. Was the wedding rosary and subsequent scavenger hunt an elaborate, last-ditch match-making attempt? Had Granddad truly lost his mental faculties, and with his dying breath taken a befuddled gamble to make her happy?

Father Niall held out his hand. "Come to my office, then, and I'll get it for you."

Like everything that had happened during the past twenty-four hours, her theory didn't jibe. Professional hit men wouldn't have attempted to kill her over a marriage rosary and Bible verses.

They followed Father Niall down the hallway to a wildly cluttered office. He unlocked the bottom drawer of his desk, riffled the contents. "Ah, here." He straightened and handed Sabrina another Tyvek envelope.

Postmarked Sacramento, the bulky, heavy envelope bore the same date as hers. But it was addressed to Father Niall at the church...and had been opened by him.

Sabrina glanced at Grady, and he nodded.

Her pulse kicked as she reached inside and withdrew a battered hardcover book. She scanned the brown embossed cover, then hurriedly flipped through the pages. No secret compartment, no stashed envelope, no letter. *Nothing.* "Granddad sent you a *Bible* to give me?"

"William's note said to tell you it's your guide. He wanted you to know how proud he is that you're carrying on his legacy."

"*Oh.*" Her shoulders slumped. Considering everything she and Grady had been through, Granddad's message, while well meant, was anticlimactic. "Thank you, Father Niall."

"Take heart." The priest patted her shoulder. "Your grandfather is at peace."

They said goodbye to Father Niall. On the way out Grady stopped at the bank of candles. "Hey, can't hurt." He lit one and she followed suit. They stood silently, heads bowed. While she was at it, she added a more personal petition. She needed all the help she could get.

She walked with him to his Jeep, climbed in and settled the Bible on top of her purse at her feet.

He pulled into traffic, and she watched him effortlessly shift and steer. She had watched in awe as his hands had tenderly fed an orphaned kitten with a doll's bottle. Watched in pleased surprise as they'd carried a bouquet of daisies to her bedside when she'd broken her wrist sliding in after a home run. Observed in admiration as his hands had performed inventive and often dangerous science experiments.

Every poignant memory in her life was touched by Grady.

Neither spoke until they were heading out of town. She rolled her head to ease taut muscles. "Where do we go from here? We've hit a dead end."

"Have a little faith."

Sabrina wearily leaned back, closed her eyes. "In what, Grady?"

"In your grandfather." His voice went soft. "In me."

She so badly wanted to believe in Grady. Believe in *them.* Believe that love eventually triumphed and some people were gifted with happily-ever-after. But it was getting damn hard. "At the moment my faith is a bit shaky."

"Gran always said, 'Faith isn't really faith until it's all you're clinging to.'"

If she lost hope, she might as well check out now. Life without hope wasn't worth living. "You're *right.*" She opened her eyes, ashamed of her momentary lapse. "And Granddad used to say, 'Don't let the bastards win.' I am *not* giving up this easily." Not on Grandad. Not on Grady.

"That's my girl." His smile lightened her heart. "Let's start at the beginning and work forward."

"The California Senate is in Sacramento, and Granddad was checked into the motel under an alias."

"If his poking around disturbed the Men in Black, it's likely he stumbled across a conspiracy or some sort of corruption."

"Corruption in a government organization? Surely you jest."

His snort of laughter was interrupted by a sharp inhalation. His eyes narrowed at the road. "And there it is."

She jerked her attention out the windshield. An overturned truck blocked the road. Two other drivers had stopped and were helping the truck's driver light flares. "It's a wreck."

His glance swept the mirrors. "No, it's an ambush."

"How do you—"

"Experience." He slammed down the brake and clutch, geared into Reverse and whipped the wheel around. The Jeep lurched backward and spun a one-eighty turn. Grady stomped the gas and sped in the opposite direction.

A quarter mile ahead, a semi rumbled from a side road and straddled the highway at an angle.

"Hang on!" Grady yanked the steering wheel sideways and the Jeep careened off the pavement, bumped through the ditch and into a field. "God bless four-wheel drive!"

She looked back. The rear panel of the semi slid upward and three motorcycles with black-leather-clad, black-helmeted riders roared out and raced toward them. "Grady! Motorbikes!"

"Dammit!" He rocketed the Jeep toward a cluster of bushes. "Who *are* these people?"

She clung to the roll bar. "I don't want an introduction."

"No worries, darlin'." He grinned fiercely as the Jeep tore through the terrain, and dirt jettisoned over their pursuers.

Two bikes split off and edged up on both sides. "They're gaining!"

"Bastards, trying to cut me off." One hand on the steering wheel, the other wrenching the gear shift, Grady swerved toward the motorcycle on his side. "Get the windows up! And grab my gun—back waistband."

Grady had only left the windows open a scant inch. She stabbed the window button, but the biker on her right edged close enough to thrust black-gloved fingers through the opening and attempt to shove it down again.

She released her seat belt, snatched the heavy Bible and pounded his fingers. "Get off, creep!" He jerked away, steering out of reach.

"And thank you, Grandpa, for the Good Book."

A thump jarred the back bumper, and the third biker climbed up the back of the Jeep. "Grady! Leech at six o'clock!"

"I see him. Get the gun!"

She struggled to lean over the console amidst the wild swerving. "Why aren't they shooting?"

"Dead men can't answer questions. They want us alive. We're not so picky."

Sabrina fumbled at his back waistband. As her fingers closed around the grip, a jagged knife blade speared through the ragtop roof between them. A gloved fist sliced the knife downward, narrowly missing Grady.

Sabrina screamed and he ducked, rocking the Jeep and throwing her sideways. The gun winged out of her grasp and onto the back floorboards.

Grady swore, and his hand clamped onto the attacker's wrist. His steering grew even more erratic. "Okay, they want *you* alive."

"I dropped the gun!" She hung over the edge of the seat, feeling frantically for the weapon.

"Forget it. Help me out here."

The two bikers at their sides had caught up and stood on the running boards, clinging to both doors. They raised steel rods and smashed the windows. Safety glass shattered into glittering webs and crumpled inward, opening fist-size holes.

Gloved hands thrust inside, and the man beside Grady brandished a gun. "Pull over!" The throaty command echoed eerily through his helmet.

Grady grunted, still fighting a one-handed war with the knife bearer. "Sure thing, Darth Vader." The Jeep arrowed through a gap between two pines, and a sturdy trunk grazed the assailant, knocking the man free of the vehicle.

Sabrina unlocked her door and shoved her shoulder into it. Her door crashed open and limbs on the second tree caught her attacker and flung him to the ground.

"Nice going, honey!" Grady laughed. "The Force is strong within you."

"You're craz—" The Jeep jolted out the other side of the clearing and onto a rutted logging road, throwing her halfway out the open doorway.

Sabrina yelped and scrabbled to hang on, but her fingers slipped off the leather seat. Dirt and rocks rushed past beneath her. She couldn't hang on. Couldn't stop her fall!

Flailing in vain for a firm hold, she screamed as she pitched headfirst out of the Jeep.

Chapter 8

8:00 a.m.

The rushing road blurred, inches from Sabrina's face. She slammed her eyes shut, bracing for impact.

"Sabrina!" Grady's hand grabbed the back of her hoodie and yanked her inside.

He'd had to release the knife-wielding attacker to save her. The knife slashed the ragtop, and the man's helmet and upper body speared through. Grady dodged the blade, and Sabrina grabbed the assailant's arm.

The guy was too strong to restrain for long. Hitting him with the Bible would only slow him temporarily. And she couldn't find the gun in time. The solution struck her like an answer to a prayer...and maybe it was. "Grady, faster!"

No questions. He merely geared up and punched the gas.

Sabrina lunged at the dash and mimicked motions she'd seen Grady perform a hundred times. She hit the button that unlocked the bolts and flipped the hydraulic lever to raise the ragtop. The top ratcheted up a foot, then another, and wind caught canvas.

A grinding mechanical shriek split the air, metal twisted and the canopy ripped off and sailed into the sky—carrying their assailant with it.

Stunned, Grady stared into his rearview mirror. Then he looked at her, threw back his head and laughed. "*Yee haw!* Did you *see* that dude soar outta here?" He grinned, his eyes sparkling. "You are *awesome,* woman!"

She didn't feel awesome. She felt like throwing up. That knife had been too close to Grady. "Th-thanks," she managed.

The Jeep bounced over another rut. Her door rebounded and loosely latched, rattling as they sped down the primitive track. She buckled her seat belt, no small feat with numb, quivering fingers.

Grady rapidly put distance between them and the attackers. After several miles, he pulled the Jeep to the shoulder. "Secure your door."

She opened her door and yanked it shut again, shuddering at the glimpse of boulders and tree stumps. If Grady didn't possess incredible reflexes, she'd have been ground into hamburger.

"You're not hurt, are you?" He leaned over and wrapped warm, muscular arms around her.

Trembling, she closed her eyes and let him hold her. She needed to hear his heart beating, strong and vital.

"Sabrina? You all right?"

Aside from gargling stark terror for the past fifteen minutes? "I'm…um…yes. Fine. I'm fine."

He kissed her forehead. "Your agile brain saved our butts."

She dragged in a breath, and her pulse chugged down to double digits. "You gave a decent accounting yourself. Even if you are nuts."

"Appreciate the official diagnosis." Chuckling, he jumped out and rummaged on the back floorboards for his gun, and she leaned over the console to watch. He disappeared behind his seat. "I needed three hands today, though. Lucky for me you were here to lend one."

"The reason you're under attack is *because* I'm here. It's *my* fault you almost got shot." She shuddered. "Or knifed."

"Guilt?" he growled. "You aren't responsible for my safety. Guilt's not an option."

"*Ahem.* Pot, meet kettle."

"Baby, if it wasn't stormtroopers on motorcycles, it'd be terrorists, smugglers or drug dealers. Some lunatic is always itching to take a crack at me." He jammed the pistol in his back waistband. "I even fly without training wheels now."

He climbed into the Jeep. He cupped her cheek, and his thumb stroked her face. "I couldn't have asked for a better partner today. You kept your cool, and your improv under fire was inspired."

"I'm sorry I fumbled and dropped the gun." She grimaced. "Not that I know how to shoot. If I'd tried to use it, I might have caused a disaster."

"Not when I'm in charge of disaster control." The engine roared to life, and he pulled onto the road. "I'm taking over where your guardian angel left off."

"I think that ship has sailed, Captain Solo."

Grady sped to his houseboat. After he disarmed his alarm system and performed a security check, he told her to grab a snack while he scouted the property.

Sabrina set her purse on a chair and shrugged out of her hoodie. Bemused, she examined the contents of Grady's fridge. Behind the Guinness and root beer, she found fresh veggies, organic fruit and sunflower-soy protein bars. She smiled, oddly reassured by the stash of health food. Her fearless flyboy wasn't as laissez-faire about his well-being as he appeared.

When he called her outside, she snatched up her purse and carried protein bars and a bottle of apple juice to him. He thanked her and wolfed them down while he escorted her into the meadow beside the houseboat. She looked around the clearing. He'd chosen the spot with care. The helicopter protected them on one side, the houseboat on the other, and the river angled across the front.

He'd draped his jacket over a post. The muted sage of his T-shirt teased silver highlights from his eyes, the luminous green pools as deep and compelling as the sun-dappled river in the distance.

She reluctantly broke eye contact. "Seems like a weird time for a picnic."

"I'm solving a problem, and the sooner the better." He pulled the Glock from his jeans.

"I know I've been a pain, but isn't shooting me rather messy? Think of the paperwork."

He grinned. "I'm not the shooter. You are."

"That would be a big *no*." She backpedaled. "I don't want to hold death in my hands."

"Someone is pretty damned determined to get to you." He held out the gun. "Take your *life* in your hands."

"When you put it that way..." She set her purse in the grass and gingerly wrapped her fingers around the thick grip. "It's larger than I realized. And weighs a *ton*."

"Just hold it until you feel comfortable with the weight and balance."

"Please tell me there's a safety button that stops it from accidentally discharging."

He stepped behind her. Sunshine bathed her head and bare arms, and Grady's big, solid body radiated warmth at her back. "This is a Glock 20, favored by law enforcement and military personnel. There's no safety. It's combat ready."

"Yikes! No wonder you're standing behind me! Take it back!"

"Relax, safety features are built into the firing sequence. Keep your finger off the trigger until you've committed to shoot." He showed her how to chamber a round. "She's locked and loaded. The bullets punch in with enough velocity to penetrate seventeen layers of sheetrock. Don't fire unless you have a clear background."

She gulped. "I don't like this."

"Once you've practiced enough, it'll feel like second nature." He moved closer, his hard-muscled thighs snug against her bottom. His knee nudged her legs apart. "Widen your stance or the recoil will knock you on your butt."

He slid his arms around her. His body surrounded her. His hands encircled her wrists, his cheek settled against hers. "Lock your elbows and sight down the barrel at the targets I lined up."

His nearness spiked her senses, and fear evaporated. He smelled scrumptious, the uniquely Grady scent of warm, clean man and refreshing citrus. She inhaled deeply, loving the feel of him strong and steady behind her. Loving his bristled cheek pressed intimately to hers.

A new sensation stole her breath, deeper than the camaraderie they shared, more potent than the desire arcing between them. Something richer. Stronger.

Exhilaration blossomed inside her and tingled through her veins. Not from the lethal weapon she held in her hands. The powerful, glittering energy radiated from her connection to Grady.

"Sabrina?"

The world refocused. Once more she heard Grady's smoky voice, felt his warm breath in her ear and grew aware of the hard, heated length of him against her back. The Glock wasn't the only huge weapon in play.

She blinked. "Sorry, what did you say?"

"Concentrate, sweetheart. I might not always be around, and knowing this could save your life."

He was teaching her to protect herself, planning for when he left. "I've been taking care of myself for years." Sabrina clenched her jaw. She would fight for him, harder than she'd fought for anything.

"Normally, this weapon shoots fifteen rounds. Mine is fitted with a floor plate for two extra, and if there's one in the chamber, you get eighteen. Now don't pull the trigger, squeeze with one smooth motion."

The explosive roar and jerk of the recoil startled her, but Grady held her steady. "If you have to shoot someone, commit fully. Use everything you've got, empty the clip."

"That wasn't as scary as I thought."

"Good, keep practicing. Stay focused on the target."

"Oh, I will." Sabrina leaned into him and gloried in his indrawn breath, the leap of his heart. If she had her way, she wouldn't be the only one whose fears would dissipate, given enough familiarity. *I'll use every bit of ammo at my disposal.*

And I fight to win.

Sabrina disintegrated four juice cartons, six Guinness bottles and Grady's self-composure before her cell phone chimed and halted the torture.

Grady palmed his gun and stepped back so she could retrieve her purse. He wiped his perspiring face on his forearm and studied the verdant landscape. For early summer, it was as hot as the outer hinges of hell.

He emptied the chamber, stuffed the Glock into his waistband and smiled wryly. There was far less room in his jeans since he'd started teaching Sabrina to handle his weapon. He glanced at the sweet feminine curves he'd been snuggled against, and his belly clenched. Target practice had never been an erotic exercise before.

She wasn't bad with a firearm, but Sabrina was hitting *his* bull's-eye every damn time.

Grady swore beneath his breath. He was trapped in his own personal purgatory.

Sabrina disconnected the call. "That was Christina at Mercy. Your mom just arrived at the hospital, but Christina couldn't flag her down before Maureen dashed upstairs. If we hurry, we can probably catch her."

Grady scanned the perimeter, debating the wisdom of going mobile again. He could leave a message with the switchboard and hope his mom checked in before she left. However, the pros who were after Sabrina seemed hesitant to expose themselves, attacking in isolated situations. They'd already scoped his route and attempted an ambush. Alex's backup and Grady's security system had secured the houseboat so far, but an assault was only a matter of time.

The smartest tactical plan was to move into a police safe house.

He loaded up on ammo and had her pack an overnight bag. When she headed for the Jeep, he steered her toward the chopper. "You said you wanted to fly with me."

Her brows scrunched. "I thought we were going to the hospital and then a safe house."

"Not in a topless Jeep that's been ID'd and compromised. Mercy has a three-chopper helipad, and the bird will be closer if we need to bug out in a hurry."

Grady strapped her in and placed miked headphones over her ears. He jogged to the pilot's seat and jumped in. As he donned his earphones and powered up, she stared around the interior, eyes wide. "I hate to appear finicky, but where are the *doors?*"

"I flew her doors-off for my earlier mission. When I got the orders with your name, I didn't waste precious minutes reattaching them." *Thank all the saints.* He went cold again thinking about how close she'd been to death.

He contacted aircraft control with his flight plan, throttled to flight speed and unlocked the controls. He pulled pitch and the chopper zoomed skyward, the rotor wash kicking up dust. Pulling into a steep vertical climb, he rolled left to miss the trees ringing the field. A battle maneuver that had saved his ass more than once. *Crank and yank.*

Sabrina's yelp echoed in his earphones. Her complexion had

turned Army-issue green and moisture dewed her upper lip. Damn. he hoped she didn't wig out midair with nothing between her and the ground but a seat belt. "Whoa! You all right?"

She slowly turned her head. "Peachy."

He rubbed her shoulder. "Don't worry, your straps are secure. You won't fall."

"You'd better hope not," she whispered. "Because I'll come back as a pissed-off zombie and stalk your ass."

He grinned. "You're an interesting shade of green." The best cure for Sabrina was a challenge. "You're not gonna wreck my nice leather upholstery, are you?"

"Not…unless…you…hurl…first."

He'd been on the receiving end of that über determination a few times too many. "The day that happens is the day I dress up like Dorothy from Oz for a drag revue in Vegas." His grin widened. "Oh, yeah. Been there, done that. Still have the pinafore."

She swallowed and wrenched her attention from the speeding cityscape. "I'd have paid a million bucks for a ticket to that little show."

"Zoe has a video." He patted her. "Breathe, sweetheart. We'll be there before you know it."

Sabrina breathed, relaxed and stopped looking like she was gonna pass out on him. Soon she was leaning out in her seat to catch the view. "What a head rush! No wonder you love it!"

He'd thought flying the wild blue yonder was the ultimate head rush…until he'd kissed Sabrina.

After the short flight, he landed on Mercy's rooftop. Christina said Maureen had gone to Wade's office.

Upstairs, Sabrina poked her head inside the doorway and withdrew. "Maureen is in there alone."

"I won't leave you unguarded. Come with me."

"I'm right outside the door. If anyone looks at me cross-eyed, I'll shriek to high heaven."

Grady hesitated. Until he stepped inside that room and asked his mom, until Maureen told him otherwise, she was fine. After, there was no going back. "How does she look?"

"Sheesh, do you want syrup with that waffle?" Sabrina gave him a push. "Go see for yourself." She sat cross-legged on the floor and pulled the Bible from her purse. "Unless you need me to hold your hand, I'll page through Granddad's Bible and see if I can pick up any clues."

Sabrina wasn't the only one who responded to a challenge. "Excellent idea." He squared his shoulders and strode into Wade's inner sanctum.

The trauma surgeon rated a corner office with a huge window overlooking the city. Maureen had her back to the door. Her trim figure flattered by a lilac pantsuit, she was leaning over the massive walnut desk and writing on a notepad.

"Mom."

Maureen whirled and her Emerald Isle eyes lit up. "Grady! What a wonderful surprise!" She rushed to hug him. "Lord, I've missed you, boyo."

Feeling nine years old again, Grady cleared an unexpected tightness from his throat. "I've missed you, too." Her coloring was as vibrant as always, and the ever-present hint of mischief lurked in her buoyant smile. But deeper lines etched the corners of her eyes and around her mouth. She looked a bit older and wearier than she had seven months ago. His stomach bottomed out. "Mom—"

"When did you get in? Have you seen your brothers? They've been on a major call-out."

"I flew in around oh-nine-hundred yesterday. Haven't caught up to Aidan or Liam, but Con and I had a brief discussion this morning."

"Hmm, did you now?" She patted his jaw. "The...*discussion* was apparently long enough for you to catch a fresh bruise."

He rolled his eyes. "Mom." He caught her hands in his. "Are you okay?"

"I'm right as rain. But you look tired...and stressed. Have you slept at all since you got back? When did you eat last?"

"Never mind about me. Something happened to you. What was it?"

"Your brother tattled on me, did he?" Her flame-colored brows lowered. "I skidded into a bit of a rocky patch in late December, but it's long past."

The butterflies in his gut morphed into Blackhawks. "Are we talking pebbles or boulders?"

She tugged her hands from his and paced the length of the room. "You're not going to let this rest, are you?"

"Would you?"

"You're not *my* mother, boyo."

"No, but you're mine. The only one I have. Now spill it."

"Don't get cheeky with me, Grady Stephen. I'm still able-bodied enough to switch your behind."

When he folded his arms and glowered, she sighed. "I suppose if I don't come clean, one of your brothers will rat me out. The flu bogged me down for a few weeks and left me with a nagging cough." She propped herself against the desk. "An X-ray revealed a spot on my lung, which turned out to be a mass."

Time hung suspended. All the oxygen seemed to have been sucked from the room, and he couldn't hear over the roar in his ears. His mind buzzed with a thousand questions. He hunted desperately for words but couldn't speak.

"See, now, this is exactly why I didn't want to say anything." His mother briskly rubbed his arms. "Don't look so stricken. Dr. Blanchard removed the tumor, and the biopsy eventually came back benign. All's well that ends well."

"How—" he cleared the hoarseness from his throat "—how long did you have to wait to find out?"

"From start to finish, the whole business took about four weeks."

His vital, seemingly invincible mother had undergone major surgery. Had suffered a terrible scare. And he hadn't been here. Hadn't even known. *"Damn it all to hell."*

Maureen frowned. "And I'm still perfectly able to scour your tongue with Irish Spring."

"Yes, ma'am, sorry." He scrubbed a hand over his face. What if the diagnosis had been dire and—God help him—he hadn't made it back in time?

"I'm sorry, Mom." He swallowed nausea. Swallowed fear and pain and regret, and imprisoned them deep inside. "Sorry you went through a rough time. Sorry I wasn't here for you." Sins of the past vibrated in the air between them. *I'm sorry I let you down when you needed me the most. Then and now.*

"Stop thinking you failed me somehow." Her voice was gentle. "Son, you have to live your life the way you see fit. But if you want the truth, the person you're shortchanging is *yourself.*"

"I sure as h— I *did* fail you, Mom."

The compassion in her eyes nearly demolished his control. She smoothed his hair. "You've been tearing around the globe, seeking something. Have you ever considered that what you're looking for is right beneath your nose?"

A frustrated breath burst from him. "I don't know what I'm looking for!"

"The key is already in your possession, Grady. You just need to summon the courage to unlock the door."

Woman-speak. As mysterious and indecipherable as hieroglyphics. He'd left Riverside seeking the unattainable. Something that always shimmered just out of reach. He'd left behind the painful memories. The disgrace of his weakness. "I don't get it."

"No, you don't *want* to get it. But you've a clever brain behind that cute, dimpled face. Stand in one spot for more than five minutes and exercise it."

Grady frowned. He'd rather just go conquer the SWAT obstacle course. A hard, sweaty, physical challenge usually exhausted his demons into silence. But the obstacle course—and evasive inner quiet—had to wait until he fulfilled his duty to Sabrina.

Sabrina entered the room, followed closely by Wade. "I'm sorry to interrupt, but Dad needs to talk to us."

Wade saw Maureen and checked. "Hello, Maureen. When did you arrive?"

"Wade." For a fraction of a second a look passed between them. "I was just leaving you a message."

The weirdest feeling assaulted Grady, almost as if— He shook his head to clear the fog and the moment passed as quickly as it had come. *What the hell?* His mom's confession had rattled him more than he realized.

Smiling, Maureen hugged Sabrina. "Hi, sweetie. How are you? It's been a while since you've stopped in for tea and a chat."

"Yeah, things have been…insane lately."

"I have a new Bailey's Irish Cream cake recipe."

"Ooooh. I'm so there."

"I'll call you." Maureen turned to Grady. "I should get downstairs. They've asked me to cover a shift. Will you be in town long enough for a family dinner?"

No censure colored her tone, but Grady felt like a jerk at her assumption he was immediately taking off again. Even though that was his plan. "I'll be around some. I'd like to see everybody."

Wade gestured. "Stay, Maureen. This concerns you, as well. It's the reason you were brought on duty." He thrust his hands into the pockets of his lab coat. "We have—" he glanced at Maureen, then Sabrina "—a situation."

The hair on the back of Grady's neck rose. He'd never seen Dr. Spine-of-Steel fazed by *anything*. But the tension lurking beneath Wade's pseudocalm expression sent his senses screaming. Had the spooks who were after Sabrina breached the hospital? Grady moved to her side, put his arm around her. "How serious?"

The edgy set of Wade's mouth hinted at…fear. "Those two men admitted into the ER died from toxic epidermal necrolysis."

"Yes," Sabrina said softly. "I know."

Her father put his hand on her shoulder, and Grady's pulse spiked. Wade's hand was trembling. "What killed those men is an accelerated form of the disease. They were infected just seventy-two hours ago." Wade cleared his throat. "The TEN we witnessed is viral. And highly contagious."

Chapter 9

9:00 a.m.

Sabrina gasped. "*Impossible!* TEN is not communicable!"

"This strain is." Wade frowned. "After I administered morphine to the conscious victim, he was able to whisper information before he coded. Those men were virologists at a classified laboratory. They isolated a mutant strain of TEN and engineered it as a genetic DNA modification piggybacked on a virus. V-10 is highly contagious. Brutally lethal. The mortality rate is ninety percent."

Maureen paled, staggered. "My sons."

The blood drained from Grady's head. "My brothers were at the incident site in Eastern Oregon." Grateful for Sabrina's staunch presence at his side, he groped for his mother's hand and offered silent support. "They were exposed."

Wade thrust a chair forward. "Sit down, Maureen. There's no need to panic."

His mother snapped ramrod straight. "No, thank you." Though she was pale, her clear reply clipped out. "I do not panic, Dr. Matthews."

Admiration sank into Grady as a hint of a smile ghosted across Wade's mouth. "Of course you don't. Forgive me." The surgeon returned the chair. "There's a good chance Aidan, Con and Liam will be fine. V-10 is highly contagious, but transmission occurs through body fluids. No first responders are at high risk unless they touched the victims or their blood."

"Like my fellow paramedics," Grady said.

Sabrina gulped. "And Dalton."

Grady squeezed Sabrina's shoulder. "Those guys aren't rookies. Or reckless. They'd have followed biohazard protocol and gloved-up." He looked at Wade. "How soon can you tell if anyone is infected?"

"An antigen usually appears in the blood within twenty-four hours of exposure. I've notified emergency personnel to report for testing."

Maureen pursed her lips. "Are you declaring code orange and executing quarantine?"

"At this stage, I'm only isolating those who had immediate contact, and we're not going public."

Grady nodded. "Mass hysteria would cause as much harm, if not more. But you might not have a choice for long. FBI and Homeland Security are gonna be all over this."

Wade's expression was grave. "There was an assault on the lab, which accounts for the gunshot casualties. The attackers might be infected themselves, or mishandle the V-10 and let the virus accidentally escape. Or this incident could be a launchpad for terrorists. We have to prepare for the worst. That's why we've called in available medical staff."

"How can I help?" Sabrina asked.

"Right now, by staying out of the way." When she protested, Wade held up a hand. "The last thing the hospital needs is additional security issues. If the V-10 spreads, there'll be plenty of work. Until then, I want you somewhere protected."

"Sabrina, as much as it tortures me to admit it—" Grady eased away in case she vetoed him with her elbow "—I agree with your father."

She snorted. "That's a first."

Wade kissed Sabrina's cheek. "I need to go. The CDC wants samples from the victims."

"Hold the elevator, Wade." Maureen hugged Sabrina, then Grady. "I'd best get moving, too. The ER needs all troops on the front lines. Grady, track down your brothers and keep me posted."

"Yes, ma'am." Grady held on to her a moment longer. If the V-10 spread, his mother would be working in the heart of crisis central, surrounded by the deadly virus. "Be careful, Mom."

"Don't be worrying about me, boyo." She ruffled his hair, then strode toward the door. "We ex-Army nurses are tough old broads."

He dredged up a cocky grin. "You're not old."

His mother's laughter trailed her down the hallway.

Scared but trying to hide it, Sabrina turned to him. "What's the plan?"

"What we do best. Improvise. Did you pick up any clues in the Bible?"

"It's stamped by the Gideons, the type of Bible found in hotel rooms. I started scanning pages from the beginning, but didn't get far before Dad showed up."

"Keep looking. We're missing something."

Grady accessed his TCU and called Riverside PD to obtain the location of the nearest safe house. Nobody was available to grant authorization.

Next, he tried Aidan again. His big brother picked up on the third ring. "Aidan, about damned time. What's your 20?"

"Grady. It's been a while." A pause. "Why, what's *yours?*"

"By your pissed-off tone, I'm guessing the same location. Mercy Hospital."

Aidan cursed. "You picked one helluva day for a family reunion, baby bro."

"My timing is nothing but impeccable." If the monster was loose, his brothers would need him. This time he would be there. "I assume Liam and Con are with you. What floor are they conducting the blood tests on?"

"You were always too smart for your own good. Don't bother. Security won't allow you through the perimeter."

"You know me better than that, A-Man." He hung up on his brother's frustrated growl.

There weren't enough forces in heaven or hell to keep him from seeing his brothers. Less than two minutes later, he and Sabrina grabbed an elevator.

Downstairs the atmosphere reeked of dread. He didn't recognize the young cop guarding the door. Grady flashed his Riverside

PD badge and spoke the absolute truth. "Dr. Wade Matthews ordered the SWAT teams to report for tests."

"Main corridor past the desk, Officer O'Rourke. Police to the right. EMTs to the left."

The observant officer's shoes were spit-shined, his uniform creases knife sharp. Unlike many people around them, he didn't look frightened. The thought of taking Sabrina inside the isolation ward had bugged Grady, but he hadn't seen an alternative. Now he eyed the guy's shoulder patch. "How do you like it down there in the third precinct?"

"They keep me busy."

"You know Kaminski, in Vice?"

Humor flickered in his gaze. "Doesn't everybody?"

"Old Stan owes me one for saving his ass on that crack house bust that went FUBAR last fall."

"You're *that* O'Rourke?" A grin banished the remote cop face. "Man, oh, man, any truth in the stories?"

"Afraid so." Grady indicated Sabrina beside him. "This is Sabrina Matthews, Dr. Wade Matthews's daughter. There're a couple of badasses in suits real interested in eliminating her. You make sure that doesn't happen."

"You got it."

Sabrina frowned. "I should go with you."

Grady turned to her. "The way our perps have been flying under the radar, I doubt they'll try anything. I won't be long. Keep searching Bill's Bible."

"I wasn't concerned about myself." Her teeth worried her lower lip. "Promise you won't pull any demented stunts in there."

"Your idea of demented or mine?"

She sighed. "Dimples, you wouldn't recognize demented if it bit you on the butt."

"If I had time to think about that, I might be insulted."

He strode past the checkpoint. The staff had segregated small groups behind glass-walled cubicles. Grady passed the area containing Ronnie Nguyen, Kim Swanson and Dalton James and offered an encouraging thumbs-up.

The fireman returned Grady's salute with a gesture that wasn't exactly a thumbs-up. Kim waved. Ronnie nodded, still shell-shocked. Nguyen and Swanson were good medics, always willing to fill in on short shifts. Kim was working her way through medical school, and Ronnie supported elderly parents.

Grady found Aidan and Liam imprisoned with Hunter Garrett, the SWAT sniper, and other team members. The men were gathered around a low table, playing poker. There was no sign of Con.

Murphy, Liam's German shepherd K-9, sat outside the glass wall with his nose quivering.

"Hey, hound dog." Grady scratched Murphy's ears. He hoped like hell Con's absence didn't mean the worst. Fighting trepidation, he switched on the intercom as his brothers walked to the glass wall. "Where's Con?"

"He got here first, tested negative and split," Aidan said. "Bailey's BP is elevated, and the doc put her on bed rest. Con had to get back to her." He scowled. "You shouldn't be here, either."

"There's no danger as long as I don't have contact with anybody's blood. Besides, I gotta take one for Team O'Rourke. I'm Mom's designated snitch today."

"Lucky you." Liam lifted his palm to the window.

Willing his hand not to tremble, he pressed his palm to Liam's through the glass in a brief high-five. "Anything I can get you?" The question was as futile, as freaking *useless* as he was. Helpless fury clouded Grady's vision. His brothers were trapped, waiting to hear if they'd been infected. There was nothing he could do for them. He hated that his brothers were beyond his reach. Beyond anyone's help.

Aidan waved at their glass prison. "We're as cozy as chimps in the zoo." Though his tone was casual, worry edged his brown eyes. "Have you run into Zoe?"

Grady cleared the thickness from his throat. Neither brother would thank him for going maudlin on their asses. "Not so far."

"I hope to all the saints she's nowhere near this mess."

"I hear ya." Shared concern passed between them. Knowing Zoe, they couldn't count on it. Grady sank his fingers into Murphy's thick ruff. "I know it's a lousy time to ask, but I need a favor."

"Name it." Typical Aidan. His oldest brother had dispensed advice, loaned cash, bailed him out of more than one jam. And kicked his ass when he'd needed it. His brothers had never let him down.

He couldn't claim the same.

"Sabrina is with me." Grady explained the situation to Aidan and Liam. "So I need a vehicle and a place to hang until a safe house is available. I figure Aidan's high-rise with the doorman and keyed elevators is as secure as they come." He paused. "Unless you think it'll be too dangerous for Zoe?"

Aidan snorted. "Zoe would have my head on a pike if I even thought about refusing on her account." He tugged a key ring from his scrubs pocket and sent it through the airlock transfer. "*Mi casa es su casa.* I'll hitch a ride with Liam."

"Appreciate it." All three shared another silent exchange. Grady took his cue from his brothers' stoic demeanor. They were maintaining, and so, by God, would he. *Stick to business, and keep your damned emotions out of the equation.*

Liam scrubbed a hand over his jaw. "How much of this is public knowledge?"

"It's on a need-to-know basis for now."

"I called Kate and told her I was back but finishing paperwork." Liam's voice went low. "We haven't said anything because we don't want to steal Con and Bailey's thunder and it's early yet, but she…we, ah,…Kate's pregnant. Just barely."

Aidan slapped Liam on the back and then swept Liam into a bear hug.

Isolated on the other side, Grady wished he could do the same. "Congrats, Liam!"

In spite of the happy news, Liam was somber. "Thanks. No point worrying her until there's something to worry about."

Grady looked at his brothers. How did they do it? How did they marry and start families…and live with the constant fear that they couldn't protect their wives and children? That they wouldn't come through for them at a crucial moment. That they'd let them down…and lose them.

What secret did they know, what strength did they have, that he lacked?

"Listen up, bro," Liam said. "If word leaks, I need you to stick around. To be there for Kate if I…can't."

Grady's heart stumbled. Even knowing his track record, Liam was entrusting him with his greatest treasure. "Count on me." He'd broken once, and been useless to his family. Never again.

He stroked the dog pressed against his legs. "Want me to take Murph with me?"

"Yeah, he'll be happier with you for the time being."

Aidan's smile didn't quite reach his eyes. "The T-bird is on parking level D. And if you put a scratch on her, I'll have *your* head on a pike."

"When did I ever?" Grady pocketed the keys and for the second time, dredged up another grin for a family member. "See you soon, girls. In the meantime, don't do anything I wouldn't."

Liam shot back the traditional reply. "Short list, little brother."

Grady rested his hand on the reassuring warmth of Murphy's head. "C'mon, Murph, *heel*."

The big dog stared at Liam and whined, and Liam signaled through the glass. "It's okay, buddy. Go with Grady."

Grady kept his hand on Murphy's soft warm head and his fear on a tight leash as he walked down the corridor.

And though his throat ached with longing, he didn't look back.

Disbelief and horror churned in Sabrina's stomach. Too upset to sit, she clutched Granddad's Bible and watched the door.

Finally, Grady emerged from the isolation ward. His face was pinched, the look in his eyes bruised. She'd seen her patients' families wearing that exact expression.

Her glance moved to the huge German shepherd who kept turning his head to stare at the door. Murphy adored Grady and vice versa, but the dog didn't willingly leave Liam's side. "Are Aidan, Con and Liam—" she swallowed hard "—all right?"

"Con is." Grady averted his glance, rejecting her sympathy. "Aidan and Liam should be cleared soon."

"I'm sure they'll be fine. Dad said their risk was minimal."

"We both know viruses have a nasty habit of mutating." His teeth ground audibly. "I should have been with them. Fighting beside them."

"Then you'd be trapped in there, too." She rubbed his shoulder. "And I…I'd be dead."

"Hey, you're shaking. And pale." His gaze whipped around the room. "What happened?"

"We need to talk."

"We'll get Aidan's T-bird, and—"

"*Now,* Grady."

"You found something," he murmured. At her jerky nod, he wrapped an arm around her. "Upstairs, your office."

The elevator ride was the longest of her life. She sat on the love seat in her office with Murphy at her feet while Grady swept the room with his TCU.

"No bugs." He tucked his device away and sat beside her. Murphy perched at his feet, brown eyes alert. "What did you find?"

"I missed it before, at the church. I was in a hurry and expecting something more obvious." Her unsteady fingers flipped pages. "Isaiah, chapter eight, verse eighteen, is underlined. 'Here am I and the children the Lord has given me.' Granddad wrote two dates beside it, the first date six years previous to the second…which is August twelfth of last year."

Grady frowned. "Sometimes people underline and date verses that speak to them or have special meaning—"

"I'm sure that's what anyone else who found this would have thought. But it's *Isaiah.*" She gulped. "The first date must be his birth date. As for the second…I'll never forget it. Isaiah died on August twelfth."

"Of toxic epidermal necrolysis. Like those men in the ER." Grady's brows slammed together. "I tossed around the theory this morning that the false appointment lured you here to witness the horror show. I dismissed it as too wild, but you said TEN is rare. This can't be coincidence."

"See these verses underlined in Exodus, about Pharaoh ordering the Hebrew babies to be taken from their parents and thrown into the Nile? There are more in Matthew showing Herod executing all the male infants." Sabrina prayed she was wrong. "And this was underlined in Jeremiah. 'A voice is heard in Ramah, weeping and great mourning. Rachel, weeping for her children and refusing to be comforted, because they are no more.'" She flipped forward. "Look at what else was underlined."

"Abigail. Benjamin. Jason. Ethan," he recited. "Elizabeth. Caleb. Luke. Bethany."

Dozens of underlined names. All with dual dates over the past ten years. "Grady, Isaiah didn't have parents. He was in the foster system, a resident of the CCC, the state care facility." She took a deep breath and went on. "The virologists were developing a viral form of V-10." Tears clogged her throat. "Assuming Isaiah's death from TEN ties in to these other children's and they were also in the foster care system, and Granddad found out…"

"If those dates signify what we think they do, someone is murdering *babies!*" Grady's eyes blazed. "What kind of sick bastards use little kids as lab rats?"

"A lot of assumptions, but they make an awful kind of sense. Please tell me we're jumping to the wrong conclusions."

"I'll tell you exactly what we're doing. We're going to uncover the truth. Find out *who* did *what*. And take them down!"

"There are drugs that can induce a heart attack. Could they have killed Granddad because he was getting too close?"

"Freaking A right," he ground out. "And exposed my brothers— and the other first responders—to this nightmare. Death is too good for the murdering bastards."

An odd cocktail of fascination and fear swirled inside her. She'd never seen this side of Grady. "You wouldn't actually—"

"What?" Several degrees of heat evaporated from his eyes and they refocused. "Sabrina, I might occasionally bend the rules…but I'm sworn to uphold the law. Even when it infuriates me." He thrust his fingers through his hair, leaving it standing up in angry spikes. "I'm a cop, honey, not a rogue assassin."

"Of course not. I didn't mean… I've just never seen you this mad."

"You haven't seen anything yet." He thought for a minute. "You have access to Isaiah's medical files?"

"Yes." She rose on wobbly legs. Murphy followed and flopped beneath her desk. "Given what we know, a random terrorist attack at the biology lab feels too convenient."

"Maybe the money-men funding the research got what they needed and staged an assault to eliminate evidence." Grady hovered over her shoulder as she sat and booted up her computer. Rage vibrated from him. "Exposing the populace is a surefire way to make a bundle of dough with the antidote."

"Infect people with V-10 to profit from suffering and death?" She shuddered. "That's so unrepentantly…evil."

He stilled behind her. "Not the first—or unfortunately the last— depravity committed in the pursuit of money and power."

He was remembering his father's murder. She half turned in her chair. "Oh, Grady—"

"No. This is way bigger than me." His voice was tight. "Pull up that data."

When the page blipped online, she read aloud. "Isaiah Elzey, DOB matches the one in the Bible. No parents listed. He talked about the foster parents he had before he got sick, but they're not listed, either." She frowned. "A *lot* of information is missing."

"His file has been whitewashed."

"I told you he was a resident of the CCC—the state-run Children's Care Center. Do you think the other names mentioned in Granddad's Bible were children who lived there, too?"

"Run a search of the hospital's records for causes of death in children between the ages of newborn and twelve for the past ten years."

"I don't know how."

"Switch places with me."

"Okay. But you need passwords to go that deep."

"This is a hospital, not NORAD." After a few moments of his rapid typing, the machine hummed, and print scrolled from top to bottom. One dark, glossy brow arched. "We don't need no stinking passwords."

He transferred the data to his TCU. "Now we download the CCC's files to cross-reference." She watched his long-fingered hands dance over the keyboard. He scowled. "Their medical records are segregated on an independent mainframe."

"What does that mean?"

"We can't access their computer unless we're physically inside the CCC. Which means we have to want the intel badly enough to commit a felony."

She watched the light of battle gathering in Grady's intelligent green eyes. "I have the sinking feeling that we do."

"Damn skippy we do." His grin was fierce. "Sabrina, my sweet, how good are you at breaking and entering?"

Chapter 10

10:00 a.m.

Sabrina groaned. "How long is the sentence if we're caught?"

"Technically, we won't be breaking, just entering." Grady launched another staccato assault on the keyboard. "We're strolling in the front door."

"I must be firing on one cylinder." She slapped her forehead. "I've sent visiting nurses and medical personnel there before. I can authorize us."

"Nope. Can't use your name. Anyone on staff might be in collusion with the bad guys."

"Then how are you planning to gain entry? The CCC has strict security. They require ID and a good reason for admittance."

Frowning, he studied the new data. "They have service contracts. Linens, food, medical-supply deliveries. Garbage pickup. But we need a cover that will let us move fairly freely around the premises."

Murphy rested his muzzle on her sneaker and heaved a contented sigh. She stared down at the dog. "Pet therapy! The bigger hospitals offer pet-therapy programs, and they've visited the CCC. They're volunteers, so the CCC won't think it's odd if we arrive on a Sunday."

Grady's hands stilled. He looked at her and his grin bounced back. "Perfect! You're brilliant."

"Or really gullible. Say this 'brilliant' plan actually works and we get inside?"

He typed faster. "Then we access the computer room, interface with the mainframe and...appropriate the evidence."

"Because robbery is sooo much better than B & E." Her mouth was dry, and she retrieved bottled water from the stash in her desk. She handed him one. "You know as well as I do if the evidence is stolen, it won't be admissible in court."

He unscrewed the cap and drank. "If we go through channels, it'll give the scumbags opportunity to destroy evidence. When we find proof of what we suspect, I'll obtain a viable confession." A muscle ticced in his jaw. "Even if I have to start at the bottom and work my way up the list."

Any smart person facing that look in her cop's eyes would confess all her sins. And pray for lenience.

A page of what appeared to be blueprints popped on screen. "Here we go. The building's floor plan, courtesy of county records."

"Specific floor plans are available online?"

"Honey, in a minute, I'll pull up a real-time infrared satellite image that shows how many warm bodies are inside and their location. It's standard operating procedure in SWAT and covert ops. Knowing exact coordinates and the enemy's manpower before you door breach is critical."

"What ever happened to good old-fashioned privacy?"

He pitched his empty bottle across the room into the garbage can. "It took a hike on the information highway."

"How did you learn all this stuff?"

"It's my job to stay alive." His eyes narrowed at the screen. "To keep my team and the civilians entrusted to me alive."

She knew he was dedicated and more than capable, but he'd rarely let her see the serious, lethal warrior. "I'm glad you're on my team."

Grady glanced at her, and tenderness warmed his gaze. "I've been on your team since the day you bailed out me and the little bulldog, sweetheart."

Sabrina bent and petted Murphy to hide the longing that invaded her. She wanted so badly for Grady to stay. Their shared bond gifted them with a rapport she'd never experienced with another person. When Grady was gone, she was missing her other half.

He transferred the final files and unplugged the cable. "I wonder if Kate's home from her class?"

"She usually works when Liam is on a long call-out. It helps keep her mind off…possibilities."

"Do you have her new studio's number?"

"Yes, why?"

"If we wanted empathy and support, we'd go to Bailey. For creative solutions we call Kate." He grinned. "When we need help finding out who hid the dirt, Zoe will be our girl."

She chuckled at his dead-on assessment as she located the number in her cell directory. "What creative solutions do we need?"

"Who better to supply us with foolproof fake IDs than a photographer? And I want the floor plan printed out to study, but not from your computer. I'll phone Kate first. I can't turn up unannounced on a cop's wife after a major call-out, especially with Murphy in tow."

"She might think the worst." Sabrina sobered. "What are you going to tell her about Liam?"

"As little as possible."

"I *hate* lying to people. I suck at it."

"I know. But we have a damned good reason, which has to stay between us for now." His sensual mouth firmed. "Liam told me Kate is pregnant."

"Oh!" She fought a brief battle with envy. "How wonderful! Liam always wanted enough kids to start his own baseball team. And your mom will be thrilled."

"Yeah. But it's early in Kate's first trimester and she doesn't need additional stress. I only told you so you'll see why we have to lie convincingly."

"I appreciate your trust. I can do it, for her sake."

On the way to the studio, Sabrina's attention lingered on Grady's handsome, familiar profile. She'd yearned to have Grady O'Rourke's beautiful babies since almost the moment she first became a woman. Would she want someone to shield her from the truth if she were in Kate's place?

Her chest tightened. Absolutely not. If women were as fragile as men thought, they wouldn't have been chosen to bear the children. But the decision was between Liam and Grady, and Kate could, and would, bust their macho, overprotective chops later.

Kate met them at the door and offered hugs. "Grady, I'm glad you're back! Sabrina, how are you?" Elegant in white slacks and a sapphire silk blouse, she looked vibrant, not appearing to suffer from the morning sickness that had plagued Bailey.

Kate drew back, and her intelligent brown eyes studied Sabrina, then moved to Murphy and finally to Grady. "What's up with my husband? He sounded…tense. Is he okay?"

"I just saw him." Grady's broad shoulder lifted in a nonchalant shrug. "As obnoxious as ever, and not a scratch on him."

Sabrina feigned interest in Kate's incredible photographs and abstract paintings. Grady possessed a knack for speaking the truth, but not the whole truth. The camouflage made it darned hard to discern what he really thought from what he said. Did he lie to himself just as convincingly?

Kate scooped a dog biscuit from the jar on her desk and offered it to Murphy. "Then why is our mutt with you?"

"Liam's tying up loose ends, and Murph was bored. He'd rather spend time with fun Uncle Grady." Grady ruffled the dog's fur as the animal wolfed the treat. "Kate, we need your formidable talents."

"You're as full of Irish blarney as your brother." Kate gave Murphy a final pat. "After Vegas, I owe you big-time. What do you want me to do, and does it involve outfitting you in drag again?"

Kate took Grady's word that he couldn't explain everything yet and set to work. Grady transferred the hospital's files from his TCU to Aidan's home computer and studied the CCC's floor plans while Sabrina assisted Kate.

In record time they possessed perfect forgeries of driver's licenses and a rival hospital's employee badges, and Murphy owned a pet-therapy diploma.

Grady drove downtown and parked Aidan's sleek black T-bird half a block from the CCC. "We want the car close, but without the staff able to read the plates. And cell phones off. Can't risk a ring at the wrong time." He handed her the car keys. "If it goes bad, bug out and don't worry about me and Murphy. We'll hold the line."

"Gee, thanks for the pep talk, Dimples." She pocketed the keys. "I thought you guys never left a man behind."

"Last time I checked, you weren't an Army Ranger." He tweaked her ponytail. "It's merely in case of a snafu. We're getting in and out—with no one the wiser. Piece of pie, baby."

"I prefer apple crisp," she muttered as she climbed out of the car.

He chuckled. "À la mode, French vanilla. With steaming Earl Grey and an even steamier romance novel."

She didn't have any secrets from him. Except one. Which wasn't very well kept. Sabrina slammed the door and marched up the sidewalk toward the four-story stone building.

Mustiness acquired by old buildings permeated the foyer. The stern, gray-haired woman guarding the front desk frowned. "You can't bring that filthy animal in here."

"Murphy is a therapy dog, ma'am." Grady's dimpled grin could have melted granite. "I assure you, he's spick-and-span."

The woman examined their IDs. Focused on Grady's trust-me-I'm-a-harmless-scamp smile, she barely glanced at Sabrina. "You and Ms. Hayes are not on the calendar, Mr. Addison."

"We scheduled our visit two weeks ago..." he leaned over the counter to peruse her name tag "...Mrs. Branson." His gaze slowly traveled over her chest, then her mouth. His eyes met hers again, and he ramped up the Irish charm. "Surely you wouldn't deprive the children because of a paperwork boggle."

"Well...our receptionist can be flighty." The woman was too busy blushing as she handed him day passes to note Sabrina's illegible scribble on the sign-in log. "Wear this in plain sight on your...chest." She cleared her throat and pressed the intercom. "Rosa, I'm sending back two outside volunteers for a pet-therapy session." She smiled at Grady. "Most of our ambulatory residents are in the day room. This floor, the wide, ah, double doors at the end of the corridor."

As they strolled down the hallway, Grady snorted. "See? As sweet as my mama's peach pie. The starchy ones have the naughtiest imaginations."

Sabrina shook her head. "You are one sick puppy."

He grinned. "Just don't squeal to my mother."

Their plan was to let Murphy spend around twenty minutes with the children, then "detour" to the computer room in a side corridor behind the front offices and download the info. Nobody would ever know they'd accessed the files.

They stopped inside the day room to observe. The musty smell was layered with the institutional odors of cafeteria cooking and disinfectant. Thirty children aged two to ten occupied the large space. Some perched on worn sofas in the corner watching an animated movie on a small television. Others finger painted at easels near the window, or constructed a building-block city on a plastic mat.

The plaster walls were long overdue for another coat of drab green paint, and stained, peeling patches on the high ceiling revealed water damage. The furniture, toys and children's clothes were clean, but tired and mismatched. Ditto the three female attendants in faded pink scrubs who milled among the children. There should have been at least six aides for this many kids. Like most government programs for children and the elderly under the departing administration, the CCC was seriously underfunded. She hadn't realized how badly.

Grady's brows lowered. "I have a huge, hairy bone to pick with politicians who prioritize buying bombs over taking care of babies."

That his thoughts were so in sync with hers should have stopped amazing her by now. "After this investigation is completed, I'm going to touch base with Maureen about a fund-raiser. We can do better by our children."

The kids spied Murphy and approached with wide eyes and questions. The aides hurried over to check their passes. Sabrina introduced herself and Grady and discovered that two of the women were Russian with barely understandable English, and the other had a heavy Hispanic accent.

Grady arrowed a silent inquiry at Sabrina and she shook her head. The attendant was much younger than the woman who'd phoned her.

He walked Murphy into the play area, and children flocked around him. Grady knelt to their level and asked their names. Murphy was extra gentle as he offered a paw to shake. "If you want to see Murphy's tricks, everybody sit in a circle."

Kids scrambled to obey, and, smiling, Sabrina joined them.

A freckle-faced boy around three years old with fire-engine-red curls declared, "I'm Mikey. You're pretty!" and plopped into her lap.

Grady winked at Sabrina. "A discerning gentleman."

She watched him automatically scan the room, a typical cop habit. His gaze snagged, tracked back to the far corner. She followed his line of sight and noticed a thin, dark-haired boy hovering in the shadows. "Get things started," she said. "I'll go."

But when she tried to lift Mikey, he emitted a screech that could have peeled the remaining paint from the ceiling. *"Nooo! I want to sit with you!"*

"Whoa, pardner," Grady drawled. "You'll scare the dog." Mikey plugged his thumb in his mouth, and the other hand clutched Sabrina's shirt.

Grady rose. His movements easy, he approached the hesitant child in the corner, and then squatted down. After several moments of sober conversation, the boy shyly slipped his hand into Grady's. Eyes downcast, he hung back as Grady led him to the circle. Though slender, his height indicated he was probably close to five years old. "Bedford has decided to say hi to Murphy."

An older boy next to Sabrina sneered. "Bedford, the bedbug."

A blonde with pigtails singsonged, "Bedbug wets the bed."

Several other kids piped up with similar taunts, and Sabrina clapped her hands. "Name-calling makes Murphy sad. He wants you to be kind to one another."

At Grady's hand signal, Murphy crouched on his belly, put his head on his paws and let his ears droop.

The children quieted, and Grady gently drew Bedford close to his side. "Murphy, pick out the coolest dude here to be my assistant." Murphy trotted around the squirmy, giggly children, tail wagging. Thanks to Grady's subtle signal, the dog stopped in front of Bedford and nudged the little boy's hand with his nose. The child looked questioningly at Grady.

"Yup, he chose you, Ford," Grady said, gifting the child with the prestige of being chosen and a new nickname. A tentative smile lifted the child's mouth, warming his peaked face.

Letting Bedford call out the commands, Grady used hand signals to put Murphy through his paces. The kids were awed when Grady sent Murphy out, gave Bedford a dollar bill to put in his pocket, and the returning dog found it in minutes.

Grady continued to call Bedford "Ford," and the other children's respect for the little boy grew…along with Bedford's confidence.

And Sabrina tumbled more deeply in love with Grady.

When it was time to leave, Mikey tearfully clung to her. She hugged him and promised to return. After saying goodbye to the other children, she stood at the door and watched Grady offer a private word to each child as he had Murphy bid them farewell.

Grady saved Bedford for last, and asked Murphy if he'd miss his new friend "Ford" the most. Murphy woofed and licked the giggling boy's face.

Excited kids gathered around Ford, the former outcast now an envied celebrity.

Grady's triumphant grin flashed, and an aching lump lodged in Sabrina's throat. She'd crushed on Grady the boy. Adored Grady the teenager. She'd respected, admired and cared about him nearly all the years she'd been alive.

Yet she hadn't quite understood what it meant to truly love Grady the man...*this man*...body, heart and soul.

She loved his roguish devil-may-care élan. Loved his lethal focus and dedication to justice. But this compassionate, tender protector was the side of him she could never forget.

She turned aside before he could see the moisture in her eyes. No matter what choice he made after this was over, no matter how far he ran—even if she had to eventually move on and marry another man—part of her would love Grady forever. The bittersweet revelation brought both comfort and heartbreak.

Grady O'Rourke would always be with her.

No matter what the future held.

The hallway doors swung shut behind them, and Grady turned to her. "What's wrong, honey?"

She cleared her throat. "Nothing."

"You don't cry over nothing."

"I'm not crying. I...have something in my eye."

"Uh-huh." He stroked her cheek. "We'll bring Murphy back again. These kids need us."

Her throat ached with suppressed longing. If he offered any more sweet reassurance, she'd totally lose it. "Let's just move on to the felonious portion of the program."

As they walked toward the front office, the elevator bell dinged and the doors slid open. An aide emerged, pushing a food cart laden with graham crackers, fruit and miniature milk cartons. Grateful for a pause to settle turbulent emotions, Sabrina sipped from a water fountain while the woman trundled past and into the day room.

The records room door lock yielded to Grady's skill with a pick, and they slipped inside. Leaving the door a scant quarter-inch ajar, he ordered Murphy to sit in alert mode. Grady grabbed a chair, booted up a PC and plugged his TCU into a port.

Sabrina listened to his fingers tap-dance as she scoped out the enclosure. Yellowed roller shades guarded outside windows. The walls were the same industrial green, and chipped metal vents at floor level indicated an ancient furnace system. "Scamming old ladies, lock picking, hacking," she murmured. "You'd be a really successful criminal."

Humor shaded his reply. "My training officer at the academy said devious minds make the sharpest cops. The Goody Two-shoes variety can't even imagine how crooks think."

Smiling, she studied black metal filing cabinets that lined the room like weathered watchmen. Faded drawer labels indicated the CCC probably hadn't transcribed older data onto computer files. She tested one, found it locked. "You must be the sharpest cop on the force."

His deep chuckle made her stomach flip. "I do my best." He made a low, satisfied sound. "I'm in. Now the data transfer."

She opened a heavy wooden door in the far wall and saw a storage closet jam-packed with more filing cabinets and stacked office-supply shelves. "How long will it take?"

"There are a buttload of files, and their system isn't exactly state-of-the-art."

"Is a buttload bigger than a RAM?" She tried closet file drawers. Also locked. She paced back, leaned over Grady's shoulder and stared at the screen. It looked like hieroglyphics. "How much more to go?"

"RAM is memory. Megabytes are units of stored info—smaller than a buttload." He drew her close, rubbing her arms to create tingling warmth. "Relax, honey, Murph will know if someone is coming before either of us does. Besides, it's a holiday weekend, and this isn't exactly Fort Knox."

He was right. Leaning into Grady, she rested her cheek on his silky hair. *Relax.* Her eyelids drifted closed. She and Grady were at home on a lazy Sunday afternoon. Her breasts brushed his muscled back, and she breathed him in…warm, clean man and fresh citrus. She nuzzled his ear, nipped the spot that made him crazy, then slid her hands down his chest, teasing up the hem of his T-shirt to stroke velvety skin. Uttering a throaty hum, Grady scooped her into his arms and loped up the stairs to their bedroom. His big, hard body followed her down onto the bed, and—

"Sabrina!" Grady hissed, and her eyelids flew open. He spun and stood. Her heart raced wildly, and her gaze slid down his body. He was showing definite interest. *Exceptional* interest.

Ohmigod, what had she done? Aroused by her daydream, had she kissed him, touched him? "Grady—"

"Shush!" He jerked the cables from his TCU, toed the outer door shut and yanked her toward the closet.

"*Wait!* Not—"

He shoved her in and followed. "Murphy, heel!" Murphy crowded in behind him, and Grady tugged the door closed. She and Grady were jammed in face-to-face, with not a millimeter to spare. "Murph alerted. Someone's coming."

Heat crawled up Sabrina's neck. Her imagination had led her way down the yellow brick road.

They fell silent as a woman's voice spoke in the room. "You…gone…until Tuesday, Ms. Schmidt," Mrs. Branson said. Her voice was barely discernible through the thick closet door. Not entirely bad. If Sabrina had to strain to hear the blatant conversation, the women wouldn't hear them, either.

A thin stripe of golden light puddled at the door's base, affording Sabrina a dim view of their tight quarters as her vision adjusted. She just hoped like hell the ladies didn't need office supplies.

"Did…organizing…children's health conference…?" Mrs. Branson asked. "New resort…Mt. Hood…very efficient."

"…aren't quite…" a higher woman's voice, even harder to hear, replied. "But…destructive computer virus…any moment. Headquarters messengered…disk…update… Came directly… I didn't…keys."

"Nice…caught…for a change. Last one…crashed system. Let…know when…lock up."

The door snapped shut. In the looming silence Sabrina

strained to hear the woman's movements, but the sturdy door panel muted them.

Hurry up, lady. Sabrina's back was against a tall file cabinet and Grady's hard, hot body pressed intimately to her front. Every time she took a breath, her breasts rubbed his muscled pecs. Every time he took a breath, his blatant arousal rubbed her lower belly.

They were both breathing too fast.

Grady's heartbeat thudded against her breasts, his ragged breath fanning her cheek. He smelled so good. Desire tingled up her spine, and her nipples tightened. Trying to ease the ache, she scrunched her shoulders…and made it worse.

Grady's soft groan vibrated from his chest to hers, and his bristled jaw grazed her cheek. "Don't," he breathed into her ear. "I'm only human."

She turned her face away from the teasing brush of his soft lips. So close. So tempting.

And saw a pair of eyes watching them from the corner.

Tiny, beady, glowing eyes.

"Erg!" Squirming, she wrapped her arms around Grady's waist, buried her face in his neck and barely stifled the strangled sound.

Grady made a few strangled sounds himself before growling in her ear, "Stop moving!"

"There's a *mouse* in here!" she whispered.

Murphy shifted. Grady was holding his TCU in one hand and steadied Murphy with the other. "No big deal," he murmured in a soothing tone that didn't fool her for one second. "Stay still. It won't hurt you."

His silent chuckle created warm, enticing friction as his body caressed hers from shoulders to knees. Her senses rioted. Her skin tingled, and liquid fire flooded her belly. Mouse? What mouse?

She heard Murphy snuffle at the rodent, felt Grady's restraining arm on the dog tense…and then the mouse squeaked and skittered across their feet.

Sabrina jerked, stiffened, and an involuntary shriek boiled up in her throat.

Grady's mouth slammed over hers, muffling the noise.

Shocked, she froze for a span of shaky heartbeats. Then, primed by her earlier fantasy, she leaned into him. And kissed him. Her tongue flirted with his, and her palms slid up the broad expanse of his back, pulling him impossibly closer.

He fumbled his TCU onto the top of the cabinet and released Murphy. His hands cradled her face, anchored her in the whirling pleasure. His satiny tongue delved deep, and another low groan rumbled in his throat.

Sabrina forgot the mouse. Forgot where she was, forgot everything. Nothing existed except the feel and scent and taste of Grady.

Chapter 11

Somehow Grady knew exactly what she wanted, what she needed. Knew when to tease and when to erotically stroke his tongue against hers.

He kissed her until her breath roller-coastered in her throat. Until her knees wobbled. Until her blood sang a wild, primitive tune, and she couldn't distinguish her crashing heartbeats from his.

Grady kissed her until she hungered for him. Ached for him.

And kept on kissing her.

His fingertips stroked her jaw, caressed her ear, trailed down the column of her neck. Gasping, she arched into him. "Grady," she panted. "I want your hands on me." He cupped her breast, kneading gently, and she sighed out a moan. "Yes."

He sought her mouth again. His hand fumbled with her buttons, parted her shirt and slid beneath her bra. His thumb flicked over her nipple, and a bolt of desire sizzled. Rocking her hips into his hardness, another low moan escaped. "More."

Grady's breathing was hoarse and ragged, and tremors shook his body. His restraint had shattered. He'd unleashed his passion…and she reveled in the hurricane.

Just like when they'd kissed in his bedroom, the amazing mind/body connection flowed between them. A spiritual bond she'd never felt with anyone else. Kissing Grady, touching him, felt so right. Felt as necessary as oxygen. His desire fueled hers, and she wanted all of him.

His mouth left her lips swollen and sensitive, her breathing frayed. He nibbled a seductive path along her jaw. Then his warm, moist breath tickled inside her ear, making her shiver as his tongue traced the outer shell. He gently bit her earlobe, and goose bumps prickled her skin.

"I want you so much, Sabrina." His husky admission resonated through her, heightened the clenching ache.

"I want you, too," she whispered against the pulse leaping in his throat. She touched her tongue to his hot skin, tasting the faint saltiness. She was already addicted to his taste. "I ache with it."

A low growl rumbled in his chest and he slid his knee between her thighs, urging her legs apart. His muscled thigh and the hard ridge of his arousal created delicious pressure. His mouth devoured hers as if he were starving. His other hand slid beneath her shirt, and both thumbs teased her taut nipples as he tilted his hips into hers. Sharp pleasure weakened her knees.

As he rocked against her, the world narrowed to swirling sensation. Sabrina's abdominal muscles contracted in anticipation. Her hips met his rhythm, answered his thrusts.

"Oh, yeah, that's it, sweetheart." Grady murmured into her ear.

She clung to him as he took her faster, higher. Grady was with her in the swirling vortex.

"Fly with me, Sabrina." The raw need in his voice made her hot and shaky, spiraled the tension tight and strong and deep inside her.

He captured her mouth in another kiss, his talented tongue making love to her with the same shattering tempo as his rocking body. Something bright and glittering and wondrous shimmered inside her. She wanted it so badly. Time suspended as she reached. Stretched. Almost there. Right—

"Woof!" Murphy's soft bark sounded unnaturally loud. Sabrina's heart slammed into her ribs, and she jumped, severing the sensual connection.

A frustrated breath exploded from Grady's throat. "Dammit!"

Shaken, disoriented, she clutched his jacket, gulping in air. Whoa. Talk about a fast ride.

Grady was shaking, too. He inhaled, visibly struggling for control. He listened, then opened the door to look. "Murphy says the coast is clear."

"Thanks, Murphy. I think." Sabrina rested her forehead on Grady's heaving chest. "I need a second to remember how to walk."

Grady shoved an unsteady hand through his hair. In spite of the interruption, his formidable arousal hadn't diminished. "What the *hell* was I thinking?"

"You weren't." She looked up at him. "Neither was I."

"I was thinking, all right, but not with my brain." Grady swore. "I've never jettisoned control in the middle of an op."

"Hey, no harm, no foul."

He looked bewildered, lost and more than a little scared. "Hell, I've never surrendered situational awareness. *Ever.*"

"You said yourself this isn't Fort Knox. Even if we had been discovered, I doubt Mrs. Branson would have shot us. Or engaged you in hand-to-hand combat. We'd have escaped."

Body taut, he pulled back. "I need to check the computer." He opened the door and strode out, taking the dog with him.

Sabrina sank to the floor, drew up her legs and wrapped her arms around them. Battling hurt, she let her head drop to her knees. Okay, it wasn't all bad. She'd lit Grady's fuse so hot he'd been moments from detonation. She inhaled a quivering breath. Her face heated. He hadn't been the only one. Inside a closet. In a public building. Completely blowing off the mouse and the possibility of imminent discovery.

But Grady's lapse wouldn't have happened if his attraction were merely physical. He was too focused, too good a cop to let his libido run the show. She'd engaged his emotions. She was making progress.

Grady's heart was finally overruling his head.

And he was totally freaked. A long sigh whispered out. If only he'd stay in one place long enough for her to complete *her* mission.

Grady disconnected his TCU, stalked back to the closet and stuck his head in the doorway. The sight of Sabrina hunkered on the floor sent his stomach hurtling to his shoes. His girl didn't easily crumble, but his brainless-wonder act had done the job. *Dammit,* he'd grabbed her and mauled her like a sailor on shore leave. He'd never lost control with a woman.

His teeth ground together. That wasn't the worst thing he'd done. He was a battle-trained combat vet, for God's sake. He'd never jeopardized a mission. Had never lost his ever-lovin' *mind*.

He'd like to kick his own ass six ways from sundown.

Grady squatted and stroked her hair. "Sabrina? We have to go, sweetheart."

She looked up, her eyes clear and bright. And dry. "I think I can walk now."

Relief trickled through him as he offered her a hand up. She quickly adjusted her bra, but her trembling fingers fumbled with her blouse.

"Let me." Concentrating on the buttons and not her silky curves, he fastened the placket.

"Stop looking like someone ran over your dog." Her voice was low but even. "I enjoyed the wild and crazy."

His gaze flew to hers. "Sabrina…"

"Surely you noticed I was cooperating. Don't beat yourself up. It was fun."

"Fun." The word felt foreign on his tongue.

"C'mon, Dimples. You know I almost…leaped without a parachute."

Yeah, he was tuned in to her wavelength like no other woman he'd ever known. Like no other person on the planet. And her passion had fired his to a fever pitch. Another few minutes and he'd have hurtled out of the airplane with her. He hadn't done anything since high school. "That was risky, stupid and dangerous."

"And exhilarating." Her lush mouth slowly curved in a seductive smile. "I think the risk added extra zing."

Hell's bells! The desire he'd barely managed to tamp down blasted back. His blood fired with the need to strip her clothes off, toss her onto the desktop and finish things between them. *Great idea, Officer Lust-for-Brains.* That would solve one problem…and create a slew of new ones.

He cracked open the door and scanned the hallway. "Let's get the hell outta here." Before he spontaneously combusted.

He stopped where the two corridors intersected to case the main hallway. "Did you catch any of the Schmidt/Branson conversation? The computer 'virus patch' that headquarters messengered to Schmidt wiped the CCC's system of all but the basic medical data. We snagged it in the nick of time."

Sabrina gasped. "Are the bad guys on to us?"

"They obviously suspect Bill tried to relay intel to you, and erasing this evidence might be the logical result. Or it could be the next phase of their plan. They'd realize the V-10 leak would launch an investigation."

They'd just stepped into the main corridor when a leggy brunette in a gray suit strode out of the day room. An aide with the now-empty food cart followed through the open doors.

The brunette's eyes narrowed. "Who are you?" It was the same no-nonsense voice he'd heard addressing Ms. Branson in the computer area.

Smiling, Grady indicated his pass, and then Murphy. "We're with the pet-therapy program."

Her brows drew together. "What were you doing in the annex? That's not the children's area."

"Yes, we discovered that." Grady infused deliberate warmth into his tone and gave her the I-only-have-eyes-for-you gaze. "We got turned around on our way out."

"There are only two hallways on this level." The brunette tapped her chin. "I've never seen you here before."

The lady obviously had ice water in her veins. "We're new and got lost." He worked the dimples for maximum effect and urged Murphy forward. "We were just leaving."

"One moment." She moved, blocking their escape route. "I'm Ms. Schmidt, the director. I'd like to speak to you further…in my office."

Grady felt Sabrina tense. The longer they were detained, the greater the danger of discovery. One signal from him, and Murphy would easily convince Ms. Schmidt to let them pass. Getting clear with the intel was their goal, yet he wanted to be able to return and help these kids. He'd resort to blowing up bridges only if his hand was forced.

"I'd be happy to join you, but my colleague has another appointment." He rested his palm on the small of Sabrina's back. "I'll walk her to the car and then meet you in your office," he lied. Once they got outside, they were gone.

"I'm headed for the front desk. I'll walk with you."

Grady assessed the woman's body language. He didn't think she was suspicious, merely overly cautious. Plan B—if he couldn't shake the chilly brunette, he'd slip Sabrina his Glock and TCU and then send her and Murphy to Aidan's. No way could the criminals already have a bead on their new transportation. The intel would be safe, and the gun and dog would protect Sabrina until Grady could extract.

A curly red head poked out the day room doorway. Seconds later an ear-splitting wail careened down the hallway. "I *said* I wanted juuuuice!" Screaming, Mikey threw himself on the floor and flailed. His sneakers kicked the doors. *Wham!* "I *hate* milk!" *Wham!*

Ms. Schmidt sighed. "Not again. Wait here." She hurried away.

"Like hell." Grady grabbed Sabrina's hand and they booked to the car.

Three minutes and four streets whizzed past without incident, and Sabrina relaxed into her seat. "Whew! Thank goodness for a convenient outburst."

"No, thank badness." Grady arched a brow. "Before we left the day room, I slipped the little imp a fiver to pitch a flaming hissy fit if he saw anyone stop and talk to us on the way out."

Sabrina burst into laughter. "You bribed a toddler into a tantrum? That's a whole new level of bad, O'Rourke!"

"I figured we might need a distraction. I'll take what backup I can get, even if he's short. Never underestimate a redhead."

"Those poor aides." She shook her head. "Apparently, ladies *and* kids like you. You should come with a warning label."

Right. *Proceed at Own Risk.* He automatically checked the mirrors for a tail. Now that they were clear of the threat, the implications of his actions rammed home. If Mrs. Branson or Ms. Schmidt had found them in the closet, it would have been awkward, but he'd have dealt with it. If the bad guys had discovered them...

Sickness welled in Grady's throat. He wanted to believe he'd surrendered to desire only because his subconscious knew Murphy would alert him. But he couldn't deny that his weak, foolish emotions had put Sabrina in jeopardy.

Grady drank in her sweet, familiar face. He loved the bright sparks of intelligence in her eyes. The merriment in her smile. The tenderness in her voice that made his gut clench every time she said his name. His pulse kicked up, and he swallowed hard.

His fear for Sabrina's safety wasn't the only thing that could bring him to his knees…and ruin her along with him.

He wrenched his attention to the road. When she'd begged him to touch her, Sabrina had fulfilled a thousand fantasies stretching back to when they were fifteen. And incited the most dangerous emotion of all. A bittersweet feeling he hadn't dared think about, much less express. The hope that he could sublimate his dread that he would let her down. That he could reconcile his doubts.

That somehow, some way, he could stay with her.

But after this last screw-up, he knew better. If he let himself care too much for Sabrina, his need, his longing would overrun him. Not only would he be unable to protect her, he'd lose his perspective. Lose himself. His emotions would smother him. Consume him. And her.

Until there was nothing left but regret.

Maybe he was a coward, or maybe he was just being smart. There was only one way for him—and Sabrina—to survive. His fingers clenched on the wheel. Leaving Sabrina wouldn't kill him, but he'd wish himself dead. He glanced at her again, and she smiled, her face open with trust, her eyes warm with acceptance.

Despair washed over him. Where would he go? What would he do? Now that he'd touched her, kissed her, held Sabrina in his arms, no adventure, no thrill, no life-or-death mission would ever replace what he was leaving behind. She was permanently in his thoughts, in his heart.

But memories wouldn't keep him warm during the lonely days and nights ahead. Grady blinked back the pressure behind his eyes. Walking away from Sabrina this final time would be the hardest thing he'd ever done.

Because this time he was fully aware of what he was walking away from.

As if sensing his inner turmoil, she went quiet. They'd never needed useless chatter. While this wasn't exactly a companionable silence, he was grateful he wasn't forced to make conversation as they dropped Murphy at Kate's studio and then headed to Aidan's condo. He couldn't speak around the lump in his throat.

And there was nothing left to say.

Carrying Sabrina's overnight bag, he used Aidan's keys to let them into the spacious apartment. There was no sign of his brother or Zoe, and Liam hadn't been in touch with Kate. Grady consulted his watch. If he hadn't heard in another hour, he'd phone the hospital.

"Don't worry, Grady, if Aidan and Liam had received their results, they'd have called." Sabrina touched his shoulder. "No news is probably good news."

He handed her the bag. "Put this and Bill's Bible in the guest room. I'll be in Zoe's office, printing data." He walked past the kitchen and dining room and through the living room. Dozens of family snapshots lined the mantel, many including Sabrina. She'd been an integral part of Grady's life. Gap-toothed grins and dirty faces after their first Little League game. Resplendent in formal wear on prom night...with her splayed "bunny ear" fingers behind his head. Tossing caps in the air at their high school graduation.

Sabrina was forever entwined with his past.

He steeled his resolve and stalked down the hall. It hurt more than he could imagine that she wouldn't be in his future.

Inside Zoe's office, her huge, one-eared tabby chirruped a greeting from the windowsill. "Hey, Evander, you holding down the fort?" Grady scratched the cat beneath the chin, then hooked up his TCU to Zoe's computer and began to print files. Sabrina soon joined him.

It was too painful to look at her and wish for something he could never have. Instead, he focused on his task. "Between the hospital and the CCC, there are reams of data. It'll take a while."

"When will Isaiah's file come up?"

"I started with it." He fanned pages on Zoe's desk.

Sabrina picked up a sheet and frowned. "Isaiah's mother is listed as deceased, and his father as 'unknown.'"

He read from another page. "His foster parents were Roger and Amy Purcell, a general contractor and homemaker. They remanded him back into the CCC's custody after he contracted leukemia."

"Isaiah mentioned them often. It sounded like they had a great relationship, but they never visited him." Her teeth worried her lower lip. "They live on Eaton Street. We could be there in a half hour—less if you drive. I wonder if they'd talk to us?"

He produced his TCU and dialed. "Let's find out." After a few minutes of intense conversation, he disconnected. "Amy Purcell will speak to us. I didn't give our names. When we get there, follow my lead on whether we're using aliases."

Grady loaded the printer with paper and left the data printing. Sabrina taped a vague explanatory note to the monitor in case Zoe or Aidan returned.

Eighteen minutes later Grady parked in front of a trim Cape Cod. Flower beds flanked one side of the expansive lawn, an incredible hand-built wooden jungle gym the other.

Mrs. Purcell met them at the door. The slender blonde in her midthirties had a gracious, if uncertain, smile and kind brown eyes far older and wiser than her face. Grady's mother's eyes had held that same look since his father had died. "Come in, please."

Comfy, overstuffed furniture graced the sunny yellow living room, and the fragrance of fresh-baked chocolate-chip cookies floated in the air. A baby wearing a diaper and pink T-shirt lay on her back on a quilt near the front window, waving her arms and babbling at wafting sunbeams. A dark-haired man was stretched in a leather recliner watching a televised soccer match.

Grady could easily picture himself and Sabrina living in the cozy scene. In an alternate universe. He slammed a mental fist into his face. *Stick to reality.* Daydreams had already cost him too much.

Mrs. Purcell gestured at the man in the recliner. "Roger, these are the people who phoned."

The guy pointed the remote at the TV, and the soccer match disappeared. He stood and offered his hand. "Roger Purcell."

Grady took Purcell's hand and his measure. Six foot three, over two hundred pounds of muscle. Gray dusted his crewcut and fine lines bracketed intelligent blue eyes. Purcell's expression was as no-nonsense as his callused handshake, but the lines around his mouth said he smiled often.

Grady's measure was also being taken. This guy was nobody's fool, and Grady had arrested enough criminals, psychos and con men to bet his life that these people were not involved in killing children. "I'm Officer Grady O'Rourke, Riverside PD." He indicated Sabrina. "And this is Sabrina Matthews, Mercy Hospital's child life specialist."

Sabrina shook hands with Mr. and Mrs. Purcell. "Your baby is adorable. How old is she?"

"Kelsey is six months old. We're fostering her." Amy's smile faded and she clasped her hands together. They were trembling. "Let's sit down. Can I get you anything? Coffee, cookies?"

"No, thank you, ma'am." Grady steered Sabrina to the love seat and sat beside her. She was trembling also. He enfolded her hand in his.

Sabrina leaned forward. "We appreciate your talking to us about Isaiah, Mrs. Purcell. I know it isn't easy. How long did you foster him?"

"Please, call us Amy and Roger." Mrs. Purcell and her husband sat on the sofa opposite them. "Isaiah lived with us almost three years. His birth mother was a drug addict who OD'd, and caseworkers couldn't find his father. We got him right after the state took custody."

Grady nodded. "Isaiah's medical records seem to be incomplete. Exactly when was he diagnosed with leukemia?"

"He was four and a half, but…" Amy smoothed her palms over her jeans. "The doctors at the CCC put him on medication immediately when he entered state care at age three. Isaiah's mother was HIV positive and his doctor claimed the medicine would boost his immune system."

Grady studied the Purcells' doubtful expressions. "You didn't agree?"

"No. He had no symptoms. No antibodies," Roger said. "One of Isaiah's nurses didn't agree, either."

"I'll need her name." Grady accepted the small notebook and pen Sabrina passed him from her purse.

The Purcells exchanged a look that spoke volumes.

"We're on your side," Sabrina assured them. "We're searching for the truth about what happened to Isaiah."

Amy looked at her husband again, then back at Grady. "Her name was Teresa Monteros."

Grady jotted the name down. "Hispanic?"

Roger nodded. "All the nurses and aides who worked for the CCC were nonnative English speakers."

"Do you have Ms. Monteros's phone number or address?"

"We kept in touch with her until recently, but she's not with the CCC anymore," Roger replied. "A week after Isaiah's death, she accepted a new position with the California children's welfare agency in Sacramento."

"Sacramento." Grady and Sabrina shared a silent exchange.

"I'm so thankful the police are checking into this." Amy swallowed hard. "When Teresa told me how Isaiah—" She choked. "That he'd...died—"

Roger's massive hands clenched on his thighs. "Promise us you're going to make those people pay for murdering him!"

Sabrina gasped, and Grady gave her fingers a warning squeeze. They couldn't let their emotions influence the Purcells' perspective and taint the interrogation. "What makes you believe Isaiah was murdered?" Grady asked.

"We don't *believe* he was murdered," Amy stated. "We *know!* The medication those doctors at the CCC prescribed was pure poison. It gave him *terrible* muscle cramps, headaches and nosebleeds, and disrupted his digestive system. Every dose made him worse." Tears spilled down her cheeks, and her husband rubbed her arm. "I would have done anything for Isaiah. *Anything.* I only wish... He trusted me, and I didn't...I couldn't..."

"Amy." Sabrina's voice was very gentle. "I was with him in the hospital. It's never easy to watch a child you love grow sicker. Nobody is judging you for returning him to state care."

"What?" Horror creased Amy's face. "We would never have returned our little boy! You make him sound like...merchandise that turned out to be the wrong fit!"

"I'm sorry," Sabrina said. "That's not at all what I meant. Foster children commonly change residences."

"We read the CCC's records." Grady tugged the copy of Isaiah's case report from his inside jacket pocket and passed it to Roger. "They claim you remanded Isaiah to state care six months before he died."

"They're lying! I questioned the doctor about the medication's awful side effects and he *insisted* I continue the regimen." Amy leaped to her feet. "Well, I didn't. I stopped giving it to Isaiah and he got better! But when his blood tests showed no drugs in his system, those *monsters* took him! They wouldn't let us visit or call." She buried her face in her hands and burst into tears. "Not even when he was dying!"

"Amy, honey." Roger dropped the papers to stand and embrace his wife. The helpless sorrow etching the big man's face punched into Grady's heart. "This has been hard for her...for both of us."

"Understandably." Grady knew too well the despair of watching your loved ones suffer a shocking tragedy...and being powerless to comfort them. "I'm sorry for your loss."

From her blanket near the window, the baby erupted in a loud wail.

Sabrina rushed to scoop up the screaming infant. She snuggled the baby into her shoulder and patted the tiny, quivering back. "Shh, sweetie, it's okay."

Grady had to look away from the sight of her cuddling the baby. Any man would be lucky to have Sabrina by his side. But she would be another man's wife. Carry another man's babies. He rose to retrieve the fallen pages...and crushed them in his grip.

"Kelsey is sensitive. Here, I'll take her." Roger reached for the infant.

Amy sniffled and wiped her eyes. "I'm sorry. So sorry. I'll pull myself together. I was just so shocked and upset—"

"It's all right." Sabrina gave the distraught woman a hug. "I didn't know Isaiah nearly as long as you, and I cared about him, too."

Grady stuffed the papers in his jacket. "Can you remember the name of the medication, the prescribing physician or the drug company?"

"I can do better than that." Amy squared her shoulders. "I kept a packet of them."

Chapter 12

Sabrina followed Amy back toward the living room, tucking the packet of capsules into her purse. "You've given us invaluable evidence."

Amy stopped in front of a closed door. "This was Isaiah's room. I haven't changed anything. I just couldn't bear to erase his presence from our lives. Not yet."

"I understand. He was...special. He had such an amazing spirit." Sabrina blinked back tears and cleared the wobble from her voice. "Isaiah didn't die alone. I was with him, holding his hand...at the end."

Amy looked at her face, then turned the knob. "I'd like to give you something else."

Sabrina followed her into the sky-blue bedroom. Twin beds were covered with bright plaid spreads. Dinosaur pictures adorned the walls, and dinosaur figurines lined the bookcase. A hitch caught at Sabrina's heart, and she pressed trembling lips together. "Isaiah was so crazy about dinosaurs."

"Wasn't he, though?" Amy unpinned one of three crayoned drawings from the bulletin board and offered it to her. "Would you...would you like a memento?"

"Oh, Amy." Sabrina accepted the green crayon drawing of a big and little stegosaurus. A smiling yellow sun filled the top corner.

She stared at Isaiah's name laboriously printed in uneven block letters at the bottom, and her eyes filled. "This is s-so generous. I'll t-treasure it."

"You took care of my little boy when—" tears spilled down Amy's cheeks "—when I couldn't."

The women embraced, grieving for the child who had indelibly touched their lives.

"Sabrina," Grady said gently from the doorway. "We need to go."

"Yes, we do." She carefully folded the drawing and tucked it into her shirt pocket, then gave Amy a final hug. "We have a lot of work ahead of us."

In the living room, Roger passed the baby to Amy. "I'll walk you out."

Grady put his hand on Amy's shoulder. "We're going to track down the people who hurt Isaiah and put them behind bars for the rest of their lives."

"Thank you, both of you. We're healing more every day, and knowing that really helps." Amy cuddled Kelsey. "Just last week, Roger was saying he wished Kelsey wasn't too young to play on the jungle gym, and we discussed fostering and eventually adopting another little boy."

"Don't get us wrong," Roger added. "We're not trying to replace Isaiah. But so many foster kids need homes."

Grady rubbed his chin. "If you're serious, we know two boys who would flourish with TLC. *And* would think that jungle gym was totally rad." He told them about Mikey and "Ford" and explained they came with challenges.

Amy smiled. "After handling leukemia, tantrums and bedwetting will be a cakewalk."

As a beaming Roger saw Sabrina and Grady to their car, Amy was already dialing the phone to make an appointment to meet the boys.

Sabrina climbed into the T-bird and hugged her purse to her chest. If she wasn't already body, heart and soul in love with Grady, the shining moment when he eclipsed Amy and Roger's sorrow with radiant hope would have sealed the deal.

When they were speeding back toward Aidan's apartment, she looked over at Grady. "Do you think Teresa Monteros is my anonymous tipster?"

"Yeah, and Bill's inside informant. I'm betting the Hispanic wedding rosary was hers. Before Bill died, he could have provided Teresa with funds and information to hire me to rescue you. He would've realized his investigation would endanger himself and the package would endanger you."

Plus, Granddad knew Grady cared about her, and the senator possessed the authority and ingenuity to discover Grady's temporary job. "Granddad would have asked her to look out for me if anything happened to him."

"With Bill dead and events escalating, she's probably in hiding. We have to find her."

"Yeah. Before the bad guys do."

"Roger said the CCC hired all immigrants. The language barrier would sure help perpetuate medication deceptions." Grady's eyes narrowed on the road. "And if the aides started asking questions, government threats of deportation would intimidate them into compliance."

"Makes perfect sense." She opened her purse to extract the packet Amy had entrusted to them. "This looks like the free samples of new medications doctors receive from drug companies to give to their patients as trial doses. There's no prescription, no doctor's name—"

Grady frowned. "And no paper trail to follow."

"Oh, there's a trail, if you know where to look." She spilled six black-and-white capsules into her hand. "Every pharmaceutical corporation stamps their medication. The white half of these capsules is imprinted with a black coiled spiral and the black half has a white number eighteen."

"Are you familiar with that company?"

"No, but pill identification programs are available online. We can look it up when we get to Aidan's."

They'd barely crossed the apartment's threshold when Zoe hurtled down the hallway. "About time, SWAT! Where have—" The petite, dark-haired pixie skidded to a stop. She was dressed in a purple peasant blouse and jeans. Her short curls were wet and her feet bare, as if she'd just showered. "Oh, it's you."

Grady smiled. "Great to see you again, too, sis."

"I got your note. Hi, Sabrina. You keeping him out of trouble?"

"Trying. But you know how that goes."

"Futile." Zoe hugged Sabrina, then Grady. "Nice surprise visit, brat." She kissed his cheek. "I'm worried about my husband. He fed me some lame story about paperwork, but he should've finished eons ago. Kate hasn't heard from Liam, either." She frowned at Grady. "Your note said Aidan gave you his keys. Is he okay?"

Grady flashed her the dimples. "You know the A-man."

"Yes, I do. Point of fact, I'm married to the guy. But that doesn't answer my question." She planted her hands on her hips. "Grady, I've been reporting live from the incident site for the past few days. I saw the victims." She shuddered. "All of them. I know the first responders landed in the middle of a classified—and horrible—sci-fi experiment gone wrong. And the authorities have slammed the lid on outgoing information."

"Aidan will be fine."

"*Will* be?" Suspicion tinged her countenance. "Why isn't he answering my calls?"

"I assume he's busy."

"Doing what, exactly?" She rose on tiptoe, nose to nose with Grady. "And don't give me one of your song-and-dance numbers."

"Zoe, chill out and listen." He grasped her shoulders. "Aidan will call you. In the meantime, he wants you to sit tight and not—"

"You're in town because he sent you here to babysit me. Why?" She gasped. "He's been exposed, hasn't he? Oh my God, I have to go."

She brushed past them, and Grady snagged her arm. "Hang on. Before you go tearing off half-cocked—"

Sabrina's cell phone chimed, and she checked the number. "It's my father. Maybe there's news." Two pairs of anxious eyes zeroed in on her. "Dad? What's up?"

"Hello, Sabrina. I assume O'Rourke is still with you?"

"Yes."

"Good." Her father paused. "I have something difficult to tell you. I hate to break the news over the phone, but…" Sabrina's heart staggered, and her distressed gaze clung to Grady's. "It's better you hear it from me. We have three cases of V-10. Unfortunately, you know them well."

"*Confirmed cases?*" she whispered.

Zoe's hand flew to her mouth. "No!"

"My brothers?" Grady's face drained of color. Like a man trapped in a nightmare, he slowly reached for the phone. "Let me talk to Wade."

The front door swung open and Aidan strode inside. He frowned at the frozen tableau. "What's everybody—"

"Aidan!" Zoe cried and launched herself into his arms.

Aidan embraced his trembling wife. "Whoa. I'm okay, baby. What's going on?"

Grady turned to Aidan. "Liam?" he asked hoarsely.

"He's fine." Aidan kissed the top of Zoe's head. "Gone home to Kate. Hunter's negative, Wyatt's negative. The team's clear."

"Then who—" Sabrina suddenly remembered the phone. "Hello? Yes, I'm here, sorry, Dad. Who's infected?"

"Ronnie Nguyen and his EMT partner, Kim." Her father hesitated. "And, Sabrina…the other case is Dalton."

The phone slid from her numb fingers, and her knees folded.

Aidan lunged and caught the phone as Grady caught her. "Sabrina?" Grady's voice echoed from a distance. "Come on, sweetheart, stay with me here."

Then she was sitting on the sofa with her head between her knees. Aidan finished the conversation with her father.

"Breathe." Squatting in front of her, Grady rubbed her back. "Easy, Sabrina. Breathe."

"Ronnie and Kim and Dalton. Dalton is—" She choked on the words.

"I know." Grady eased her up, enfolded her in his arms. "Listen to me. We're on the right track. We're going to figure out who created this monster, and get answers." He stroked her hair. "Once the lab unlocks the DNA code, they can make an antidote."

Her body temperature segued from boiling hot to freezing cold. She was shivering, and sickness churned in her stomach. "That'll take too long. Our friends…"

His embrace tightened reassuringly. "Are still alive."

"You're absolutely right." Keeping her eyes closed, she rested her head on his shoulder. For just a minute. She needed a minute. "Is the data printed?"

"It's almost done."

"Okay." She slowly sat upright and took deep breaths until the room stopped whirling.

Grady cupped her face. "Better now?"

She felt as if she'd been hit by a speeding bus. "Yes."

Aidan brought her ice water. Grady made her sip it while Aidan brewed coffee and Zoe stacked sandwiches. Evander jumped into Sabrina's lap to offer soft, purring comfort.

Grady text-messaged his mom informing her his brothers were fine. As Aidan and Zoe worked in the kitchen, Grady brought them up to speed.

When he finished, both the dedicated reporter and steely SWAT officer were as grimly determined as Grady and Sabrina to push through—no matter the consequences.

Sabrina had seen the O'Rourke clan rally around their own. If one O'Rourke was on your side, you had them all. Their loyalty and determination didn't quit.

The steadfast support reestablished her balance and her resolve.

The knowledge was both comfort and sorrow. If her relationship with Grady ended, seeing the O'Rourkes would become a painful reminder of what she could have had, and lost. She might have to give up not only Grady, but his entire family.

Fueled by coffee, Aidan, Zoe and Grady each took a stack of files while Sabrina performed an online search for the capsules' logo.

An hour later she emerged from Zoe's office. "I've got it! Serpens Pharmaceutical."

Grady's hand stilled over piled documents. "Serpens? That's a constellation—the Serpent." He would know. He and his dad had spent hours in the O'Rourke's backyard with their telescope. "Two entwined serpents is the medical symbol for healing."

"Highly ironic, seeing as how their wonder drug is killing people." Sabrina consulted her printout. "They're minor players in the industry, and based in Dubai."

Zoe drummed her fingers on the table. "Ownership could be any nationality. We've covered a lot of big corporations moving over there recently for tax breaks."

Grady smirked. "And should the company 'just happen' to be found guilty of a crime, the fact that no extradition treaty exists with the U.S. is a nice perk for their top execs.

Zoe handed her documents to Sabrina. "Let's trade. You work on these. I'll start tracing money connections. I have some contacts who will come in handy."

Grady grinned. "I figured you might."

They read data and compiled statistics, sorting papers on the dining room table.

Grady finished tallying a column and frowned. "Over a hundred children have died in the CCC's care during the past ten years, and a lot of names and dates match those in Bill's Bible."

"Obscene mortality rate," Sabrina replied. "How many are from toxic epidermal necrolysis?"

Aidan checked his figures. "Twelve."

"Wait, I need to do an Internet search." Sabrina hurried to Zoe's office and quickly returned. "The *highest normal* reported incidence of TEN is *one* in *ten thousand*. Yet, the CCC has twelve cases out of a hundred."

"Other causes of death are all over the map." Zoe read from her notes. "Liver failure. Kidney failure. Blood poisoning. Dozens of types of cancer. Eight strokes." Her brows scrunched. "All in children five and under."

Aidan slammed down his coffee mug. "Why the hell would *preschoolers* have strokes?"

Sabrina battled to distance herself from the horrible reality and process the facts. "The nonviral form of TEN is the body's adverse reaction to particular drugs. Most of these other diseases can be, also."

"All the kids were HIV positive…or their mothers were." A muscle ticced in Grady's jaw. "Serpens Pharmaceutical *is* using children for experimental drug research."

Sabrina set her cold coffee aside. "In the process of trying to find a cure for HIV, the researchers must have discovered they could isolate and induce toxic epidermal necrolysis. And then they configured a DNA modification to develop V-10."

"I wonder why there've been no hints of an antidote?" Zoe asked. "The virus isn't worth more than scientific acclaim unless they can stop it."

Aidan scowled. "The developers aren't in this for the good of humanity. V-10 would be a formidable biological weapon. They might have an antidote, but I guarantee it's highly classified."

Grady shot a look at Aidan, and private communication passed between the brothers. "The million-dollar question is…is V-10 being used *by* us…or *on* us?"

"Only time will tell." Sabrina's chills were back, and she rubbed her arms. "Unfortunately, our friends are out of time." She didn't even want to think about her dad and Grady's mom being exposed.

Zoe had some contacts who didn't like to disclose information over the telephone. She left to see them and use the newsroom's resources to dig deeply into Serpens Pharmaceuticals.

Armed with a list of former foster parents, Aidan also departed to conduct interviews.

Grady turned to Sabrina. "I want to examine your grandfather's recent bills, legislative speeches and lobbying petitions. What he was working on, and who he was working with, might be important."

"Those are public records. Granddad's ex-admin was crazy about him. I'm sure she won't mind if I phone her on a Sunday."

Twenty minutes later the fax machine in Zoe's office started spitting out more documents.

"Hmm. Look at this." Grady carried a sheaf of papers to where she sat on the sofa, skimming a transcript of one of her granddad's famous filibusters.

She rubbed her eyes. "I've absorbed so much information during the past few hours, I can't see or think straight anymore. Read it to me?"

"Senator Vaughn authored a bill last year that would have assigned impartial advocates to each foster child to oversee medical treatment. It passed the house and Senate, but the president vetoed it as 'cost prohibitive.'" He snorted. "The president claimed state governments are doing a 'commendable job' caring for foster children."

"If they're doing such a bang-up job, how come so many kids are dying?"

He dropped down beside her. "*If* this conspiracy travels all the way up Pennsylvania Avenue, we're bucking formidable odds. I'm in the fight until the bitter end, but…we might not win."

"Maybe not." She turned to him and took his hand. "But we have to savor the small victories. Even if worst comes to worst, the events of the past twenty-four hours have helped two little boys find their way home."

Grady sat immobile for so long she thought he wasn't going to respond. Then he looked over at her, his expressive gray-green eyes wistful. "No matter what the future brings, don't ever lose your optimism, Sabrina. It's a more powerful weapon than a Glock, and strong enough to deflect any missiles life fires at you."

He'd been subdued and distant since their kiss. She'd given him the space he'd asked for…and the distance between them had only grown wider. Her teeth sank painfully into her lower lip, but the words rushed out anyway. "That sounds…like goodbye."

He winced. "Sabrina…let's not—"

"No, let's." Anger and pain and fear crashed over her. "This morning, Ronnie, Kim and Dalton went to work thinking it was just another day. Now they're dying." She drew an unsteady breath and dove into dark, forbidden waters. "Let's go there, Grady. *For once,* let's damned well go there. Life is too short and death is too permanent to waste time playing games."

"Is that what this is between us? A game?"

"You tell me." Pent-up hurt and frustration exploded. "You're in and out of my life. You run hot then cold, and then just plain *run.* I know you care about me. Know you want me. And there's no doubt I lo—care about *you* and want *you.*"

He leaped up, stalked to the fireplace. "What we *want* isn't always what we *need.*"

"There you go again, putting distance between us. Enlighten me, *please.* What exactly are you so afraid will happen if you get close to me?"

Grady swore. "You were there when I found out Pop had been murdered."

"Yes. But I don't understand what that has to do with us."

"It has *nothing* to do with you." He turned his back to her. His body was trembling. *"Everything* to do with me."

She looked at the man she loved. At his tautly clenched fists, his bent head, the vulnerable, exposed nape of his neck. And saw the seventeen-year-old boy who'd lost his father to a brutal murder.

Anger and frustration evaporated, leaving raw pain. Grady's and her own, entwined so closely she couldn't separate them.

Didn't want to. "Grady?" She kept her voice soft and even. "Have you ever talked about this with anyone?"

"Talking won't change what happened."

"No, but being in pain distorts your perceptions. Venting your feelings can ease your pain."

"I deserve to feel pain," he growled.

She battled tears. If she got emotional, he'd shut down. "Why do you think you deserve to hurt?"

"So I don't forget."

"Do you believe if you don't hurt, you'll forget your father?"

"I could never forget Pop." His back was still to her. "I don't want to forget what I did. And what I didn't do."

Sabrina's heart ached. Grady was as wary and badly wounded as one of her patients. But she was trained for this. She could help him. "I remember the day your father was killed, you were playing a soccer game. Your dad was sick with the flu and had to stay home," she gently prompted. "What do *you* remember about that afternoon?"

"I…remember…you. You were sitting in the stands beside Mom. You wore white pants and a red blouse and red ribbons in your ponytail—our team's colors." He turned and propped his elbow on the mantel. Not facing her, but better than completely blocking her out. "When we won and they gave me the MVP trophy, you jumped up and down and shrieked so loudly I could hear you over everyone else."

His detailed recall amazed her. "And when everybody rushed the field, I reached you first. You hugged me and you were all hot and sweaty, but I was so happy for you, I didn't care."

"I kissed you, too." A crooked smile creased his mouth. "Got carried away by the excitement and went for it."

Her cheeks warmed. "That moment is forever burned into my brain. It's one of my favorite memories."

"Mine, too. Before everything went to hell." His mouth flattened. "I couldn't wait to show my trophy to Pop. Aidan, Con and Liam carried me in on their shoulders. I was still high on triumph. My brothers and I were chanting a semi-risqué fight song at top volume. Mom followed with my trophy, laughing her head off."

"I saw you as I was going up my front steps." And she'd laughed, too.

"We yelled for Pop to come and see…but he didn't. It was deathly quiet. No way could he have slept through the racket." He paused. "That's when we noticed the house had been tossed. Mom ran upstairs to the master bedroom. Con and I hit the kitchen, Aidan and Liam rushed to Pop's study, hollering for him." Another pause. "Then their voices…broke off."

"You could tell something was wrong."

"Oh, yeah. Con and I froze, stood there looking at one another like the first one to move would shatter. Then we bolted for the den. It was— Oh God, it was so much worse than anything I'd ever—" He closed his eyes. "Even weak and feverish, Pop gave DiMarco one helluva battle. There was blood everywhere." Grady gulped. "But Pop…his body…wasn't there. We couldn't find him."

They hadn't found Brian O'Rourke's body, or his killer, for nearly a decade. In order to declare him dead, the ME had testified that there was so much of Brian's blood in the room he couldn't have survived. "I knew it was horrible for you, but I didn't know… I can't imagine…" She hadn't wanted to imagine. Yet Grady had lived the nightmare, continued to live it for thirteen years. No wonder he still had raw places.

"Mom came downstairs, and I'll never forget the agony on her face. She tried to get into the den, but Aidan and Con had the wits to keep her out. She fought, and it took both of them to hold her back. She was screaming."

Sabrina's nails dug into her palms. Grady's memories had merged with hers, but she had to stay strong. She and her father had heard Maureen O'Rourke screaming from next door. Bone-chilling, animalistic screams.

"Blood has a distinctive smell, you know. When there's so much—spattered on the walls, soaking into the furniture, the carpet—it has a primal odor that sinks into your pores. Into your soul. The smell of all that blood, and seeing Mom fall to pieces—"

He turned his back on her again, and memories poured from him, wounds that had long needed lancing. "The pain tore me up. I…I couldn't hack it. I ran outside, dropped to my knees on the lawn and puked my guts out. That's where you and your father found me."

Biting the inside of her cheek, Sabrina let him talk it out.

"After Wade and my brothers brought me and Mom next door

to Letty's house, Aidan, Con and Liam went back to meet the cops. Your father was great with Mom. He gave her a sedative and she fell asleep. I couldn't stop shaking or crying. Wade wanted to give me a shot, too, but I was terrified I'd see Pop's body in my dreams. Wade talked to me.... I don't remember exactly what he said, but it helped. He...somehow made the unbearable easier."

Grady swallowed so hard she could hear it. "I'd always wanted to be a cop like my dad, but the reason I also took medic training was because of *your* dad."

Moisture stung her eyelids. "He'd be honored to know that."

"I remember you sitting beside me on the sofa, holding my hand. That helped, too. You convinced me to let Wade give me a smaller dose of meds that didn't put me out but calmed me down."

"I felt so helpless. I wish I could have done more."

"The meds dulled the sharp edges enough for me to find my balls and return to the house. CSI and Homicide were long gone. I stood on the front porch for fifteen minutes cranking up my courage. I had to force myself to go inside."

"Going back in there took remarkable bravery."

"Brave, my ass. I'd been sniveling with the women while my brothers dealt with the fallout. Aidan told us there was no way we were letting Mom walk into that mess. The four of us cleaned it up. Scrubbed away the gore."

She stifled a gasp. "I'm sorry. If I'd realized, I would have come and helped."

"I'm glad you didn't see it. *Nobody* should have to do what we did." He shuddered. "I've blanked most of it out, but the job took all night. We ripped up the carpet and took it and Pop's chair to the dump in Con's pickup. I had a lump in my throat the size of a boulder, and my stomach felt like it had been shredded.

"Nobody said anything until we threw Pop's torn, lumpy recliner out of Con's truck. We stood there, looking at our father's favorite chair reduced to bloody, battered refuse. Like his life. Like our lives. And we finally lost it. Put our arms around one another and cried. The *only* time I saw my brothers cry."

"They're human, they cried, Grady. They grieved for years, the same as you. Just not where you could see them."

"Hell, once the first shock wave passed, *Mom* was stronger than me. I fell apart on our front lawn, puked my guts out and bawled like a little girl in front of God and everybody." He hung his head. "I let my brothers down. Let my mom down. I let my feelings take over and I was *useless* to my family."

"Oh, Grady." No matter how cathartic, she couldn't sit any longer and watch him tear himself apart. She stood and paced to the window. "Cut yourself a break. You were only seventeen."

"I'm not seventeen anymore. And I could never bring myself to go back into the den. Even though it's been redone...to this day, I cannot walk into that room."

"You sustained a terrible trauma. Nobody can fault you." Tears blurring the view, she traced a finger down the pane. "You still have *good* memories of your dad. He loved being your Boy Scout leader, and attending school events and games. He was proud of you. He loved you so much."

"And he died thinking I hated him."

She turned, stared at his rigid back. "What?"

"Pop didn't miss my game because he had the flu. That's the reason he gave, and everyone thinks that's why." He hesitated. "He was sick, but he'd have gone anyway." Misery dulled his voice. "He didn't go because we'd been fighting."

"Teenagers and their parents argue."

"We'd been snarling at each other like two alley cats in a bag for a couple of months, since I'd announced my decision to attend the police academy after college and join the force. I thought he'd be happy and proud, like he was with my brothers. But he was livid." Grady's shoulders hunched. "Apparently, he didn't think I was cop material."

"Wait a minute. Did Brian actually *say* he didn't think you were good enough to be a cop?"

"He didn't have to. I had pro soccer scouts all over me. Pop insisted I take advantage of my soccer scholarship to turn pro." He scowled. "Can you see me hanging out in shorts with David Beckham?"

"In your father's opinion, you should have used your athletic abilities in a less dangerous profession. That doesn't mean he believed you'd be a bad cop."

"He said I lacked maturity and discipline. I proved him right."

Shame trembled in his low admission. "The day he died, I told him
I wasn't six anymore and didn't need Daddy holding my hand or
running my life. That if he was going to ride my ass about pro
soccer, I didn't want him at my game. I yelled at him to stay
home." He swallowed again. "If I hadn't lost control of my
emotions, lost my temper, he'd have gone to the game. DiMarco
wouldn't have ambushed him...and Pop would still be alive."

His voice went so quiet she could barely hear him. "It's my fault
he's dead."

"Oh, Grady!" She crossed to him and touched his back, ignoring his flinch. "You heard the testimony at DiMarco's trial. Tony
DiMarco would have come at another time and murdered your
entire family."

"But Pop wouldn't have been sick and weak. My brothers
would have been there. DiMarco wouldn't have stood a chance."

"DiMarco had four armed men with him." She rubbed his taut
trembling muscles. "'What if' can't change the past. The guilt
belongs to Tony DiMarco...and *nobody* else."

"Maybe. Maybe not. But it sure as hell was my fault that the final
words Pop took to his grave were *'I don't need you.'*" He inhaled a
quivering breath. "Our last conversation haunts me every day."

"Grady Stephen O'Rourke, listen to me." She wrapped her
arms around him, and even though he stiffened, she rested her
cheek against his back. "We have all—each and every one of us
who are mere human beings—said terrible things in anger to the
people we love. Your father was a smart man, a savvy cop and a
seasoned parent who had already guided three boys through adolescence. I know as well as you do he had disagreements with
Aidan, Con and Liam. He knew you didn't mean it."

He shook his head. "Even if that were true, it doesn't dispute
the fact that if I'd kept my cool, been more objective, the last thing
Pop heard from me wouldn't have been a cruel rejection..
shouted in anger."

Grady's tremors grew more violent, and his teeth ground
together. "After he died, if I hadn't been wrapped up in my own
pain, I wouldn't have let my family down. I was worse than useless
I was a *liability*. I didn't support Mom or my brothers. In the midst
of their suffering, they had to take care of *me*."

"That's what families do. Watch out for each other."

"We can't really, though, can we?" he asked bitterly. "Death strutted into our house in the middle of the afternoon and stole my father. And made me weak. Made me fail the people I love the most. If death has that much power, nobody is safe."

She gasped. "That's why... I get it now. The bungee jumping, rock climbing, sky diving. The reason you fight tooth and nail for each victim as a cop, for each patient as a medic. You're waging a personal war with death."

"Damned right, I am." He broke her hold and whirled to face her, his eyes fierce. "Your father gets it. Like surgeons, soldiers have to maintain distance or they can't do the job. If I let myself feel, I can't help the people who've entrusted their lives to me. I care about you, Sabrina, but I can't care too much. Because then I can't protect you, physically or emotionally."

"Can't you see... You're not trying to protect *my* emotions. Not that I *asked* you to!" She was breathing too fast, too hard. "You're hurting and scared, and you're protecting *yourself.*"

She inhaled a quivering breath. "Forever is a long time to live with regret, Grady. You think it makes you stronger not to feel? If you can't feel, you'll never be whole. No, you're not afraid to die...you're afraid to *live.*"

He thrust his fingers through his hair. "I can never go back and change what happened between me and my dad. I don't know how to fix this."

"You healer types have a real tendency toward God complexes." She forced down the aching lump in her throat. "You may hold life and death in your hands sometimes, but you're not God. Not even close. You're not responsible for who lives and who dies." She swallowed again. "You're absolutely right. This is something you can't fix."

"How do I live with that?"

"I don't know. But I'm willing to help you, if you'll let me. All you have to do is meet me halfway." She held out her hand to him.

He backed away, and dread coiled inside her. "Grady, if you can't get past this, if you can't find a way to forgive yourself and move on, you might as well have been buried alongside your father."

"I won't…let my weakness endanger you." His voice was ragged, and tears glittered in his eyes. "I *can't*."

"If you stay, I promise, I'll help you. But, Grady…if you leave again after this is over—" pain sliced into her, and she could barely force out the words "—we're done."

Chapter 13

Grady prowled in front of the picture window, turmoil eating him alive. Sabrina had been in the kitchen for fifteen minutes—pretending she wasn't crying. All he heard was scrubbing noises and water running in the sink, but he'd seen her eyes well up before she'd mumbled an excuse about cleaning and retreated.

Every teardrop fired a bullet into his heart.

He'd spilled his guts. They'd thrown their cards on the table. He should feel relieved. Instead, he feared he'd made the second-worst mistake of his life.

Dammit. He slammed his fists against the window, looked down at the city spread far below…and froze. *What the—* The building's height and thick insulation blocked outside noise, and he stared down at a silent hell.

Riverside had gone insane.

Cars clogged the streets, people jammed the sidewalks and every bridge and overpass spanning the Willamette—except the top deck of the Madison Overpass, which was under construction—was stacked with bumper-to-bumper traffic. "Sabrina!" He lunged for the TV. "Get out here!"

He turned the television on as she hurried in. He jerked his gaze from her pink-tipped nose and damp, spiky lashes. He'd made her cry more during the past twenty-four hours than in his entire lifetime.

His throat tightened. But then, only Sabrina knew how many tears he'd caused her in the past.

"What's going on?"

"Look at the city."

She peered out the window. "Holy cats!"

On the TV screen, the local anchorman sat stiffly at his desk, his face grave. Grady cranked up the volume. "Some grocery stores are experiencing outages of bottled water and food staples. Please, as we've been repeating, do not attempt to travel and block roadways needed by emergency personnel. U.S. borders are closed, and all air traffic is grounded. The president and secretary of defense have assured us there's no need for panic."

Grady scowled. "And if you believe that…just honk."

The grim news continued. "The Centers for Disease Control in Atlanta reports that small outbreaks of the mystery illness in Philadelphia, Houston, Denver and Riverside are under control, and the public is not at risk."

Grady's gut clenched, and he swore.

Sabrina gasped. "V-10 is in the population, nationwide! Do you think it *is* a terrorist attack?"

The anchorman shuffled papers. "Our elected officials in Washington, D.C., are safely sequestered and working to deliver a quick resolution. We're told representatives of Serpens Pharmaceutical Corporation have been aware of this illness for some time and were awarded a federal grant to develop a vaccine."

Grady turned to Sabrina. "It appears we have our answer."

He tugged his buzzing TCU from his pants pocket. The call was from Con's cell phone. Aidan would have passed the V-10 intel on to Con and Liam when the news hit the fan. "Yo, Con."

"Grady." Intensity edged his brother's low, even tone. "I need your help."

What had happened? Grady's fingers tightened on the plastic casing. "You got it."

"Bailey's in labor. Mass pandemonium erupted on the way to the hospital and we're trapped on the Madison Overpass. EMS can't reach us." Con's words were calm, but anxiety thrummed in his voice "You've delivered babies. You *have* to get here."

"Has Bailey's water broken?" Grady was already shrugging on

his leather jacket. Eyes huge, Sabrina spun, and he motioned her to follow. He yanked Zoe's leather coat from the entry closet on the way out the door.

"Yes, an hour ago."

He locked the door and they sprinted for the elevator. "How far apart are the contractions?"

"Four point six minutes."

Leave it to Con to be exact. "Lay her down in the backseat on her left side. Keep her breathing on track." As the floors flashed downward, he tossed Zoe's jacket to Sabrina, gesturing for her to put it on. "Everything will be fine, even if I have to talk you through the delivery." Several years ago, Grady had phone-coached Con through a birth during a hostage crisis. "We've done it before."

"It wasn't my wife and baby before!" Con inhaled rapidly, and his voice leveled again. "I need *you.* Here."

"I'm already in transit." The elevator opened, and he and Sabrina strode into the parking garage. "Give me your exact 20."

"Center level of the overpass, a quarter of a mile past exit seventeen. Jammed between a million other stalled vehicles. We're in Bailey's new car, a champagne Camry."

"ETA is less than thirty minutes. If anything changes, call. Hang tight, bro." He disconnected and shoved his TCU into his jacket.

Sabrina panted beside him as he jogged past rows of parked cars. *"No way* will we get through that traffic."

"There's always a way." He stopped beside Aidan's black Ducati, pitched Zoe's helmet to Sabrina and then tugged on Aidan's.

He slung his leg over the motorcycle's seat, and Sabrina clambered on behind. She wrapped her arms around his waist. "Somehow, I doubt a note is going to cover this one."

"Good thing drawing and quartering is illegal in this century." Grady thrust in the key, kick-started the engine, and the bike roared to life. "Hang on. It's gonna be a helluva trip."

He gunned the motor, sped out of the parking structure and into nightmare traffic. Speeding on both sides of the road, he wound through car-choked streets. Until he hit an intersection blocked by a city bus on one side and a delivery truck on the other.

"Screw this." He leaned on the horn, rocketed the bike over the curb and zigzagged down the crowded sidewalk. Pedestrians scrambled out of his way, tossing him startled looks, curses and, in a few cases, the bird.

"Yee, haw!" Grady swerved to miss a tree, then a mailbox and barreled past an outdoor café. He darted around a movie marquee by a razor's edge, and veered through a street market, skimming between crated produce and a steel lamppost.

The powerful engine growled beneath him, wind slapped his face and adrenaline glittered through his veins in an intoxicating rush. "Damn, this is fun!"

Sabrina shrieked. Her arms clamped around him in a stranglehold and she buried her face, helmet and all, in his back. "Yet you think *commitment* is scary!"

Yeah. Broken bones healed. And didn't cause one-tenth the pain of a broken heart.

After a wild, exhilarating ride, they pulled into the lot outside Mercy Hospital's emergency entrance. Every space was filled, many vehicles double-parked. Grady propped the Ducati in a flower bed. Grabbing Sabrina's hand, he dodged an influx of people as he ran for the door.

"Why are we at the hospital without the parents-to-be?"

"No sidewalks on the overpass. Besides, we can't transport Bailey and the baby on a bike."

"Then what are we—" She groaned. "Oh, no."

"Oh, yes." He skirted the ER, which was stuffed with panicked citizens. Every resident within a hundred miles suffering from an earache or sniffles was pouring in, afraid they were infected.

A throng surrounded the bank of elevators and Grady pulled rank. "Police emergency, coming through!"

The crowd parted. As the elevator bell dinged and the doors opened, three skinhead punk wannabes wearing tough-guy clothes and jittery expressions blocked his path. The front man flashed a gang sign. "We been waitin' on this car forever, yo. Y'all's don't look like no heat."

The doors were already closing, and waiting on another elevator would waste precious minutes. Grady whipped out his Glock. "This hot enough for ya, Eminem?"

"No hassle, man." Palms up, the trio retreated, and the leader cocked his veed index and middle fingers. "Peace out."

Grady steered Sabrina behind him and backed onto the elevator, keeping his gaze, and his weapon, trained on the punks. Nobody else got into the car.

The doors slid shut, and Grady shoved the gun into his waistband.

Sabrina's gilded brows arched. "Dramatic much?"

"We don't have time for tweaker crap."

On the rooftop, they raced to the chopper. Grady buckled Sabrina in, then tore around and jumped inside. He donned headphones, tossed Sabrina a pair. Thank all the saints, medical distress calls rated precedence from air traffic control. He performed preflight in record time, throttled up, pulled pitch and the chopper leaped skyward.

The sky buzzed with aircraft. A Cessna 152 shot into his peripheral vision and banked too sharply to his left. "Dammit!"

Grady cranked and yanked, and Sabrina's gasp echoed in his earphones. "Yikes! That was close!"

"Every news organization in the city is jamming airspace." He'd rather fly rotor-to-rotor with gunships in a firefight than jockey through a fleet of vultures hell-bent on five-o'clock exclusives.

When the massive concrete overpass came into view, Sabrina shifted. "Um…Grady?" She stared at the gridlock far below. "Where are we going to *land?*"

He pointed. "In the only traffic-free zone in a sixty-mile radius."

"It looks awfully…narrow." She swallowed. "Ah…what about construction workers?"

He looked down at the jagged, half-finished Madison Overpass jutting over the Willamette River. "*If* any workers hung around after hearing the news broadcasts, they'll move. People tend to haul ass when they see a three-ton whirlybird coming down."

She moaned. "I can't watch."

"Piece of—"

She flung up her hand. "If you even *mention* food, your leather upholstery will become an endangered species."

He chuckled as he maneuvered through strong crosswinds buffeting the river. The challenge was almost enough to make him forget what had happened between them earlier.

His humor fled.

Almost.

The skids kissed concrete, and Sabrina eased one eyelid open. "Are we...alive?"

"So far."

She glanced around. "How do we get to Con and Bailey?"

Grady shut down the engine. "We're gonna rappel over the side of the bridge."

"No, seriously—" She stared as he yanked on his gloves. "You *are* serious."

"As a major myocardial infarction." He handed her a pair of gloves. "If the scenario goes FUBAR, I'll need someone with a cool head and medical training."

They climbed out of the chopper. River-driven wind shoved at Grady's back as he uncoiled rappel cables and donned his harness and a backpack of medical supplies. When he buckled a harness on Sabrina, she was shaking. "Cold or scared?"

"B-both."

"I've done this hundreds of times. I won't let anything happen to you." He drew her close. "Trust me, Sabrina."

Her eyes locked on his, and the absolute faith in the glowing brown depths made his heart stumble. "I always have."

"You won't be on your own. We're going to tandem rappel." He steered her to the edge of the overpass and clipped their harnesses into the cable. "Remember, Bailey's life—and the baby's—are on the line."

Sabrina's chin firmed. "You can count on me."

Grady couldn't stop himself from planting a quick kiss on her luscious mouth. "I always have."

He boosted her onto the ledge and climbed up beside her. Trembling violently, she stared at the choppy green waves far below. He cupped her cheek and brought her gaze back to his. "Wrap yourself around me and hold on tight. Our weight will make the descent fast, and it'll feel like we're free-falling. No matter what happens, don't panic. And don't let go of me, because you'll skew us off balance. Got it?"

"Don't worry." She nodded slowly. "I'm not *about* to let go of you."

"I won't let you fall, Sabrina." Braking arm braced on the taut cable, boots braced against the concrete railing, he suspended them backward over the precipice. "Ready?"

"Oh God." She inhaled. "As I ever will be."

"Rappelling." He dropped over the edge. Sabrina gasped and tightened her grip. Even weighted by the sobering responsibility for her safety, hurtling through space at breakneck speed over open water sent a thrill up his spine.

At the middle tier of the overpass, he braked hard, letting their momentum and the wind rock them toward the ledge. "Nearly there," he said into Sabrina's ear. "We have to swing a little." When his boots touched the railing again, he pushed off.

They swung out over the river, then back, soaring in perfect tandem. Sabrina's arms clung around his neck, her legs around his waist, her body intimately plastered to him. Her heartbeats galloped against his chest, her warm, rapid breaths tingled down his neck. The rush was almost as exhilarating as their interlude in the closet.

Almost.

The third arc swung them over the railing into the overpass and he released more cable. His boots scraped asphalt, hit solid ground. He rubbed Sabrina's back, then surrendered to the temptation to pat her bottom. "You can turn me loose, now, honey."

She shakily gained her feet and looked at him. "You. Are. Irre-deemable." But she smiled.

Grinning, he unhooked the cable and looked over at dozens of astonished gazes staring at them from gridlocked vehicles. "Tell me that didn't give you a tingle."

Her smile widened into a sparkling grin. "Maybe…one."

"Well, all right, then." He stripped off his gloves, stuffed them in his pocket. "Corruption has to start somewhere."

Con and Bailey were six car lengths ahead. Grady opened the back door of their Camry. "Somebody here order a pizza?"

Con was sitting against the opposite door, cradling Bailey with his body. She was propped on her left side, with her cheek against Con's chest. His brother smirked, but relieved gratitude warmed some of the worry from his dark brown eyes. "Extra sauce, hold the ham. Quite an entrance, bro."

"Guaranteed to arrive in less than thirty minutes, or it's free." Grady shrugged off the backpack and passed it to Sabrina so he could climb into the car. "Hey, Bailey. It's a beautiful day for a birthday party. A Gemini baby, just like Uncle Grady."

His sister-in-law's heart-shaped face was flushed, and damp strawberry-blond curls stuck to her temples. Her blue sundress clung to her body, the fabric limp with perspiration. She smiled at him. "Heaven help us."

He motioned for Sabrina to get into the front seat with the backpack. "I'm going to take your vitals." He took Bailey's pulse. "How are you doing?"

"All right, considering," she replied. "But I'd rather not give birth in my brand-new car."

Grady accepted the blood pressure monitor from Sabrina, strapped the cuff around Bailey's upper arm and pumped. "Seems my niece or nephew has an independent agenda. I warned you about O'Rourke genes." He listened through the stethoscope Sabrina handed him, released the air and read the dial. And wasn't reassured.

Keeping his expression neutral, he looked at Con. "How far apart are the contractions?"

"Three point four minutes."

Bailey gasped. "Here comes another one."

Grady placed his palm on her abdomen to gauge the strength of the contraction.

"Uh! I have to push!"

"Don't," he instructed. "The baby is too high up, and we don't know how dilated you are yet. *Don't push.*" He waited while Con helped his wife breathe through the pain.

"Good teamwork, guys." He gently palpated her distended abdomen. Something wasn't right. "Bailey, can you turn on your back for me?"

She complied, and he rechecked the contours beneath his hand. His fears confirmed, his mouth went dry. *Dammit!* Not here. Not now. His glance snagged on Sabrina's and her eyes narrowed. She always had been able to read him too easily.

"I need to touch base with your doctor. It's SOP. Be right back." Avoiding the sudden alarmed questions that sprang into his brother's face, he patted Bailey's hand. "You're doing great. When the next contraction hits, don't push."

Grady stalked to the rear of the car and kept going until he was out of Con's visual range before tugging out his TCU. He couldn't get through to the hospital. He couldn't raise an operator to attempt to break into the line. And 911 was looping a recorded message that the system was overloaded. He swore viciously.

"What's wrong?" Sabrina asked from behind him.

"Bailey's BP is spiking, and the baby is breech. I can't reach a doctor to coach me. It's just me. *Me!*"

She touched his arm. "I'm here, Grady."

He whirled. "Dammit all to hell! I can't do this!"

"Take it easy. You've delivered other babies."

"Not a breech birth, especially with complications!" He raked his fingers through his hair. "Not my brother's child. A baby that shares my family's heritage, my blood. A baby that's too close to my heart." Grady swallowed hard. "Bailey needs a *cesarean.* We're in the middle of the *freeway.* No doctor, no ambulance, minimal equipment—"

"We'll manage."

"If I let my brother's wife or child die—" he choked.

"They are *not* going to die." Sabrina grabbed his upper arms. "I have faith in you. Con and Bailey have faith in you. You are the ace of improvisation." She shook him, hard. "You can do this! Now get your ass back to the car and handle it!"

Sabrina's confidence was a slap of cold water, dousing the inferno of fear. Gulping deep breaths, he sprinted to the Camry.

Con was paler and sweating more profusely than his wife. "Grady…" His lips trembled and he clamped his teeth together. "What the f—"

"Your son or daughter threw us a curve ball. The baby is breech…which calls for a new game plan." Grady explained what was about to happen. "Bailey, I know it's really tough, but you cannot push. Just pant through the contractions, understand?"

Fear glimmered beneath the surface, but her mouth firmed. "Absolutely."

"If—" Con swallowed hard. "Grady, are you positive—"

"A hundred percent. We have no other choice." Grady looked at Sabrina, waiting for him outside the car. Then he held Con's gaze, offered a silent vow. *I know, brother. I know what you're terrified you'll lose. And I'll give my life to ensure it doesn't happen.* "I promise, I will get you through this."

He rested his palm on Bailey's abdomen and leaned down. "Hey, kiddo, this is your uncle Grady. If you'll *please* wait thirty minutes to arrive at the party, I'll buy you a Ferrari."

The baby kicked beneath his hand, and Grady smiled in spite of his anxiety. "Deal."

He jogged back to the edge of the overpass, yanked on his gloves and clipped his harness into the cable.

Sabrina blew him a kiss. "Be careful."

"Keep them calm, and keep Bailey from pushing."

"I will."

"I know you will." He saluted her, pushed off and climbed back up to the helicopter.

When he reached the chopper, he hovered it above the bridge and sent down the rescue basket on its reinforced cable. Grady couldn't fly and attend to Bailey. He couldn't leave Sabrina unprotected on the freeway. And Bailey was going into surgery and needed her husband at the hospital to make decisions if she couldn't. He had to scoop up all three.

A quick call between cell phones confirmed Sabrina was aboard the rescue basket and he winched her up. He pulled up Bailey next, and while Sabrina was settling Bailey in the back of the chopper, he retrieved Con.

Then he flew like never before. Grady listened in his headphones as his brother and Sabrina gave Bailey calm, focused support. It was the longest fourteen minutes in history.

He had aircraft control override Mercy's communication system and radio ahead, and the instant the chopper settled on the helipad, a trauma team rushed out with a gurney.

They crowded into the elevator, he recited Bailey's stats to the OB nurse and then he and Sabrina ran behind them to the surgical floor.

The big double doors swung shut behind his brother and Bailey. And then all Grady could do was wait.

And pray.

Stomach churning, he stalked to the window. Had he gotten them there in time?

Sabrina followed. "You okay?"

"Why wouldn't I be? I'm not the one having the baby." He'd been shot, knifed and had taken shrapnel from a rogue grenade…but *damn*…he'd delivered enough babies to know if given a choice, he'd never put himself through that hell.

"C-sections go pretty fast, but I'd like to check in on Dalton while we're waiting."

"No problem." Given the situation, he couldn't resent her concern. "Phone the nurses' station and ask."

She placed the call, then hung up, frowning. "Only family is allowed."

"I'm sorry, Sabrina. I know you care about him."

Moisture flooded her eyes. "I just can't bear the thought…"

"Don't." He pulled her into a hug. "It won't help him or you."

She rubbed her cheek on his chest, melting his heart. He should resist touching her. But he couldn't.

All too soon he'd never touch her again.

Avoiding crowded waiting rooms, they walked the halls, detouring downstairs to the cafeteria. Sabrina got coffee. Grady's stomach was too jumpy.

When they returned to the surgical floor, he consulted his watch, and anxiety crawled up his spine. Almost two hours. They should have heard by now.

Sabrina peeked into the waiting room as they passed again. "Grady! Zoe's on TV!"

They hurried inside.

"This is Zoe Zagretti, with an exclusive live report from Ethan Burke's vacation home on Mt. Hood." Zoe used her maiden name on camera to protect her and Aidan's privacy.

The camera panned back to show a spacious lodge living room. Ethan Burke, a charismatic, fortyish politician, sat on a leather sofa beside his polished, blond wife and seven-year-old son. "The esteemed attorney and high-ranking presidential adviser was in town to chair a regional conference on children's welfare when the current crisis arose." Zoe turned to Burke. "Mr. Burke, why have you chosen to remain in Riverside, rather than return to the capital?"

"Riverside is one of the cities affected by this tragedy, and I'm here to offer the cabinet's full support, with the president's blessing. We want to assure our citizens the danger is minimal, and my presence proves that." His steady blue gaze looked directly at the viewers. "Stay off the roadways and remain calm. I'm not running scared, and neither should you."

"Or maybe the entire city is quarantined," Grady muttered. "And the president doesn't want the possibility of infection anywhere near D.C."

Sabrina elbowed him. "Cynic."

Burke smiled into the camera. "I'm working closely with the White House, and we're preparing a press conference to announce the latest developments. We'll deliver breaking news to you as soon as possible."

Zoe asked a few more questions, signed off, and then the screen switched to the local news anchors.

Sixty seconds later, Grady's TCU buzzed with a call from Zoe's cell phone. He hit the connect button. "Just caught your latest exclusive."

"There's a lot more stuff I can't say on camera...yet. I'm on the move and this has to be fast, so listen up," Zoe said, rapid-fire. "I touched base with Aidan, and he's collected statements from other foster parents that jibe with the Purcells'. Three months before Senator Vaughn died, he refused a hefty donation from lobbyists pushing for less restrictions on pharmaceutical research. Guess who didn't turn them down?"

"Ethan Burke?"

"Nope, not Burke. He raised the banner for children's causes again after Senator Vaughn died, and he's been open and cooperative." Her voice lowered. "It goes *much* higher. Directly to the vice president. Deeper digging uncovered a major Serpens stockholder...also the vice president."

"Then we're outgunned with money and manpower."

"Oh, it gets better. Before I went on air, I received a call from a senior agent with Homeland Security. He ordered me to drop the investigation or face arrest."

"Dammit, Zoe, this is dangerous territory. Be careful."

She snorted. "Look who's talking. Gotta go. I'll call with updates."

Grady stared at his blank TCU screen as dread filtered through him. He'd once skied down Mt. Hood barely ahead of an avalanche. The ominous, heavy rumbling at his back felt much the same. He steered Sabrina into the corridor and filled her in. "This is getting hairier by the second. I'm gonna call Riverside PD and secure that safe house for you."

Her eyes flashed amber fire. "While you, Zoe and Aidan endanger *your* lives? This is *my* fight…more than any of you. Those monsters killed Lord knows how many defenseless children. They killed a little boy I cared about. Killed my grandfather."

"Sabrina…"

"No! My personal safety doesn't mean squat when men we've elected into office—men who are *supposed* to represent 'We the People'—are getting away with murder!" She stabbed his chest with her index finger. "I don't care how powerful they are. We have truth, right and good old American justice on our side." Her eyes blazed, her cheeks flushed and her body trembled. "Dirty money and dirtier politicians can bite us!"

Grady's hands fisted against the urge to grab her and kiss her speechless. Damn, he loved it when Sabrina got fired up with righteous fury.

He loved her loyalty. Loved her fearless dedication to truth and fairness. Loved her intelligence, humor and the soft vulnerability she revealed only to him.

The breath slammed out of him.

He loved her.

He'd known he loved her. Had always known. He'd just never acknowledged his feelings. Never given them form, or voice.

Sabrina had been dead-on accurate…he hadn't run only to protect her.

Grady stared at the girl he'd known most of his life, at the woman he loved beyond all reason, and his heart turned over. He had a huge decision to make. Did he keep his emotions barricaded and save himself?

Or did he lower his shields, battle his terror and fight the armies of hell for the woman his soul was empty without?

Chapter 14

7:00 p.m.

Time. He just needed more time.

His pulse roaring in his ears, Grady turned aside. And saw Con standing motionless at the end of the hallway.

His brother's blue surgical scrubs were soaked with sweat, his eyes were glazed, his face white.

"Con?" Grady sprinted to him. "Is Bailey—"

"I have never...in my life...seen anything..." Con swiped an unsteady hand over his face. "Bailey's fine." He broke into a wobbly smile. "We have a baby girl. Seven pounds, twelve ounces...squalling her head off."

Grady whooped, hugged his brother, pounded his back. "That rocks, bro!"

Smiling, Sabrina kissed Con's cheek. "Nice job, Dad."

"Dad." Con exhaled. "Whoa."

Grady stepped back. "Bailey come out of surgery okay? No side effects from anesthesia?"

"The anesthesiologist did an epidural. He didn't want to use general because of her high blood pressure." Con gulped. "The obstetrician said... Grady, if you hadn't flown them in, my wife and baby wouldn't have—"

"They're okay." Grady shook his head. "It's all that matters now."

"Thanks to you." Con clapped Grady on the shoulder. "I… uh…shouldn't have lost my temper and slugged you before."

"The wake-up call was overdue." Grady shrugged. "I shouldn't have been AWOL when Mom was sick."

"You've been waiting awhile to meet your niece. We wanted time alone first."

"Understandable."

Con grinned. "Ready?"

"Lead the way." Grady slid his arm around Sabrina's waist, and they trailed Con down the corridor and into Bailey's room.

Bailey reclined in bed, cradling a tiny, pink-wrapped bundle. She looked damn good considering she'd had major surgery… while awake. Grady shuddered. He'd seen the size of those epidural needles, had observed a C-section. No wonder Con looked shell-shocked. "Hey, sis. How are you feeling?"

"Much better than when you saw me last." She smiled. "Thank you, Grady, from the bottom of our hearts. Words aren't enough."

"Sure they are." He winked at her. "I won't ask for your first-born."

"As if we'd give her away." She offered up the impossibly small bundle. "You can hold her, though."

"I don't think…"

Sabrina elbowed him. "Don't be a coward."

"Er…all right."

Con lifted the alert infant into his arms and stroked her cheek. "This is your uncle Grady. The one who owes you a Ferrari." He carefully handed the baby to Grady. "Meet Brianna Rose O'Rourke."

Brianna, in honor of their father, Rose for Bailey's favorite flower. "Hello there, princess. Happy birthday." Grady looked down at the dusting of red curls, tiny rosebud mouth and serious blue eyes that warily assessed him, and an aching lump lodged in his throat.

"She's beautiful," Sabrina breathed.

Grady glanced at Sabrina, tumbled into her soft amber gaze. "Yes, she is."

His heart stopped, then kicked into a thundering tattoo. What he truly wanted had never really been in doubt.

He didn't have a clue how to handle the terrifying responsibility. But he could sure as hell scrap his pride and learn from someone who did.

"Your turn." He carefully passed the baby to Sabrina. "Ah, Con." Grady gestured at the door. "A word."

"You bet." Con kissed his wife. "You'll be okay if I step out for a minute?"

"I'm not going anywhere." Bailey smiled at Sabrina. "Sabrina, Brianna Rose and I can indulge in girl talk."

Grady paced the hallway, unsure how to begin.

Crossing his arms, Con leaned against the wall. "I'm the one who just became a father, and *you're* green around the gills. What's eating you?"

"I...lost it today," he confessed. "I flipped out on the bridge. I...was... I was scared, Con."

"Ya think?" Con snorted. "Hell, we were *all* scared, Grady." His brother grimaced. "I haven't stopped being scared. I'm freaking terrified right this minute. I will, in all probability, never *stop* being terrified until my final breath."

Grady stared at his big brother. "But you and Aidan and Liam don't... You aren't—"

"Holy crap, bro." Con straightened. "You think we're superhuman? Have you watched Aidan when Zoe is embroiled in an investigation? He gets so intense you could snap him in half. And even after Liam was exposed to the virus, his biggest concern was Kate." Con put his hand on Grady's shoulder. "You were scared, but you came through for me. For us. You saved my wife and child."

"Thanks to Sabrina." Grady swallowed. "When I unraveled, she yanked me together. *She* ordered me to get my ass back to the car and handle the situation. She was...amazing."

"I'll be damned." Grinning, Con stepped back. "You *finally* caught a clue. The rest of the clan had Sabrina pegged as yours years ago."

Apparently he'd let fear blind him in more ways than one. "Guess I lagged out of the starting gate."

"Now you're up to speed," Con prompted. "What are you waiting for?"

Grady propped his palms on the wall and let his head drop. "How do you do it?" he blurted. "How do you marry the woman you love, bring children into the world, knowing you can't protect them? Knowing you can't keep them safe?" He slapped the stucco so hard his hand stung. "How do you fight an invisible enemy?"

"One battle at a time, little brother," Con replied. "And you never stop feeling like your heart's being squeezed in a giant fist." He sighed. "Sometimes…you just gotta walk by faith."

Terror roiled back as Grady turned to face his brother. "I'm not sure…my faith is strong enough."

"I guarantee, it's not. Not alone." Con shook his head. "Did you *see* my wife today? Even about to give birth on a freeway, she was rock-solid incredible. You should have seen her in the OR." He smiled. "O'Rourke men only fall for exceptional women. And having that remarkable woman by your side is worth every second of doubt, pain and fear."

"Would you say the same if things had gone differently?" Grady hesitated "If we'd…lost them?"

"Hell, yeah. Nobody's future is certain. *Right now* is all we get. My wife and child could have died, and there wasn't one single thing I could do. Except call you."

He went cold. "Exactly why I freaked. The responsibility—"

"Wasn't all yours." Con rubbed the back of his neck. "It wasn't you alone who saved them, Grady. It was you…and me…and Bailey…and Sabrina…and even my baby girl, who fought the odds like a champ. If—" He gulped. "Yeah, if I'd lost them, it would have blown me to pieces."

"How do you *live* with that?"

"Because if the worst happened, you'd be here to prop me up. Aidan would be here. And Liam. And Mom and Zoe and Kate." Con spread his hands. "And you'd all be there to support Bailey and Brianna Rose if fate caught up with *me*. We're family. We've got each other's backs."

Grady lowered his gaze. "You guys had my back when Pop died. But I…I wigged out then, too. I didn't pull my weight."

"That wasn't you on your knees beside me scrubbing away blood all night? You stayed with Mom while we talked to the cops, big whoop. You didn't miss much."

Obviously, his brothers had a different slant on that night. Sabrina may have been correct about pain skewing his perspective. "But if Pop had gone to my game… If I hadn't…" He sucked in air that stung like acid. "Pop got killed because of my stupidity."

A heartbeat of silence ticked past. Another. Con slapped him on the back. "I need a caffeine hit. Take a walk with me."

They walked to the vending station at the end of the corridor. Con fed quarters into a soda machine and then frowned at him. "Is that what this is about? You're still beating yourself up over butting heads with Pop?"

Grady started. "You knew we were fighting?"

"So you and Pop had a dust-up or six. Didn't we all? When I was fifteen, I informed him he didn't know squat about real life." His brother barked out a wry laugh before sobering again. "Pop wouldn't thank you for the sackcloth-and-ashes crap. In fact, he'd be the first to kick your ass and tell you to snap out of it."

Con handed him an icy can of root beer. "None of us hold you responsible. Why the *hell* are you blaming yourself?"

Grady fumbled, dropped the soda. "You *all* knew? Even Mom?"

"Damn, Grady, we're not deaf or blind." Con scooped up the can and steered him toward two upholstered chairs parked beneath a window. "Sit."

Grady complied. "He didn't think I'd be a good cop. Which made me more determined to prove him wrong."

"That's a load of bull. Pop had been framed and was stuck riding a desk, and a lot of the brotherhood in blue believed him guilty." Con handed him the root beer, then popped the tab on his cola. "He saw that you had a shot at something he thought was better, a job that wasn't about blood, betrayal and death."

"That's not what being a cop is about."

"No, it isn't. But we deal with a crap load of it, don't we? Pop temporarily lost hope and surrendered to bitterness. He was our father. Bigger than life. We respected him, admired him and damn near worshipped the ground he walked on. But he was only a man, Grady…like us. We're not infallible, invincible or indestructible."

It was Grady's turn to sigh. "How did you figure all this out?"

"I had a few extra years to grow up with Pop. But my wife pounded a few lessons into my thick skull, too." Con chugged his cola. "Bailey also taught me asking for backup is a sign of strength, not weakness. I wish like hell you'd spoken up before."

Oddly light-headed, Grady slowly put down the soda he didn't want. "I was…" The admission took every iota of strength he possessed. "I was…too ashamed of myself."

"Well, get over it." Con set aside his soda can. "Do you remember what Mom said at Pop's memorial service?"

"That entire week is nothing but fog."

"She said, 'Nothing in life is random. Everything happens for a reason.'"

"Why, then? *Why* was Pop killed?"

"Nobody said we'd *know* the reasons." Con rested his elbows on his knees and leaned forward. "We might never know. But you have to trust yourself, Grady. Trust your woman. Trust your love for each other. And ultimately, we don't have the final say. So we have to trust in a power far stronger and wiser than ourselves."

Warmth seeped through him. "Sabrina said pretty much the same thing."

Con grinned. "She's a smart woman. Listen to her."

"Yeah." Con had always been the brother with the best grip on slippery emotions, but it sounded as though Aidan or Liam would have given similar advice. Grady and his brothers had far more in common than he'd ever realized. He returned Con's grin. "Maybe I should."

"Marriage and fatherhood are one hell of a trip." Con stood and playfully cuffed him upside the head. "But if you want the ride, boyo, you gotta pay for the ticket."

Did he want the ride? Grady walked Con back to Bailey's room. For the first time, he didn't feel the urge to flee. Didn't feel fear. Instead, the faint stirring of hope brushed his heart.

He and Sabrina said goodbye to Con, Bailey and Brianna Rose, and then stepped into the elevator. They'd traveled one floor when it jerked and stalled, the alarm bell clanging. The lights went out, and the dim yellow auxiliary light flickered on. Grady snatched up the emergency phone. "Anybody there?"

"Syrone Spencer, security office."

"Spence, Grady O'Rourke. Why is Mercy's head of security answering the phone? And more important, what the hell is wrong with five east's elevator?"

"Hey, Grady, you're back! We're balls-to-the-wall with the

rush." After a brief pause, Syrone returned. "Looks like the heavy traffic blew a circuit. We'll have a crew on it ASAP."

"Great. In the meantime, kill the alarm."

"On it. Hang tight, O'Rourke."

The alarm went silent. Grady reached for Sabrina's hand. "Thank you. I couldn't have managed without you today."

"Yes, you could have. You'd have pulled it together because you had to. That's what you do, Grady. You save people."

"And you saved *me,* sweetheart. You didn't give up on me today." He cleared his throat. "You didn't give up on me the past *decade,* even though I behaved like an ass."

She grinned. "I have a stubborn streak."

"Thank God for that." He tugged her into his embrace and captured her mouth.

Grady wrapped his arms around Sabrina and unleashed his emotions. He poured everything he had, everything he was… everything he wanted to be into his kiss. And the sweet, poignant hope growing inside him.

When he finally lifted his mouth from hers, Sabrina staggered. "What…" She blinked, inhaled shakily. "Wh-what did you and Con smoke out there in the corridor?"

Con's words rang in his ears. *All we have is right now.* "We need to talk—"

The roof panel slid open and a blond man in black coveralls dropped into the car with them.

During the seconds it took Grady to assess the man's cold blue eyes, hawklike features and gloved hands—and shove Sabrina behind his back—the guy had a pistol pointed at his heart. "Cooperate, and you don't die."

Grady scowled. "This isn't my first time downtown, pal." Sabrina whimpered behind him, and Grady reached back to touch her hand. Then his fingers closed around his gun, and he whipped it out, aimed it at the man's face. "Let the lady walk, and *you* don't die."

"You understand my weapon's capability, Officer O'Rourke. You know my bullets will rip through your body and into hers."

"I've got a point-blank cold shot to your brain stem." Grady's voice lowered with quiet menace. "You won't have time to blink."

"You willing to chance her life on it?"

No. But he was willing to risk his. Grady's finger depressed the trigger just enough to engage the override. One smooth pull would do the job. "Sabrina! Floor! Now!"

"Move, and he dies!" their assailant countered.

Grady's every sense was on red alert, his hearing magnified, his vision crystal clear. He stared into the eyes of death—and was ready. More ready than he'd ever been. "Sabrina, get down!"

"I can't," Sabrina whispered. "Grady, I can't let you die for me."

The man smiled without humor. "The lady isn't as brave...or foolish. Hand over the gun. Slowly."

Swearing, Grady complied.

The man tucked Grady's gun into his coverall top and confiscated the backup gun from his ankle holster. But he didn't catch the throwing stars strapped to Grady's forearm beneath his jacket. "Step out from behind him, Miss Matthews."

When Sabrina obeyed, the man jammed the gun into her ribs, and her terrified gaze locked on Grady. "I'm sorry."

There was no room for fear. Glittering rage obliterated every other emotion. "It'll be okay, sweetheart."

The man stabbed buttons, and the car descended to the third floor, where they boarded a service elevator.

Grady ground his teeth in helpless fury as their assailant forced them through a side exit to the parking lot and into the back of a large black van with tinted windows. Blondie kept the gun between his body and Sabrina's, and the few people they passed only saw three acquaintances walking to a vehicle.

Three more armed men were inside the van, along with Aidan's Ducati. Grady was shoved onto a bench on one side, Sabrina on the other. Their abductors didn't bother to hide their faces. The significance wasn't lost on him. He hoped Sabrina was more naive.

Blondie saw Grady eyeing the bike. "You're known to disappear to parts unknown for months at a time. Without a word. You took off on the bike and..." He waved.

Grady kept his expression stoic as his arms were wrenched behind his back. Plastic hand restraints were produced, and the second man cinched the first loop tightly around Grady's right wrist. Grady inclined his head at Sabrina, being subjected to the same treatment. "She doesn't disappear on people."

"No…" Grady wanted to carve the sneer off the bastard's mouth as the guy sadistically twisted his left wrist in a prelude to forcing his hand through the second loop. "But she could easily contract a mysterious virus."

Snarling, Grady launched off the bench. He plowed a left hook into the man's jaw. As he staggered, Grady yanked out a throwing star and slashed at the man's exposed jugular. The blond ducked and the blade sliced his cheek instead. Grady rammed a knee into the guy's gonads before the other three men jumped him.

Grady heard Sabrina cry out. Then a blow slammed into his skull and the world went black.

As a wave of icy water slapped Grady's face, he jerked to consciousness. Coughing, he shook his head. A headache pounded his temples, and every muscle thrummed with pain. His hands were bound behind his back, his upper body tied to a wooden chair. He was imprisoned in a standard interrogation room. According to the clock above the two-way mirror, he'd been out—he blinked to clear blurred vision—around forty minutes.

"Welcome back." The blond man smirked. "I hope you enjoyed your nap. It'll be your last respite."

He couldn't let himself think about where Sabrina was or what their captors were doing to her. The Army had trained him to survive and escape. He'd aced it once before. In order to save Sabrina, he had to do it again.

His jailer slammed a water pitcher onto a nearby table, and Grady smiled at the sight of the guy's gashed cheek and pronounced limp. "Bite me, Blondie."

"John will do." The guy stood in front of him and folded his arms across his chest.

"John *Smith*, I presume? Typically original for a Fed." He snorted as "John" arched his brows. "It's obvious that you're government issue."

John backhanded him. The warm, coppery taste of blood pumped adrenaline, and rage, through his veins. *He'd* had the satisfaction of drawing first blood. "Your face must hurt."

John leaned down, hit him again. "Before I'm done, you'll spill your guts."

"Straight from the 'Badasses for Dummies' manual." Grady spat blood into his assailant's face. "That's as close to my guts as you'll get."

John deliberately wiped his face on his sleeve. Then he snatched a cattle prod off the table and jammed it into Grady's stomach.

Grady's body jerked uncontrollably as liquid fire scalded every nerve ending. A scream balled at the back of his throat, and he locked it behind clenched teeth.

The agony finally eased as John pulled back the prod. "Talk."

He dragged air into lungs that felt singed. "Sure. How 'bout those Seahawks?"

John rammed him with the prod, longer this time. The searing torment lasted an eternity, and Grady couldn't suppress a groan.

John smiled. "Not so cocky now, huh?"

Grady coughed. Dug deep to steady his voice. "Untie me, and we'll see who's the tough guy."

"Do you like pain? All you have to do is tell me what you know, and I won't hurt you any more."

"I once spent three days as a 'guest' in Afghanistan. I've been tortured by the best, Blondie. And you're amateur hour." Grady stared into dispassionate blue eyes. "You can juice me up until I'm my own night-light, but I'm not telling you squat."

Blondie raised the cattle prod to eye level, and Grady braced for a more painful assault.

Don't anticipate. Just endure.

Blondie abruptly shook his head. "I have a better idea. Let's invite your girlfriend to the party." His fingers lovingly stroked an obscene parody on the cattle prod, and chills knifed up Grady's spine. "Women are softer and much more…sensitive."

Bile flooded Grady's parched throat, and he threw himself against his bonds. "Do it, and you die. Slow and ugly."

Noise erupted in the hallway. As shouting men pounded past the door, John swore. "I'll be right back. Try not to miss me too much, O'Rourke." He stalked outside.

"In your twisted dreams." Grady rocked the chair closer to the wall. His upper body was bound tightly, but his feet were free.

Propping the chair at an angle, he gained enough leverage to stand. Then he bashed the chair legs into the wall with desperate force. Over and over, until the wood groaned and the legs and seat splintered.

He yanked at the seat back until it clattered to the floor. The extra space loosened the cords enough to work them up past his forearms.

A grenade detonated outside the building at the same instant gunfire erupted in the corridor. He had to find Sabrina! Teeth gritted, he struggled harder, pushing the ropes up enough to shrug over his head. Then he stepped through his bound hands and brought them in front. His captors hadn't replaced the plastic restraints, dammit. They'd be tough to break.

Grady felt his pockets and his heart sank. The bastards had taken everything, including the Swiss Army knife his father had given him on his thirteenth birthday. Not only could he have used the tools to cut the restraints, but the memento was irreplaceable.

The yelling and gunshots traveled outside the building. An internal dispute...or something more sinister? Staying low, he eased the door open a crack. A dozen men wearing black fatigues and military boots sprawled bloody and lifeless on the hallway floor. There were no identifiers on their uniforms.

He crawled into the corridor and patted down the first body. One of them had to carry a knife. He searched three before finding cigarettes and a disposable lighter in a shirt pocket. That would do. Hands cupped, he thumbed the lighter and angled the flame backward. He cursed but held steady as it seared his wrists. The stench of melted plastic mingled with cordite and blood, and the restraints popped apart.

Grady shoved the dead man's 9mm pistol into his waistband, palmed another and sprinted down the corridor, sweeping every room for Sabrina.

Then he heard her screaming. She was outside in the firefight.

Exploding through the doors at a dead run, Grady rolled to evade a blitz of gunshots. He flung himself behind a truck parked in front of the building. If the terrain and vehicle license plates were any indication, he was on some sort of covert base in the Oregon desert. The bad guys must have flown them out while he'd been unconscious.

On the opposite side of the fenced compound, Sabrina was fighting a huge, cammo-clad, Kevlar-hooded man trying to carry her toward a rough airstrip. She and her captor were taking fire from men positioned behind outbuildings. Her abductor was alternately attempting to subdue her and shooting back. Grady's pulse kicked into overdrive. If the guy took off with her in one of the small planes, Grady might never find her.

If the stupid bastard didn't get her shot first.

Grady tugged the second pistol from his waistband and zig-zagged in pursuit. His chase drew bullets previously directed at Sabrina and her captor. Returning fire with both hands, he rolled again, regained his feet and flattened against a shed. He peered around the corner, and a bullet from Sabrina's captor screamed past his cheek and slammed into the metal siding.

The man had reached a twin-engine turboprop and was forcing Sabrina inside. Cursing in English and Gaelic, Grady glanced around the compound, then grinned. Dodging a hailstorm of bullets, he raced to the parking lot.

Hotwiring the Ducati took a hair longer while simultaneously shooting. The plane's engines rumbled to life seconds before the motorcycle's. Grady's first pistol clicked empty, then the second. He shrugged and tossed them over his shoulder. He couldn't shoot and ride at the same time, anyway.

Grady hopped aboard the bike and raced toward the turboprop bumping down the runway. Pouring on speed, he caught up, then veered alongside. The aircraft was prepped for skydiving, with an open side door. Sabrina was belted into one of the rear passenger seats. She saw him, and her face blanched.

Grady glanced ahead. They were nearly out of runway.

Nearly out of time.

He swerved closer to the plane. Sabrina's frantic head shakes said she'd probably guessed his plan.

Grady gave her a thumbs-up.

She yanked off her seat belt and scrambled to the door. *"Grady, no!"*

He'd have mere seconds. One slip, and he'd be a grease spot on the runway.

Worse, he'd lose Sabrina forever.

Grady steadied the bike into a straight glide and jumped up, balancing his feet on the seat. As the plane lifted off, he let go of the handlebars and leaped for the opening.

His fingers gripped the bottom of the doorway and clung, and the plane soared skyward with his body dangling in midair.

Sabrina shrieked, grabbed the collar of his jacket and boosted his momentum enough for him to clamber inside.

Panting, he sprawled on the floor. "Piece…of pie."

She pummeled him. "Are? You? *Insane?*"

He grinned. "You're welcome." The grin faded as he sat up and sent his glance over the interior. Six seater. No weapons. A jumper's first-aid kit.

And Sabrina was wearing the only parachute.

The guy in the pilot's seat tugged off his earphones and stalked to the rear of the plane.

Grady looked up at the biggest soldier he'd ever seen. The man's shoulders dwarfed the tight space, and his biceps were the circumference of Grady's thighs. He'd removed the Kevlar hood and wore the only other parachute. His head was shaved, his olive skin darkly tanned, his obsidian eyes flat. Predator's eyes that bored into Grady with lethal intelligence. Showed no mercy.

This wasn't a man. This was a killing machine.

"You gonna be a problem?" The question rumbled out as deep and ominous as thunder.

"Depends." Slow and easy, Grady stood, shielding Sabrina with his body. "You gonna give me a reason?"

"You don't affect my mission, I don't terminate you, O'Rourke."

So he wasn't a rogue operator angling for quick bucks from Sabrina's kidnapping. "What's your handle?"

"Viper."

"Okay, Viper. You don't hurt Sabrina and we won't have a problem."

"Hurting Miss Matthews isn't my objective."

Sabrina shifted uneasily to Grady's side. "Um…Mister… Viper…shouldn't you be flying the plane?"

"It's on autopilot."

Grady kept his voice and expression neutral. "Where are we headed?"

"My bunker in the Wasatch Mountains will be secure until the virus runs its course."

Sabrina cleared her throat. "Thank you for rescuing us, but we can't go to Utah. This virus is endangering our family and friends. We're gathering…information that could save them."

"There's nothing you can do. Trying will make you dead, like your grandpa."

She started. "You knew Granddad? *How?*"

"He helped me. I owe him."

Grady studied the knives, grenades and ammo clipped to Viper's military-issue utility belt. A pistol was holstered at the man's right thigh. Grady wouldn't last a millisecond if he made a move toward it. "That's why you rescued Sabrina. You raided the base."

"Affirmative."

The man hooked his thumbs in his belt loops, and Grady saw the tattoo on his right forearm. A triangulated lightning bolt with a sword thrust through it. More of the puzzle fell into place. *De Oppresso Liber.* Free the oppressed. The motto of Delta Force. "Did you commission me to extract Sabrina Friday night?"

"She'd been targeted for a hit, and I had to run another op."

Sabrina frowned. "I've seen your tattoo somewhere. Wait…" She fumbled with the button on her blouse pocket and withdrew Isaiah's drawing. The big stegosaurus bore a tiny crayon replica of Viper's tattoo on his right leg. Sabrina looked up at Viper. *"Who are you?"*

Viper slowly reached for the drawing. Holding the picture carefully between his massive hands, he stared at it. Anguish flickered in his eyes, and then those big hands started to tremble. "I'm… Isaiah's father."

Sabrina gasped. "The authorities said—"

"They lied. About everything." A muscle ticced in Viper's jaw. "They killed my son."

Grady tensed. The events of the past few days suddenly made terrible sense. "It was you who decimated the lab. Then you called Sabrina to the hospital so she'd see the virologists."

"They had to be stopped. Everyone has to know what they've done." Viper was still staring at the drawing. "An eye for an eye."

The turboprop bumped through an air pocket, and Sabrina's

hand sought Grady's. She was trembling. For the first time in Grady's life, he was in way over his head. The huge, grief-stricken man in front of him was a deadly, highly capable trained assassin... and not entirely sane.

Grady entwined his fingers with hers and feigned reassurance he didn't feel. "We're working on that. But we need to return to Riverside."

"It's too late." For a fraction of an instant, Viper's gaze brushed the canisters on his utility belt. "They'll confess their sins...or die."

Grady's breath caught. "You have more of the virus."

"And the advantage. I took the only antidote."

Sabrina jolted, and Grady squeezed her fingers. They were juggling live grenades, and one misstep could blow up in their faces. The only weapon he had was reason...and a father's love. "If the virus spreads or mutates, a lot of innocent men, women and children—like your son—will die, too."

"Collateral damage is a fact of war. The traitors who are in power understand that."

"Viper," Sabrina said softly. "Isaiah wasn't collateral damage. He was a little boy. *Your son.* I cared about him, too. Please, tell me about your son. I'd like to know more."

Respect and admiration wound through Grady. Her request would encourage Viper to make a personal connection.

"Me and his mom weren't married. Gwen had it rough, but she was okay. She was good with him, until she got into meth." His entire focus was concentrated on the picture, as if he were seeing his son's face. "I used to take him to the park. Isaiah liked to swing. He liked strawberry slushees."

"And dinosaurs," Sabrina said.

"Yeah." The twin engines hummed loudly as Viper paused. "I fought for custody, but my name wasn't on his birth certificate. And I had to do everything between deployments. When Gwen OD'd, the state took Isaiah." His teeth clenched. "They said I couldn't take care of him because he was sick. I didn't know where they'd put him. But he wasn't sick. Not until they started feeding him poison. Your grandfather found other kids with the same symptoms. I know what my son went through."

"How did you meet my grandfather?"

"Senator Vaughn visited a base when I was stationed overseas. He was a straight shooter who battled for kids. After Isaiah... died...I went to the top with my questions, but the officials just handed me more lies. I asked the senator for help. He talked to people, dug around. He was working with a reporter who helped him. Right after the guy located the lab, he died in a hit-and-run 'accident.' Bill told me he was gathering intel, but the people involved were powerful—and dangerous—and he alerted me to watch my back."

"And mine?" Sabrina asked.

"Yeah. They tried to make the senator look like he was crazy. When he got too close, they killed him, too. I mustered out and took a job at the lab as a security guard. The vice president owns a majority share in the company, you know. While I was fighting, killing for my country, traitors were torturing and killing my son." Viper looked at them, and his eyes were colder than the wind whistling past the open door. "Now I have all the power."

The hair prickled on the back of Grady's neck. "What do you plan to do with it?"

"The news is being suppressed, but the other coordinates I infected were all Serpens Pharmaceutical laboratories. I planted virus bombs with remote triggers. I opened the cage and let their monster loose. To put it back, the vice president has to come forward by oh-nine-hundred tomorrow. He has to admit what he's done."

"And if he doesn't?"

"Then New York gets infected. Los Angeles. And D.C. Bombs are positioned, timers set. The penalty for treason is death. He'll either confess...or die." Viper's attention shifted to the picture again, and his finger unsteadily traced the letters of his son's name. When he looked at Sabrina, tears glittered in his eyes. "Can I have this?"

"Of course," Sabrina said gently. "I'm so sorry. I understand the hell you went through. I was with Isaiah when he died, and I know how much losing your son hurts."

"You saw it. He suffered."

"I know it's spare comfort, but your son died with courage... and a final act of kindness for someone else. Killing thousands of innocents won't bring Isaiah back. It won't right the wrong they did to your son. Don't tarnish his memory," she pleaded. "Don't become like the people you despise."

"You're trained in strategy," Grady added. "In weapons and combat. Help us lock the men who murdered Isaiah behind bars forever...the honorable way."

"I tried. Senator Vaughn tried. You tried. They're beyond men's laws."

"Nobody is beyond the law," Grady insisted. The small aircraft rocked, and Sabrina clung to his hand. "We're close. We'll get proof."

"They told Isaiah I gave him away, ordered him not to talk about me. My son died believing...I deserted him." Viper's rumbling baritone broke as he pointed to the tattooed drawing. "I didn't protect him, but he didn't forget me. I can't desert him."

Grady understood Viper's anguish and regret all too well. "Isaiah's picture shows he still thought about you. Cared about you." He caught Viper's gaze. "Don't throw your life away. Do the right thing for your son. The right way."

"I remember having principles." Viper stared at Grady. "You're not gonna let me go, are you?"

Grady didn't answer. He didn't need to.

Viper's big hands tenderly folded the drawing and tucked it inside his fatigue shirt, next to his heart. He bowed his head at Sabrina. "I owe your grandfather honor. I owe you gratitude."

Grady's taut shoulders relaxed. They'd gotten through to the guy. Sabrina's tremulous smile wavered in his peripheral vision, and he flicked her an encouraging look.

Viper sighed. "But I don't owe *you* nothing." His fist ploughed into Grady's face, knocked him flat.

Reeling with pain, Grady heard Sabrina scream. He grabbed on to the seat and pulled himself upright. *"No!"*

Viper dragged Sabrina to the door. "Count to five hundred and then pull your rip cord." Shoving the first-aid kit into her hands, he pushed her out. Viper saluted Grady. *De Oppresso Liber."*

Then he pivoted and leaped out of the plane.

Chapter 15

His gut tight, Grady stumbled to the doorway. Flying a fixed-wing aircraft was nothing like a chopper. He had seconds to execute his plan. And possibly, himself.

The vice president would never confess. That antidote was their only hope.

He looked down and saw Sabrina free-falling in midair, Viper below her. Neither chute had deployed yet.

Grady breathed a prayer and hurtled out of the plane.

Clamping his arms to his sides, he torpedoed downward. Within seconds, he hit terminal velocity. He squinted into the blasting air and aimed for Viper's trajectory. He flew past Sabrina, slammed into Viper and clung to his parachute straps.

The men battled for position, tumbling toward the earth a hundred miles per hour.

Grady fumbled for the ripcord. Viper head-butted him. Grady lost his grip, and Viper somersaulted away. Grady flipped backward, and dove, catching Viper as he straightened. If one of them didn't open the chute within the next thirty seconds, they'd both die.

Grady clamped on to Viper's torso with his legs, clung to the chest strap with his right hand, and yanked the ripcord with his left. Brown nylon streamed upward, and their bodies jerked as the chute snapped open.

Two men could land using one parachute. Grady glanced at the ground hurtling toward them. But with a huge guy like Viper and chute deployment delayed, they were gonna auger in.

At the last second, he twisted Viper beneath him to cushion the impact. Grady slammed into what felt like a brick wall. Starbursts of pain exploded inside him.

And then the world went dark.

Descending toward the desert, Sabrina saw the blur of tangled bodies fall. A scream locked in her throat. *Grady!*

The men crashed to the ground below in a geyser of dust. The momentum flung Grady thirty feet to Viper's right, both men sprawled motionless in the sand.

The scream burst free. She dropped the rescue kit and writhed in the harness, but couldn't force a quicker landing.

She hit the ground. Her legs buckled. She rolled, clambered to her knees, wrestled free of the chute. It was taking too long!

Sabrina stumbled to Grady. Dropping to her knees beside him, she pressed trembling fingers to his neck. A slow pulse throbbed, but he wasn't breathing.

She began the cycle of breathing for him...a lungful of air every few seconds.

In the distance, the plane plummeted to earth. A loud *kaboom* vibrated, erupted into a fireball. Oily smoke stained the horizon. The smoke and flames would be a beacon for rescuers. And the bad guys.

"C'mon, Grady!" She gave him another breath. "Come back to me!"

She pressed her mouth to his and gave him another infusion of precious oxygen.

"Listen to me, Grady."

She filled his lungs again. "Please! Please *breathe!*"

Another breath. Then another. Grady's body jerked, and he coughed, then inhaled raggedly.

Her own heart resumed beating and she stroked his cheek. "That's it. Good, one more. Breathe."

His dark lashes fluttered, drifted upward. She stared into stunned gray-green eyes. "I've got you, Dimples. You're all right." Love, tenderness and searing pain balled in her chest. She swallowed hard. Dredged up a smile. "Leave your blue tights and cape in the plane?"

He chuckled weakly, then groaned. "Ow."

She skimmed her hands over his body. "Does it feel like anything is broken?"

"Feels like *everything* is broken." He gingerly flexed his limbs. "Don't think anything is." He tried to sit up, groaned again. "*Viper!* Gotta—"

"Oh, no, you don't." That she was able to push him flat told her how weak he was. That she'd totally forgotten the other man told her how far gone *she* was. "You rest. I'll check on him."

"Dammit, I can get up." He struggled, then his head fell back and his eyes closed. "In a second."

"Stay put. I can handle it."

She hurried to Viper and knelt at his side. He'd hit a rocky outcropping. He was unconscious, his breathing labored. Blood streamed from a gash on his forehead and trickled from his nose and ears. Her stomach clenched. He'd suffered severe head trauma. "Viper?"

She pressed gentle fingers to his neck. His pulse was light and thready. "Viper? Can you hear me?"

He moaned and his eyes slitted open. "Can't... Isaiah."

"Easy, it's okay." She scrambled to the first-aid kit, grabbed a gauze pad and hurried back to press it to his forehead.

"Mission," he slurred. "You. Finish."

"Shh. Everything will be okay." But she wasn't so sure.

His fingers plucked at his shirt. "Picture..."

"Right here." She unbuttoned his shirt. The picture was soaked with perspiration, splotched with blood.

She placed it in his hand, and his fingers crumpled around it. "Son." A tear trailed down his broken face. "Failed. Him."

"You did everything you could." She swallowed a choking lump in her throat. "You loved him. And he knew that."

"Isaiah," Viper whispered. Light flickered in his eyes and a faint smile ghosted across his mouth.

The pulse beneath her fingertips stuttered, stopped. As Viper's gaze blanked, a drifting breeze fluttered Isaiah's drawing, caught loosely in the huge, limp hand.

Sabrina closed Viper's eyes.

Tears blurred her vision, and she bowed her head. "I hope you find peace."

"Sabrina!" Grady hissed. She jerked her head up to see him weaving toward her.

She met his horrified gaze. "I know he committed terrible crimes. But I can empathize with a grieving father."

"Did you touch him?"

"Yes, I had to—"

His face was bone white, his eyes tortured. "Where's the first-aid kit?"

"Grady—"

"Where's the rescue kit?"

She inclined her head. "In front of that big rock."

"Get up." He staggered toward the kit.

"What in—" She rose, looked down at Viper. Her blood froze.

The utility belt around Viper's waist was twisted and broken, the crushed canisters ruptured. What she had thought was perspiration was the virus. V-10 had soaked into Viper's shirt. Into the picture. She stared at her palms.

Into her hands.

Carrying a bottle of peroxide, Grady limped toward her, and she backed away. "Don't!"

"I need to dump this on your hands. Wash them off."

He advanced, she retreated. "We both know that's useless."

"The antidote is gone. We have to try! Have to give you a fighting chance!" He stumbled over a rock and nearly went down. "Stop running away from me, dammit!"

"I won't contaminate you!"

"I'm not giving up if I have to chase you through the entire frigging desert."

No, he'd never give up. Even hurt, he'd catch her. Running, she circled back, snatched the gun from Viper's holster. Gripping it in the two-handed stance Grady had taught her, she aimed the pistol at his chest. "Stop!"

He lurched to a halt. "You would never kill me."

"No." She gulped, lowered the barrel three feet. "But a bullet in the leg will slow you down."

He limped toward her. "You won't put a bullet in me, sweetheart. You don't have it in you."

"You're right." Despair clawed at her. "I could never shoot you." She pressed the muzzle to her temple. "But I will shoot myself. Right now, if it keeps you from getting infected."

He flung up his hands. "Sabrina, *no!*"

"Stay right there."

"Put the gun down, sweetheart," he pleaded hoarsely. "It'll be all right. Trust me."

"Not this time." She was shaking so hard, she could barely hold the heavy pistol. "I finally get it, Grady. I finally understand the desperate need to protect the one you love. I'd rather die than see you hurt."

"I'm not running from you anymore." Sorrow shadowed his beautiful green eyes. "You go, I'm coming along."

"Calculated risk."

Grady was shaking, too. "Sabrina, you need to clean your hands. Just lower the gun."

"I'll rinse them off if you'll promise you won't touch me." She inhaled. "And don't lie to me…because you'll never get another chance."

"I won't." His Adam's apple jerked convulsively. "You have my word."

Sabrina kept her eyes locked on his a moment longer. When she dropped her hand to her side, Grady's breath heaved out. She squatted, laid the gun in the sand. Grady walked to her, kicked away the pistol and held out the peroxide.

"This is useless." But she poured the foaming liquid over her palms.

His lips trembled, and he pressed them firmly together. "We have to believe it's not."

Three hours later Grady paced his cramped quarters in the isolation ward. He glanced at Sabrina, locked in the glass room next to his. Like him, she was dressed in blue scrubs. She sat cross-legged on her bed, her head bent over Bill's Bible. Kate had run by Aidan's apartment and delivered it to Sabrina at her request.

Waiting in the desert with her had been the longest thirty

minutes of his life. He'd built a signal fire from scrub brush and
the matches from the rescue kit. Air rescue had called in a biohazard containment team. He and Sabrina had been separately quarantined and airlifted to Mercy, put through decontamination
protocol and then secured in isolation. They were awaiting the
results of their blood tests.

Grady didn't think he'd touched the V-10. But since he'd ini-
tially landed on Viper, and didn't know when the canisters had
ruptured, he wasn't sure. In any case, the spill at the scene could
have easily have carried to him on the breeze, or from Sabrina's
hands or clothing. Even without direct contact.

One droplet of concentrated live virus was enough.

After they were admitted, Wade had delivered the heart-
wrenching news that Ronnie Nguyen and Kim Swanson had suc-
cumbed to the virus. Dalton was in critical condition.

Sabrina hadn't cried. She'd refused a sedative and attempts at
comfort. She'd completely withdrawn, and Grady couldn't coax
her to the speaker in the adjoining wall.

Was she protecting her heart…or his? Either way, it was making
him crazy. He needed to talk to her. Needed to touch her.

Needed her.

He stalked to the outside window. The governor had called in
the National Guard to disperse traffic, stop looting and protect city
officials working around the clock. A curfew had been imposed.
Except for patrolling soldiers, the streets were empty. News reports
said citizens were sequestering themselves.

Dan, their nurse, entered the corridor and accessed the outer
speaker beside the airlock transfer. "Grady, do you need anything?
Food? Juice? More water?"

"No, thanks." How could he eat when fear was chewing up his
guts? The thought of Sabrina suffering, dying, left an icy void inside
him. He couldn't imagine living the rest of his life without her.

He didn't want to live without her.

Dan's hazel eyes were warm with compassion as he nodded
toward Sabrina. "Is she doing any better?"

"Not that I can tell."

"Dr. Matthews wants to run more tests. He'll see Sabrina first,
because you have visitors. We're sending a few at a time."

Grady's pulse kicked. His family. "Okay."

Wade entered dressed in a hooded biohazard suit and carrying syringes. He went into Sabrina's room and pulled the privacy curtain.

Expecting his mother or brothers, Grady was dumbfounded when Ethan Burke appeared, accompanied by two burly bodyguards and an armed National Guard escort. Burke strode to the speaker. The politician's hair was coal black, and no lines marred his tanned face. "Officer O'Rourke, how are you?"

"Maintaining. I thought they only allowed family inside."

"The president wanted me to personally thank you for tracking down and apprehending the individual responsible for this heinous crime. At great risk to yourself. The president is considering a medal."

Grady wasn't even close to being done taking names and kicking asses. "I don't want more medals. I want answers."

"So do I. And we'll get them."

Grady weighed his next words. "Even if it means challenging power brokers who could make or break your career?"

Burke's eyes narrowed. "I know honesty is considered old-fashioned in current politics, but I've based my career on my values. People are dying. Nothing is more important than lives."

Truth or polished PR? Time would tell. "If you're serious, I might be calling you."

Burke nodded. "My service will put you through, day or night. Thank you again, Officer O'Rourke." He departed.

A few minutes later Aidan entered with Zoe. "Well, this is one scrape I can't extricate you from, baby brother."

"Hey, it's only slightly worse than getting expelled for brewing rocket fuel in the junior high science lab. Ah...about your Ducati..."

"Let me guess. It's now the world's largest paperweight."

"I'll buy you a new one."

Zoe tucked her arm in Aidan's. "Stay tough, brat. We're boxing them in. And Serpens Pharmaceutical says they're close to a breakthrough with an antidote."

"Let's hope they're not lying about that, too. Aidan, how's Mom?"

"Worried, naturally. But she's determinedly positive and keeping busy with work."

"I know you'll watch out for her if..."

Aidan scowled. "We're not going there."

"If it does go there, I want you to take care of…arrangements. So Mom doesn't have to."

"The only thing I'm gonna arrange is your face if you don't knock that crap off." A tremor went through his brother, and his voice lowered. "But you can count on me."

Zoe blew him a kiss. "The fight is far from over."

"Give 'em hell, Grady." Aidan smiled, but his face was etched with concern. "As only you can."

Con came in next, by himself. "Bailey is sorry she can't be here, but they won't let her in so soon after surgery."

"It's okay. Tell her that her priority is taking care of herself and my niece."

"She sent this." Con put a Celtic Woman CD and portable player through the airlock.

He swallowed the lump in his throat. "Thank her for me."

"Thank her yourself as soon as you're cleared. You and Sabrina hanging in there?"

"We have the whole family pulling for us." Grady stroked his index finger over the CD case. "And the outcome is in hands bigger than ours, isn't it?"

"You did get what I was trying to tell you before."

"Yeah." He looked up, met his brother's steady brown gaze. "Thanks, Con."

Con touched the glass. "Keep the faith, bro."

After Con departed, Liam arrived with Kate…and Murphy. "Hey, Grady. Aidan and Zoe briefed everyone. We're on it, 'round the clock."

"Good to know."

Kate rested her hand on Murphy's head. "Can we bring you anything?"

"Since a six-pack of Guinness is out of the question, I'd like my own clothes. And my guitar."

"Okay, I'll hurry back." Kate kissed Liam, waved and rushed out.

Liam bent close, and Murphy put his paws up and pressed his nose to the glass. "Grady, you can beat 'em at their own game. Hell, you've made a career of knocking the odds on their arse."

He summoned a grin. "Yeah, don't start divvying up my CD collection yet."

Liam's hearty smile didn't disguise lurking worry. "I have a couple of hot leads to run down. We're gonna nail their asses to the wall, little brother."

Grady watched Liam stride out. They'd all made a point of not saying goodbye, but everyone was aware this could be the last time they'd speak.

His brothers would stand with him. Or if worst came to worst...*for* him.

Knowing that was his greatest comfort as he braced to see his mom.

She bustled in and flipped on the speaker. "Well, me boyo, this is a pretty kettle of fish. I'd no sooner sprung your brothers from solitary than here you are."

He should have known better. She'd never let him see anything but encouragement. "In it up to my ears, as usual. Sorry to worry you, Mom."

"Grady. I worry because I love you." His mom patted the glass, as if she could touch him. "Your father and I have always loved you. We've never been anything but proud of you. Every moment of your life."

Moisture scalded his eyes. "I love you, too, Mom."

"All right, then." She shook herself, cleared her throat. "Dan says you're refusing food. I'll bring you and Sabrina sandwiches and salads from the cafeteria and you'll eat them. You need to stay nourished and hydrated. You'll both be fine."

His mouth curled in the first genuine smile. "Yes, ma'am."

After Maureen left, Wade entered, took Grady's vitals and drew more blood. Food was delivered, as well as his guitar and a nylon duffel of clothing.

Sabrina hadn't opened the privacy curtain, and Grady was alone. Isolated. Forced to stop running and face his own mortality for the first time, Grady took stock of his life. And didn't like what he saw.

Solitary independence was what he'd sought for ten years. Now he hated it.

He'd been a moron.

He depressed the button on the speaker connected to her room. "Sabrina? How are you doing?" Silence. "Talk to me, sweetheart."

Grady coaxed, cajoled and threatened to throw the bed through the wall, but she didn't reply.

He pounded his fists on the glass. Dammit! He'd spent a decade constructing barriers between himself and his family. Between himself and Sabrina. And now that he'd lowered them, he was imprisoned and helpless behind walls he couldn't batter down.

The curtain opened and Sabrina stood on the other side watching him, her palms planted on the glass.

He got up and pressed his palms to hers through the barrier, and she burst into tears.

He longed to touch her. Needed to comfort her...but he couldn't. "Baby, don't cry."

"I'm going to die, Grady."

"No!" Terror writhed in his belly like a nest of snakes. "You're *not*. Nobody is going to die!"

"Ronnie is dead. Kim is dead. Dalton is dying."

"Sweetheart, listen to me." He swallowed hard. "Don't let fear overtake you. After Pop died, I ran for ten years because I let fear control me. Not fear of intimacy. Not fear that I'd hurt you, though that was part of it. My biggest fear was needing you. I was afraid of losing the one thing in this world that matters most to me...you."

"Oh, Grady." She sobbed harder.

He inhaled an unsteady breath. "I spent a decade running from pain—which deprived me of my greatest joy. I promise you will never be alone again. I will never leave you again."

Sabrina bit her lower lip so hard she drew blood. She leaned her forehead on the glass. "But I might...have to leave you."

"You're a part of me. And I, you." He embraced her the only way he could, with his gaze. "I thought the ultimate enemy was death. But the *real* enemy is despair. You stuck with me all this time. Don't give up on me now."

Chapter 16

1:00 a.m.

Grady leaned on the sill beneath the window in the isolation ward, staring at the night sky. Light trapped in towering high rises beat against the blackness, and a crescent moon speared pale swords across the dark slash of river.

He and Sabrina had stood at the central wall talking for hours. They'd shared memories...and avoided mentioning the future. When she'd swayed on her feet, he'd urged her into bed.

Wade had been by several times to check on them, but hadn't reported their test results. The verdict had to be in by now. The fact that neither had been discharged said it all. Fear and love tangled inside Grady until he couldn't separate the two.

He had thought he needed more time. Always believed he and Sabrina would have plenty of it. Instead he'd wasted his life trying to outrun his problems. And stupidly carried his baggage on his back everywhere he'd gone.

He couldn't squander what might be his final hours in sleep.

"Hey, Pop." Grady looked at the moon and far-flung stars. "It's been a while since we talked. I know now that a few harsh words couldn't destroy the bond we shared."

He blinked until his vision was clear. "Somehow, if there was some way you could let me know you hear me...that you forgive me..."

Waiting, Grady gazed up at the stars.

But no answer came during the long night.

When dawn's pale fingers gripped the horizon and crept over the city, Sabrina stirred. Grady walked to the dividing wall. "Morning, sweetheart."

She sat up, and his heart wrenched. Even across the room, he could see the fevered flush on her cheeks.

He sprinted for the intercom, hit the call button. "Sabrina's running a fever! Get in here!"

The day nurse hurried into the corridor. "The doctor is donning protective gear. He'll be right in."

Stiff with fear, Sabrina stumbled to the partition. "Grady."

He went to her, stabbed the speaker button. "You're gonna be okay."

She leaned on the glass. "I'm scared."

"I know." He offered his palm. "But Serpens is working on an antidote. Zoe said they were close."

She aligned her palm with his. "Promise me something."

His throat was as raw as if he'd swallowed ground glass. "Anything."

"If I…don't win the battle, promise you won't run from your family again. Or the possibility of love. Don't let the past dictate your future anymore. I want you to be happy, Grady."

Sabrina was his past. His future. He would never love another. Never be happy without her. "I told you, I'm done running. Stand your ground, Sabrina, and so will I."

Her eyes welled. "I'll do my best."

Outfitted in biohazard suits, a doctor and nurse shuffled into the hallway, then entered Sabrina's room. The nurse drew the curtain.

"No!" Grady slapped the glass. "Don't shut me out!"

He paced, waiting, watching.

After an eternity, they exited Sabrina's room.

Grady rushed to the outside speaker. "What's happening to Sabrina?"

The doctor turned. "She needs to rest."

"Open the curtain so I can keep an eye on her."

The doctor shook his head. "You need to rest, too."

Swearing, Grady thrust his fingers through his hair. He couldn't just sit here. He had to do something. But what?

After the medical staff checked his vitals, he prowled like a caged tiger for another twenty minutes until his bedside phone startled him to a halt. He snatched up the receiver. "O'Rourke."

Static crackled over the line.

His fingers clenched on the phone. "Hello. I can hear you breathing."

"Mr. Grady O'Rourke?" asked a woman's heavily accented voice.

His pulse stumbled. "Yes."

"I tried to reach Miss Sabrina, but the operator said she is not receiving calls. I have been seeing the news. I have...information you should know."

Grady fought to keep his voice calm. "You can trust me."

"*Sí.* My important friend, he told me this."

"Tell me what you know."

"I must speak with you. My friend, he said never to say over the telephone. Never longer than sixty seconds, or they trace me. I have much to tell."

He swallowed his impatience. "I can't leave. You'll have to come to me."

"People watch. I will be killed."

"I swear on my life, my brothers will protect you." He inhaled. He had to reassure her before she got spooked and hung up. "There are three of them, armed to the teeth, and a German shepherd police dog."

A brief hesitation. "Ask Miss Sabrina, Genesis three, twenty-two. I will wait there thirty minutes, that is all."

A click, and then the dial tone buzzed.

Grady stalked to the partition, hit the speaker. "Sabrina, can you hear me? Teresa Monteros just called. I need you to look up Genesis, chapter three, verse twenty-two in Bill's Bible."

After heart-shaking minutes, the privacy curtain parted. An IV had been inserted in Sabrina's left arm. Bill's Bible was open in her trembling hands. "'Man has become like one of us, since he knows good and evil,'" she read. "'He must not take the fruit from the tree of life and eat. Then he would live forever.'"

"The tree of life. Supposedly an apple tree. Does that mean anything to you as a rendezvous point?"

Golden brows scrunched. "Yes! The oldest apple tree in the Pacific Northwest is growing at Fort Vancouver. Granddad used to take me to the apple festival every year."

"You go back to bed and rest. I need to call my brothers. They'll pick her up at Fort Vancouver and bring her here."

Call completed, Grady retrieved the duffel Kate had brought and set it on his bed. If he was meeting an informant, he wanted to be dressed. His own clothes would make him feel less a patient, more a cop. He unzipped the bag…and froze.

Pulse pounding in his ears, he stared at the garments inside. And the Swiss Army knife on top.

His Swiss Army knife.

He knew it was his because the grenade shrapnel that had left a small scar on his right hip had also nicked the casing.

Grady cradled the knife in an unsteady palm. He'd never been without it since Pop had given it to him seventeen years ago. He'd used the scissors to cut tape for Sabrina's bandage. He was sure the knife had been in his pocket when he and Sabrina had been kidnapped. Equally sure it hadn't been in his pocket when he'd escaped.

He'd asked his father for a sign.

His breath caught.

No way. There had to be a logical explanation. Maybe the knife had slipped out of his pocket at the houseboat, and he hadn't noticed. His brothers' wives knew the O'Rourke tradition. Kate had probably seen his knife lying around and figured Grady would want it.

Somehow the convoluted justification seemed more far-fetched than believing his resourceful dad had found a way to give him another gift. Something far more precious than a knife.

Hope.

Grady closed his eyes, bowed his head and finally laid his fears—and his father—to rest.

His heart lightened, and the smothering weight lifted from his chest. He tightly clasped the battered knife. "Thank you, Pop."

Resolved and refocused, he carried his clothes into the bathroom and dressed. Then he flipped on the television for the latest news.

Forty-five minutes later, Aidan, Con, Liam and Murphy escorted in a slender Hispanic woman. A black scarf covered ebony hair and large sunglasses protected wary dark eyes.

Grady left the speaker on so Sabrina could join the conversation. Zoe revealed what her investigation had discovered.

Then Teresa told Grady everything she knew. When she finished, she frowned. "But I do not have any way to prove this."

Neither did he. Yet. "Will you testify at a trial?"

"*Sí.* Enough people have died."

A war council was held, ideas exchanged. Theories were formulated and refined.

Afterward, his brothers agreed that hiding Teresa in a safe house was the best option and departed to arrange the transfer.

Leaving the speaker on, Sabrina curled up in bed, and Grady strummed his guitar and sang to her until she fell asleep.

Grady watched the news, paced some more. Prayed a lot.

When the answer hit, he jerked to a halt. *Damn,* it was dangerous. And not just to himself. But hell, life wasn't about being safe or comfortable. He would always be willing to take risks—but from now on, only for the woman he loved.

He thought everything through. Sketched a tactical plan. Reviewed details a second then a third time before placing a conference call to his brothers.

He hung up with a lump in his throat the size of a baseball. His brothers were willing to put their careers—and their lives—on the line for him.

Grady tugged the knife from his pocket. "Here's to you, Pop. *Sláinte!*" He unscrewed the faceplate from the keypad door lock, snipped wires, reconfigured schematics. In less than five minutes, the glass panel slid open and he was in the corridor.

Then he finessed the lock outside Sabrina's door...and walked into her room.

Her eyes flew open and she sat up in bed, gasped. "What are you *doing?*"

"I have a plan we need to discuss."

"No!" She scrambled off the bed. "Stay away!" For his every forward step, she took one back. She flung out her hands. "Wait! The morning you saved me from getting shot, you vowed something."

He halted. "What?"

"You said you wouldn't leave unless I asked you to. Well, I'm asking. No, I'm *begging*. Leave. Get out of here."

"Sorry, sweetheart. I can't do that."

Her back hit the wall. Avoiding the IV tubing, he carefully grasped her arms, and she slid to the floor. "Please, Grady, *don't!*"

"Shh." He went to his knees and gathered her into his embrace. "It's all right." He stroked her hair, kissed away the tears sliding down her face. "I know exactly what I'm doing."

He explained, and her expression blanked with shock. "Grady, are you sure?"

"More than I've ever been. About anything." Tilting up her chin, he captured her mouth in a gentle kiss.

She went stiff, but didn't fight him. Her skin was warm, her mouth hot beneath his, her lips soft and pliant.

When he released her, she was shaking. "How can you take such a risk?"

"Because I have to." He smiled. "Let's get into bed."

He scooped her up and settled her in the bed, then climbed in with her. She curled into him, and her heartbeat pounded against his. "Oh, God, if you're wrong…"

"Just another calculated risk." Grady tenderly rubbed her back. After a decade on the run, he'd finally found peace. "Even if we lose the battle, Sabrina, we'll have won the war."

The following morning, Grady surfaced from a dreamless sleep with a throbbing headache and his body burning. Eyes still closed, he smiled. He smelled Sabrina's sweet fragrance, felt her soft curves spooned to his. Their combined body heat threatened to incinerate the sheets.

The medical team had freaked when they'd discovered him in her room. Since there was nothing anyone could do after the fact, they'd allowed him to stay. He nuzzled her silky hair. A National Guard squadron couldn't have thrown him out.

Sabrina moaned softly and rolled to her back, and Grady opened his eyes, looked into hers. The warm whiskey depths were glazed, and an angry red rash scorched her limbs. His heart gave a shaky flip. "Are you in pain, sweetheart?"

"My skin stings like I have the mother of all sunburns."

"I'll call the nurse." Grady rose without touching her tender skin. He slid the chair next to her bed, where he sat to await the doctor. Other than his fever and headache, he didn't feel bad.

Yet.

The doctor entered for morning rounds, charted vitals and injected morphine into Sabrina's IV. Grady swallowed a couple of ibuprofen to knock out the headache and reduce his temperature.

Once they were alone again, Grady phoned Aidan. "Phase one complete. Initiate phase two."

Aidan's gusty exhale rang in his ear. "You really did it."

"Viper's V-10 bombs are detonating in other cities. It's Armageddon, bro. No surrender, no retreat."

Grady hung up, returned to the chair and gently took Sabrina's hand. Her gaze was sleepy from the pain meds…and dark with terror. "I'm afraid for you."

Not half as much as he was for her. "I'm gonna be fine."

Tears welled. "I don't want you to die."

"I'm not too excited about it myself." He forced a grin. "Remember our secret blood oaths?"

"The ones we sealed with spit instead of blood because I was afraid to cut myself…only I was too squicked out to actually spit? Yeah."

"I won't die if you don't." He removed his hand from hers, kissed his palm and held it out to her.

Her wobbly smile broke his heart more deeply than the tears. "Deal." She kissed her palm and solemnly shook with him.

Holding her hand, he leaned close. "Fight, Sabrina. Rouse that stubborn streak and stay alive. For me. For us."

"Don't worry, I'm not about to give up. St. Peter will have to drag me kicking and screaming through the Pearly Gates."

Grady tenderly brushed a kiss on her sizzling-hot forehead. "That's my girl."

Fifteen minutes later Aidan and Con strode into the corridor wearing black battle gear and SWAT caps. Aidan carried a large black duffel. He extracted identical clothing and passed it through the air lock to Grady. "If I had any lingering doubts about you being crazy, baby brother, they're blown."

Grady grinned. "Nobody lives forever. Blaze of glory and all that rot."

He changed inside the bathroom, tugged his cap low and strolled out. Standing beside Sabrina's bed, he leaned down. "Well, honey, off to another boring day at the office."

She chuckled weakly. "You look superb in that uniform, Dimples. If you didn't get demerits for being late, I'd jump you."

He touched his lips to hers. "Great idea. I'll hold you to it."

"Grady." She clung to him. "Be careful. Come back to me."

"I always will. Just make damn sure you're here when I do."

"I will be." She kissed him long and slow, making his heart kick.

Grady had to clear his throat before he could speak. "Sabrina, I love you."

She burst into tears. "I've waited so long to hear you say that. I love you, too."

Unwilling to release her until the last possible moment, he held her tight. "Remember, no matter what happens, nothing will ever separate us."

Grady stalked to the door. He didn't jury-rig the keypad, because the company had added a tamper alarm when they'd installed a new lock yesterday. He could have gotten around it, but time was wastin' and he'd learned the code while covertly observing the service tech. The tech had been so rattled about working in a bio-hazard unit, he'd set a land-speed record.

Grady turned to leave, and looked back at Sabrina. She smiled and blew him a kiss. He saluted her, then deliberately strode down the corridor. He had to banish her from his thoughts to do his job.

He had to leave her one last time in order to save her.

Liam leaned on the counter at the nurses' station chatting up the ladies, while Murphy, his partner in charm, poured on the cute-doggy routine. Grady kept his cap low and his head down, and nobody noticed that three tall, dark-haired men in uniform left instead of two.

Around the corner, Aidan summoned the huge service elevator, used for transporting patients on gurneys and multiple medical teams to and from the roof. Con held the car for Liam and Murphy, who joined them moments later.

The wide double doors shut, and silence hummed inside the car. Grady yanked on black tactical gloves. Aidan opened the duffel, doled out weapons. Flash-bang grenades clicked into belts, pistols slid into holsters, ammo magazines snapped into assault rifles.

Each brother had his own prebattle thoughts. As the numbers ticked upward, they mentally prepared for combat.

The doors slid open, and shoulder to shoulder, the O'Rourke brothers stepped onto the rooftop.

Chapter 17

Grady jogged beside his brothers to the helipad. He was warm, but the headache had dulled. His reflexes were sharp, mind clear. He would never fly dangerously impaired. And as long as he didn't touch—or kiss—anyone, there was no danger of spreading the virus.

Six SWAT officers walked out from behind the chopper, and he lurched to a stop. He scanned the lineup. Riverside PD's entire Alpha Squad, present and accounted for.

Grady's breath hitched. "This is an unsanctioned op. Your asses are on the line, and so are your careers."

"We've been briefed." Wyatt Cain grinned. "No way are the Fighting Irish stealing all the thunder."

"Besides," Hunter Garrett drawled. "There's nothin' to watch on TV but news reports."

The guys would rag him until doomsday if he bawled like a little girl, but, *damn*. The entire team had thrown in with him. "Let's get this show on the road, ladies."

They spent fifteen minutes reviewing the operation.

Grady rolled up blueprints. "The National Guard is protecting the building. There'll be bodyguards. Federal agents. You guys know the score." He glanced around the solemn circle. Every man was his brother. "So do I. I want everyone's word that if I go down, nobody touches me."

He drilled stares at Aidan, Con and Liam. *"Nobody."*

Grady made them all swear a vow. Officers who were sworn to uphold the sanctity of life and the letter of the law reluctantly promised they would let him die rather than risk infection.

Ten warriors stood in a silent circle, the responsibility of their mission heavy in their hearts.

"Hell." Liam ruffled Murphy's fur. "We're dead men walking, anyway. If we live through this, our women are gonna kill us."

Grady snorted. "And Mom will fire the first shot."

Laughter broke out, and they boarded the chopper.

The team donned throat mikes and tactical headsets. Grady throttled to flight speed. "Skying up!"

The flight to the roof of the KKEY news tower seemed excruciatingly long. And unbearably short.

The team disembarked, then tugged on Kevlar hoods and clipped cables into rappel harnesses. A K-9 harness allowed Murphy to rappel with Liam.

The men braced backward on the skyscraper five hundred feet above the city.

"Alpha One, standing by," Con, the team's leader, barked into the headset.

As each squad member verbally checked in, Grady rolled taut shoulders. "Pop," he murmured. "If you're inclined to help out, now's the time to bring it."

"Double Z," Aidan said. "Are you in position?"

Zoe had gained access with her employee pass. "Standing by," she answered from inside the building.

"Rappelling!" Con said.

"Rappelling!" Grady replied. The call echoed eight times in his headset as they leaped. He hurtled ten floors, then braked in front of the huge windows.

"Fire!" Con commanded.

Gunfire bit into the glass above head level. Windows shattered, and the team swung inside and landed on the floor.

"Down!" the squad yelled at stunned people packed into the large room. "Everybody on the floor!"

Aidan and Hunter sprinted out the door, headed for Zoe's post.

"Doc Holliday, three o'clock!" Liam barked into Grady's headset.

Grady pivoted and aimed his assault rifle at a soldier brandishing an M16. "I wouldn't."

The soldier raised the gun. A snarling Murphy charged and knocked aside the weapon.

Grady kicked the gun out of range. "On the floor."

"Alpha eight, clear," Aidan reported from downstairs.

Finally Grady heard Con say the magic words. "Green light."

Boots crunching glass, Grady stalked through acrid gun smoke past rigidly prone bodyguards, the governor, the mayor, city councilmen and prostrate reporters and cameramen.

His boot nudged Ethan Burke, cowering on the carpet. "Get up."

Quivering, Ethan clambered up. "Wha-what do you w-want?"

"To shake your hand." Grady removed his left glove. He tugged out his Swiss Army knife, and sliced his palm. He advanced on the retreating man, gripped his arm and then clasped his hand.

Burke stared at his blood-smeared palm. "I d-don't understand."

"You sold your soul, Burke." Grady yanked off his Kevlar hood. "Now there's the devil to pay."

"O'Rourke?" Burke stumbled. "What have you done?"

Grady smiled. "Infected you with V-10."

"It's a bluff! They wouldn't release a contagious victim!"

"The doctor will verify. I'll wait." Grady clenched his fingers over his bleeding palm. "You might want to hurry. The longer you're exposed, the uglier it gets."

"*Help!*" Burke scrubbed his hand on his suit. "Bring me the antidote! *Now!*"

Grady shrugged. "There isn't one."

"No," he sobbed. "You're wrong!"

"Interesting." Grady addressed the cameramen. "You were invited to broadcast a press conference. Fire up your cameras, boys. Ethan Burke has a helluva story."

The cameramen scrambled up. News cams settled on shoulders, and lights blazed on.

Grady spoke into his tactical mike. "Double Z, do you see Burke on the monitors?"

Zoe's face appeared on the wall screen. "Crystal clear. The telecast will transmit live, nationwide. Nobody will interfere." She gave him a thumbs-up. "Say when."

Grady stared at Burke. "March your sorry ass to the podium and talk. Every detail. Every name." He glanced at Zoe and grinned fiercely. "When."

From her hospital bed, Sabrina watched television news anchors discuss the V-10 crisis. She'd retrieved Grady's scrub shirt and clutched it like a lifeline. Any minute.

If he'd succeeded.

After a rant about Grady's disappearance, her father had donned a biohazard suit and come to sit with her.

"He knows what he's doing, Dad."

"O'Rourke is exposing Lord knows how many people for another irresponsible stunt."

"Grady understands the risks. He'll be careful."

"That'll be the day." Wade's scowl didn't conceal his worry. Sabrina's symptoms had progressed rapidly. "What's your pain level?"

On the pain scale, one was minimal, ten was excruciating. "A three," she fudged. Even dulled by morphine, her skin and muscles *burned.* And her stomach cramped as if a rodent was gnawing on it. But they both knew what she was facing.

The TV went black, and Sabrina's pulse leaped. Zoe's grave face appeared. "This is Zoe Zagretti with live, breaking news from Riverside, Oregon. Mr. Ethan Burke, the president's top adviser, is in KKEY's studio with an important message." She nodded. "Mr. Burke, you're on the air."

Ethan Burke stumbled to a podium, his complexion gray, hands trembling.

In spite of her pain, Sabrina smiled. O'Rourkes one, bad guys zilch.

Ethan fumbled with the microphone. "I'm here to set the record straight." He exhaled. "For twelve years, Serpens Pharmaceutical has been conducting research using the V-10 virus. A Serpens laboratory discovered V-10 while attempting to develop a drug to cure children born with HIV. Doctors working with the pro-gram…ah…" Burke cleared his throat. "Some doctors prescribed unproven medications to foster children. Side effects occurred, and there were unfortunate fatalities."

The politician's gaze skittered off-screen and he gulped. Sabrina knew he saw a green-eyed avenging angel wearing battle gear. *Go, Grady.*

Burke soldiered on. "Specifically, over three hundred foster children died." His fingers whitened on the podium. "A week ago, Serpens sold the patent for V-10 to the government to use as a biological weapon. The corporation received five hundred million dollars. Yesterday, the president signed an exclusive contract with Serpens…two billion dollars upon delivery of an antidote. The contract funds Serpens' research for the next seven years and grants Serpens Corporation and its officers exemption from antitrust laws.

"The truth is—" Burke adjusted his crimson tie as if it were strangling him "—the vice president of the United States and I convinced the president to sign the contract. We're…partners. Major stockholders. We, ah, buried our ownership in offshore investments."

A quivering breath. "This is the president's final term. The vice president intended to announce his candidacy for president, with me as his vice president. Winning an election requires millions of dollars."

As he paused, a twitch vibrated his right eye. "Uh…we were aware of the tests on foster children and the consequences. We…arranged the death of Senator Vaughn when he investigated our corporation. We tried to…eliminate his granddaughter because he passed on information. V-10 was released into the population because…of…our failure to come forward."

His gaze flickered off-screen again, and he blanched. "Um…I secretly stockpiled the antidote, which the vice president and I withheld for distribution until after…the contract was signed. And, uh…until more people…ahem…to increase market demand."

Burke raggedly named individuals involved in the conspiracy. "I…uh, apologize to…everyone affected by this tragedy for my…lapse in judgment." Shoulders bowed, he trudged off camera.

Zoe signed off, and the screen cut to local anchors.

Wade stared at Sabrina. "O'Rourke knew this?"

Grady had done it! "He uncovered the information, yes."

"But why ensure he was infected?"

"Our word against theirs. We needed a confession." Sabrina told Wade everything. "Grady wasn't positive they had an antidote, but he accepted the risk. To save me. To save everyone."

She sank into her pillows, and Wade's forehead furrowed. "You're getting tired."

"My throat..." *feels like I swallowed needles* "...is...dry. Could I have some water?" Battling weakness, she sipped. "Teresa Monteros was a CCC nurse. She was there three years ago when Burke adopted his son. The boy survived V-10, and she overheard the doctors telling Burke they could create an antidote using the child's antibodies."

"Burke adopted the kid as an insurance policy? Cold-blooded bastard." He smoothed her hair with a gloved hand. "Sabrina, you don't have to—"

"I'm okay," she lied. Awful lassitude crept over her. She was terrified if she drifted into sleep, she wouldn't wake up. She wouldn't keep her promise to Grady. "Teresa didn't comprehend the implications, but after Granddad contacted her, they figured it out."

A cough racked her, and she sipped again. "Viper didn't know about Burke's son or Teresa. Teresa said Granddad was concerned because Viper was increasingly obsessive."

Another painful coughing spell hit. She removed her hand from her mouth...and saw blood. *"Dad?"*

"Lie down." Wade's eyes were wild, but his voice was soothing as he placed an oxygen mask on her. "O'Rourke has the antidote. Hang on." He stabbed the intercom, barked orders.

The room whirled, spears stabbed her chest. *Grady.* All she had to do was wait. Stay strong. Her fingers entwined in Grady's scrub shirt. Survive until he returned.

Just like she always had.

Desperation thrummed inside Grady as he retrieved the antidote from Burke's safe and flew the chopper back to Mercy. The rest of the team had taken Burke to the police station.

Sabrina was dying.

He could feel the connection between them weakening.

In the isolation ward, Wade was bent over Sabrina's bed. Grady rushed to her side, and his heart crashed into his ribs. Her eyes were closed. Blisters had appeared on her face and arms. A ventilator was breathing for her.

"*Sabrina?* Baby, I'm here."

He handed Wade the antidote. "Can she hear me?"

"I don't know." Wade's lips trembled as he walked to a cabinet. "She's been unresponsive for thirty minutes."

"Sabrina." Grady carefully slid his hand beneath hers. His heart wrenched again as he saw she'd been clinging to his shirt. "We did it, sweetheart. You're gonna be all right."

Wade injected the antidote into Sabrina's IV, then turned to Grady. "Your turn."

He shook his head. "Not until I know she's okay."

"Grady, the sooner—"

"I made her a promise. If she's going, I'm going with her. We'll be together in this life…or the next."

He looked down at Sabrina. Bloody tears leaked from her eyes and stained the pillowcase.

Wade put a gloved hand on Grady's shoulder. "She hears you."

Grady dragged the chair next to Sabrina's bed and took her hand again. Wade had another bed wheeled in as he left to administer the antidote to Dalton. Though fire scorched Grady's skin and his limbs were rubbery, he refused to leave Sabrina's side.

He rested his head on the sheets. "Fight, sweetheart. You can do it. You didn't give up on me before. Don't let go of me."

He talked nonstop until his throat felt raw. When he reached for a glass of water, the nightstand veered away. "No!" The room spun. "I won't leave you!"

Grady fought with every ounce of remaining strength. But a torrent of pain dragged him into darkness.

Grady drifted into awareness. There was no sound. No movement. Bright light pierced his vision.

He remembered the fiery torment of hell. Remembered hoarse screams torn from his raw throat. His mother, weeping. His grim, silent brothers guarding him. A dim recollection of Father Niall quietly reciting Last Rites.

He felt no sorrow.

No pain.

Was this the ever after?

He raised his hand. Hmm. He had a body…and it was beeping.

Grady blinked, his thoughts cleared. *"Sabrina?"* He sat up, and his gaze whipped around the white room.

He was in the isolation ward. Sabrina lay in the next bed, pale and still, no longer on the ventilator.

Grady jerked out his IV, then reached beneath his hospital gown and yanked off monitor wires. He staggered to her bedside. "Sabrina!"

Her eyelids floated up. A slow smile drifted across her mouth.

"You're all right!" He resisted the urge to scoop her up. "You're alive!"

Wade strode inside, sans biohazard suit. "Hey, now. What's with ripping out your IV, cowboy?"

Grady grinned at Sabrina and watched her eyes light up. "She's okay?"

"She's alive." Wade gestured. "Get back into bed."

Grady swayed, then casually leaned on the railing surrounding Sabrina's gurney. "I'm good."

Wade snorted. "Well, you're back to normal."

"Why isn't she talking?"

"It's been a long seventy-two hours. Sabrina was hit harder, and her throat is still healing."

Grady brushed a kiss on her forehead. "She'll be fine."

Sabrina squeezed his hand and nodded.

"We're not sure about permanent damage." Wade sighed. "We're lucky to have her at all. We almost lost her."

Grady looked into Sabrina's eyes, and the love glowing in the amber depths made his heart do a slow roll. "You could never be lost." He put her hand on his chest. "You were always right here."

Sabrina walked out of the rehab wing three weeks later. After her final checkup, she'd stopped to see Dalton, who was still recovering. One of a handful who'd survived a prolonged bout with V-10, he seemed uncharacteristically bitter.

Worrying about him was easier than dwelling on her test results.

She paused to collect herself before joining Grady. Her rock. He'd encouraged and pushed her through recovery and physical therapy.

After the hospital had discharged her two weeks ago, he'd moved her into his houseboat. He'd slept on the floor beside the bed. Catered to her every want. When she looked into his eyes, she saw love. Complete commitment.

But now she had to tell him… Her throat clogged. She would not surrender to despair. Not after everything they'd been through.

Rounding the corner, she halted as her father approached Grady. They'd called a wary truce during her illness. "Sabrina with the doctor?" she heard her father ask.

Grady tensed. "Yes."

"How's she doing?"

"Excellent." Grady's shoulders squared beneath his mocha shirt. "Dr. Matthews, I love Sabrina. I know you never thought I was good enough—"

"Hold on." Wade frowned. "Step into my shoes as a father. What if you lived next door to four raging teenage libidos…and the daredevil of the lot was interested in *your* only daughter?"

Grady's right hand dropped to his waistband where his Glock normally rode, and Wade laughed. "Exactly. Plus, you weren't one for sticking around, and I didn't want her hurt. It was nothing personal." He extended his hand. "You've proven yourself. 'Thank you' is hardly adequate for everything you've done."

Grady's handsome face warmed as he accepted Wade's peace offering. "You were right to warn me off. I wasn't ready to commit to her then."

"You've grown into a fine man, Grady. Sabrina is happy."

"I'll try my best to keep her that way, sir."

Blinking back tears, Sabrina joined them. She was deliriously happy with Grady. But he was destined for disappointment.

During the drive to his houseboat he kept glancing at her. "You're quiet."

"Sorry. I have…things on my mind."

"Dalton?" His concern was genuine.

"Partially. He's not himself."

"He's been through a lot." Grady's hand embraced hers. "So have you."

"I'm all right." She stared out at the bright June morning. "When we get to the houseboat, we have to discuss—"

"If you're worried I'll be upset because the doctor isn't sure you can conceive…" He squeezed her hand. "Don't."

She whipped around. "You *knew?*"

"I'm a medic, remember?" Muscles ticced in his jaw. "Internal bleeding does damage, sweetheart. The doctor didn't want to say anything until she ran more tests."

"I saw the way you held Brianna Rose." Her voice was still husky when she got emotional. "I know we haven't talked…" *Don't assume and make him feel trapped.* "We…haven't decided…anything. But how can you be okay with this?"

"Sabrina, all I want is you. And the only sure thing is right now." Smiling, he raised her hand to his lips. "We'll cross that bridge if and when we have to."

Relief warred with dismay. He didn't appear disappointed. She knew he wouldn't leave her again. But his refusal to consider the future sounded too much like the old Grady.

Chapter 18

Grady escorted Sabrina to the table on the houseboat's deck. "The captain called while you were with the doc. He wants me at the station to discuss concluding my leave of absence. Will you be okay?"

"Of course." Maybe he *was* thinking about the future. "Any word on the fallout from Burke's arrest?"

"SWAT is cleared for duty." He grinned. "Every government official is scrambling for distance from Burke and the VP. The governor claims he and the police chief planned the takedown. And the president is yammering about medals again."

"You guys deserve them." She scowled. "But Mr. President should forgo the pomp and circumstance and examine his cronies more closely."

"Spinning this is gonna give everyone in D.C. permanent vertigo." He kissed her. "How about a picnic supper when I get back?"

"Sounds fun." She smiled. If he was fine with enjoying the present, so was she. "Perfect weather."

"See you in a while. No working. I'll grab food on the way home."

"I'm completely recovered. And I feel great."

"Just relax. I mean it." With a jaunty wave, he strode away.

Sabrina gazed at the river. She and Grady were alive. In love. It was enough. Why was she uneasy? Jittery and distracted?

She perused a magazine, wandered the deck, then checked her watch. After painting all twenty nails petal pink, she went upstairs to dress for the picnic.

Surrendering to the temptation of Grady's decadent shower, Sabrina luxuriated in hot spray. She left her blow-dried hair loose, the way Grady liked it, then donned lacy undergarments and a celery-green sundress.

She padded downstairs and was slipping on high-heeled sandals when Grady climbed out of the Jeep. Sabrina shaded her eyes and watched him prowl down the dock.

He moved with the predatory grace of a man who was comfortable in his own body...and knew its power. Rolled shirtsleeves bared sinuous forearms. Faded jeans hugged lean hips and muscular thighs. The breeze played in his dark hair, and his eyes sparkled with mischief and humor.

His knowing grin made her stomach swoop. Tension invaded her limbs. Her restlessness wasn't a side effect of recovery. Grady had treated her with careful concern, but she'd been yearning for him again.

Well, she would prove to him she was totally healthy. Starting now.

He held out his hand. "Hello, gorgeous. Ready?"

"Yes." She held his gaze. "I've been ready for a long time."

The tension from her body hummed into his. "Okay...food's in the car."

"Mmm. Good." She watched the pulse leap in his throat. She wanted to put her teeth right there and nip. Before the night was over, she would nibble every inch of his delicious bod. "I'm starving."

He inhaled sharply. "Let's get to it, then."

She grinned. "Yes, let's."

Grady pulled the Jeep out onto the highway. "Sorry for the delay. The station was a zoo, and then the deli took forever."

She rested her palm on his thigh, smiling when his muscles twitched. "I'm sure there's a way you can atone."

"Uh...honey..." He slid her hand to his knee. "Trying to make me wreck?"

She so wanted to wreck him. All innocence, she blinked. "Where are we going?"

He shot her an amused glance. "You'll see."

Before long, he pulled to the curb at the end of their old block. Right in front of the spot where they'd first met.

Carrying a picnic basket and quilt, Grady led her into the park. He spread the quilt in an alcove beneath the trees. "Remember this place?"

"How could I forget? We spent half our lives here as kids."

In the basket were chilled bottles of pomegranate tea with turkey avocado subs, pasta salad and fruit. They lingered over the food and talked about everything and nothing in a conversation thrumming with innuendos.

Watching her with an intensity that made her tingle, Grady fed her a bite of juicy watermelon. Awareness jolted Sabrina. Before the night was over, she would finally belong to him.

Time passed in teasing talk and scorching glances. The sensual hunger in Grady's eyes ate her up as he folded the quilt. "Ready for dessert?"

"Very."

She was disappointed when he parked in front of the coffee shop across from their former high school. She'd thought he'd meant a different dessert.

He treated her to Amaretto cheesecake and coffee, with a side of smoldering glances.

The next stop was the library where they'd once done homework together. Sabrina grinned. "We're taking a stroll down memory lane."

Holding hands, they sauntered through the library. He retrieved a wrapped package from the order desk, and she opened it to discover a book of nature poetry.

"It's yours. I bought it from a dealer."

"Thank you!" She hugged him and earned a scowl from the librarian.

Next was the deserted high school soccer field. Grady produced a beribboned bouquet of daisies from behind the bleachers. "Wanna go steady?"

She chuckled. "Can I have your letterman's jacket?"

He gave her a slow, deep kiss. "Everything I have is yours."

They sat on the bleachers and kissed until she was breathless and trembling. Grady was none too steady on his feet, either. He'd managed to recapture the fun and innocence of their youth...while carrying out an erotic seduction.

He drove downtown to the ritzy hotel where they'd pulled their prom shenanigans, and handed his keys to the parking valet. This was it.

Instead of getting a room, he escorted her to the bar. At a cozy corner table, they listened to music from their graduation year, sipped champagne and shared hot kisses.

She was thoroughly puzzled as they left the hotel. Maybe he thought she'd be more comfortable in familiar surroundings.

He navigated streets edged with misty blue twilight. When he parked at the O'Rourke family home, she frowned. "We're visiting your mom?"

"She's at an out-of-town rowing competition. She said we could borrow the house."

They were going up to his old bedroom? There was familiar, and then there was...overkill.

But he didn't take her inside. Instead, they walked to the backyard, and Sabrina gasped. The massive oak tree on the edge of the wooded lot glittered with hundreds of tiny white lights. "Grady, what did you do?"

Grady bent in a sweeping bow. "Welcome to Castle O'Rourke, m'lady."

Sabrina slipped off her sandals and preceded him up the ladder to the huge treehouse. She gazed around the large enclosure. A beige area rug warmed the floor. Multitudes of potted daisies fringed the perimeter, some on small tables beside clusters of white pillar candles. Head-high walls were open to the roof, affording a panoramic view of lighted branches against the midnight-blue velvet sky.

Grady stripped off his shoes and socks beside the entrance, and then lit dozens of candles. In the far corner, she saw a thick mattress dressed with snowy white linens.

Sabrina clasped her hands. "This must have taken *days!*"

Moving behind her, he wrapped his arms around her waist and nuzzled her neck. "You like?"

"You're...incredible!" She leaned into his heated strength. "So much thought went into arranging everything."

"You deserve a courtship."

A pop ballad swirled; he'd switched on a portable CD player. He spun her around. "May I have this dance?"

She slid her arms around his neck. Their bodies swayed, and she breathed him in. She'd recognize his scent blindfolded. His breath feathered her temple; his heart thundered against hers.

Past sorrows and regret fell away. Grady's embrace wrapped her in joy, and time spun into a shimmering cloud of soft music and sensual motion.

There was nowhere she'd rather be.

The poignant notes of her favorite ballad drifted out. Grady's heartbeat kicked, and a tremor rippled his body. "Sabrina..." Staring into her eyes, he took a breath. Stepped back.

Then he went down on one knee.

Sabrina looked at the man she loved, kneeling at her feet, and the world stopped.

He enfolded her hand in both of his, and she started to shake, too. "Sabrina, when I was a boy, you were my companion. When I was a teenager, you were my confidant. Since I became a man, you've been my champion."

Smiling, Grady inhaled raggedly. "From the moment I set eyes on you when we were five years old, there's never been anyone else. I've trusted you with my life. My dreams. And now I entrust my heart to you."

He swallowed, and dampness sparkled on his dark lashes. "From now on, when I run, I will always run toward you. I want to spend not just today, but every day with you...for the rest of our lives. Be my best friend. My lover. My wife. Forever."

Speech became impossible with her heart lodged in her throat.

Grady squeezed her hand. "Sabrina?"

She found her voice. "Yes! Yes! *Yes!*"

"Whew!" He pressed a shaky hand to his chest. "You scared me." He withdrew a ring from his pocket, slid it onto her finger and then stood.

Sabrina stared at the sparkling diamond, shinier than the stars. Smaller glittering diamonds encircled the platinum band. *"Oh!"* She burst into tears and flung her arms around his neck. "It's perfect!"

"Your love saved me, Sabrina. From my fears. From myself." He kissed her. "I brought iced champagne to celebrate."

"Nice!"

"I arranged things so we could spend the night in comfort, but there's no pressure, sweetheart. If you're not up for it, we can dance and talk—"

"No. We've waited long enough."

Pressed intimately to him, she felt his body jerk. He walked to the bedside table. "We haven't discussed what we want to do about kids, yet, but I…uh…brought protection. Just in case, no pressure," he repeated hastily.

"It's sweet that you considered every detail." She peered into the drawer. "Geez, Dimples, *four boxes?* Ambitious much?"

Those sexy dimples flashed. "I never do anything halfway."

"Yeah, I know." She bit her lip. "Do you want children?"

"When you're ready."

"Seeing as how the doctor thinks I might have difficulty conceiving…and…we went through so much to be together…I'd rather not put any more barriers between us."

"Neither would I." His voice was husky as he stepped behind her. Brushing aside her hair, he kissed her nape.

A shiver skated up her spine. "Grady?" She snuggled into the hollow of his shoulder. "I've waited a long time for you."

Kisses trailed down her neck. "I'll try not to disappoint."

The single shiver rippled into multitudes. "I mean, um, I *waited* for you. Just kissing other guys felt all wrong. I couldn't bear to let another man touch me when I longed for you."

He went still. *"Sabrina?"* She turned her head to meet his stunned gaze. Grady did a slow blink. "I'm…blown away. Honored. I don't—"

She muted his protest with her lips. "You can stop talking now."

Deep laughter rumbled against her back. "Yes, ma'am."

Warm lips cruised her neck to her shoulder. He repeated the sensual glide, began again. Goose bumps prickled, and her shivers returned. His teeth caught the tendon where her neck and shoulder joined and gently nipped.

Grady kissed her neck, back and shoulders until she was whirling in sensation. His talented mouth teased her ears, making her nipples pebble. Making her breasts ache for his hands. "Mmm." His deep voice vibrated inside her. "You taste so damn good."

"Grady, touch me."

"I will. Soon." His body was hard and hot behind her, as taut as a bowstring. *"Everywhere."*

Sabrina's knees went weak. "What happened to fast and wild?"

His chuckle was warm in her ear. His tongue darted inside. "We'll get there."

Her groan was a plea. *"Grady."*

Easing away, he unzipped her dress. As he skimmed the garment downward, he kissed down her spine, to the small of her back. The dress puddled at her feet, and she stepped out of it. Grady's hands spanned her hips, his mouth lingered just above the waistband of her panties.

"Oooh. So not playing fair!"

"What's not, honey?" Hot kisses roamed up her spine until he was standing behind her once more.

"I want to touch you, too."

One hand on her shoulder, he walked around to face her. His fingers trailed down her arm, and he caught her hand. "As you wish." He kissed her palm, then placed it on his chest. His heartbeat raged beneath her palm, and passion glittered in his gaze.

As she unbuttoned his shirt, his fingers slid into her hair and he watched her face. Never breaking contact, he lowered one arm, then the other, letting her bare his torso. Sabrina drank in toned muscles dusted with dark hair. The man she'd loved her entire life. She placed a kiss over his heart. "Magnificent."

Groaning, he crushed her to him. One big hand cradled her head, and his lips found hers. He licked her lower lip, gently bit. When she gasped, his mouth covered hers and his tongue slid inside. His essence surrounded her. His silky tongue enticed hers to dance, as if kissing her was all he'd ever wanted, ever needed.

They both trembled. Sabrina glided her fingertips over his shoulders, down his back, steely muscles vibrating at her touch. Delighted, she opened her eyes...and saw him watching her. She held his gaze, wordlessly telling him how much she loved him. Trusted him. Wanted him. Fire flared in his eyes and his breathing quickened. As he loved her with his mouth, his hands caressed her skin as if he couldn't get enough.

When he finally withdrew, she was shaking with love and need.

He combed his fingers through her hair, then stroked her back. Her bra fell away. His gaze dropped to her breasts, and his eyes darkened. "My beautiful Sabrina." Using the barest brush of fingertips, he traced her curves.

Her breasts felt heavy, her nipples tight and aching. "Put your hands on me, Grady."

Warm, callused palms cupped her, and he captured her mouth in another kiss. Strong, tender hands kneaded and stroked, teased and plucked until she was biting back groans.

"Don't hold back, sweetheart." Grady nuzzled her ear, nibbled on the lobe. "Before the night is over, I want to hear you scream my name."

Electricity jolted her nerve endings. She would give him everything she had. Everything he wanted.

His arms encircled her as his mouth meandered to her jaw. Her throat. Clinging to his shoulders, she arched her back, offering herself. Grady leisurely feasted on her curves, and her nipples tightened impossibly harder. Finally, hot, moist breath hovered above her nipple, and then Grady's tongue lightly flicked.

"Ooh." Sabrina's nails bit into his shoulders.

The exquisite sensations continued until she very nearly screamed before he drew her nipple in and sucked hard. Molten ribbons of pleasure streamed from her breasts to her belly. Moaning, she thrust her fingers into his hair, and her knees gave out.

Grady scooped her up, and she gulped in air as he carried her to the bed. He leaned on his elbows above her. Golden candlelight glimmered in the green of his irises, and bronzed his rock-hard abs into a shadowed sculpture.

He kissed her eyelids, the tip of her nose, her mouth. His lips wandered down her throat as his hand slid beneath the waistband of her panties. His fingers stroked in slow circles.

Panting, she rocked her hips. "Grady," she finally begged. *"Please!"*

His mouth tugged on her nipple at the same instant his thumb grazed her center. Molten heat surged through her veins. Sensation gathered, stronger, deeper. There were no pauses now. Just a fast, steep climb to paradise.

Her muscles clenched, her body tightened. Arching, she gasped for breath as bright, hot pleasure flooded into ecstasy.

When she surfaced, Grady was watching her. Smiling at her. He brushed a kiss on her lips. "I love looking at you. Love arousing you," he whispered, pressing a kiss to her belly. He pushed her panties down and tossed them aside.

Her fingers tangled in his hair, tugged. "Come here."

Holding her gaze, he crawled up her body. She skated her palms over his chest, down flat abs. "I need to touch you." She unsnapped his jeans, carefully unzipped the straining fly. He helped her push them down and off. He was bare beneath. She explored the hard, heated length, and he groaned.

Knowing she could make him shake and tremble with her caress was a heady rush. Warm tendrils of budding desire unfurled, and she wanted to give him more intimate pleasure. "Grady, I want to…" She whispered her desire in his ear, felt him jerk in her grasp.

"Sabrina." He groaned again and captured her hands. "Later." He kissed away her pout. "First, I'm going to taste every inch of you."

Alternating deep, hot kisses to her mouth, he lavished attention on her ears, neck and breasts. His lips tarried over her belly, and his tongue dipped into her navel. Grady made her feel cherished and adored, while arousing her to unbearable heights.

The sensitive curves of her thighs received his loving care. The backs of her knees. The arches of her feet. When he drew her toes, one by one, into the hot silk of his mouth, Sabrina's breath sawed in her throat.

Her flushed, damp skin was sensitized to his slightest touch. He settled between her thighs, urged her to open fully to him. "Beautiful." His warm whisper feathered shivers up her spine.

Then he brought his mouth to the heart of her.

The intensity, the intimacy, made her shake uncontrollably. This was Grady's mouth worshipping her. His arms holding her. His fingers gently touching her, sliding inside her.

Moaning, Sabrina clung to the man she loved as he wreathed her in pleasure.

Slowly at first, then faster, he spiraled her higher…coiled the tension tighter. Loving her with his mouth, he kept her trembling on the edge of forever…until the taut rosebuds of heat burst into glorious, scarlet blooms.

She was still glittering with sensation, her body quaking in wonderful aftershocks, when he rose above her. Grady's gaze held hers; his hands cradled her face. Slowly, gently, he filled her. Tears flooded Sabrina's eyes as she and Grady joined body to body, heart to heart, soul to soul.

His breath caught, and he froze. "Did I hurt you?"

"No," she whispered. He kissed her eyelids, and when he kissed her mouth, she tasted her own tears on his lips. "You're a part of me, now. Always."

Grady tumbled into the warm whiskey depths of Sabrina's eyes, and his heart felt as if it would burst. "Nothing will ever separate us again."

As he began the long, slow glide, she caught her breath. Watching her, he tenderly stroked her face. Sabrina's body, her scent enveloped him. His biggest fear had been allowing himself to be vulnerable. Now he couldn't imagine anything sweeter. He opened completely, letting Sabrina into his soul. Letting her see his love. No longer hiding his desperate need for her.

"Grady!" His name was an awed sigh that both devastated and thrilled him.

He'd never loved another woman before her. Sabrina was it for him…forever. He'd had sex, but had never known the joy of making love. Embracing her with his gaze, he kissed her, making slow, deep love to her body and her mouth. Their shared passion burned away everything except pure, molten perfection. Shaking, panting, he took her with him, flying faster and closer to the sun. And when Sabrina arched beneath him and cried out his name, he offered himself up.

Throwing back his head, Grady surrendered to the brilliant explosion.

When he could feel his body again, he propped on weak arms and studied her flushed face and replete gaze. "You okay?"

"Mmm." Her murmur was husky. Plump and rosy from his kisses, her lips tilted in a crooked smile. "You were *so* worth waiting for, Dimples."

He brushed damp, golden tendrils from her face. "I'm sorry I was such an idiot."

She sighed. "You can't force someone to love you. All you can do is stalk them and hope they give in."

When he chuckled, her arms twined around his neck, and her smile widened. "But you can spend the next fifty-plus years making it up to me. Starting now."

Grady smiled. "As you wish."

He captured Sabrina's sweet mouth in a lingering kiss…and then proceeded to do exactly that.

Epilogue

Riverside, Oregon
Sixteen Months Later

Grady sat in the front row of the crowd gathered on Mercy Hospital's lawn in the warm October afternoon. His heart swelled with pride as he listened to his wife—incredibly beautiful in a salmon-colored suit—dedicate the completed William Vaughn Memorial Pediatric Wing. She'd left home early to supervise arrangements, and he'd missed seeing her all day.

Sabrina finished her address, and her gaze caught his, sending a silent message of love. He gave her a thumbs-up, and then clapped and whistled louder than anyone else.

The ceremony moved to the perimeter of the building, where Grady and Sabrina, his brothers and their wives, and Wade and Maureen planted red and white dogwoods. A bronze plaque at the base of each tree bore the names and birth dates of the deceased children.

Congress had passed a law guaranteeing medical advocates for foster children, ensuring that the travesty would never happen again. Ethan Burke, the vice president and their cronies had been incarcerated for life.

Riverside SWAT and their families had been flown to D.C., greeted and feted. Grady had told Sabrina about his Swiss Army knife's mysterious reappearance, and she concurred with him.

Upon their return from D.C., they'd gone directly to the cemetery. With Sabrina at his side, Grady had left his medals on Pop's grave and said his final goodbye.

Sabrina beckoned, and Grady joined her to plant the last dogwood together. Isaiah's tree. Hands were shaken, press photos taken.

Afterward, the O'Rourkes and their friends gathered at Sullivan's Steakhouse. The restaurant on the riverfront was booked exclusively for their celebration. Grady parked the Jeep, then shrugged out of his suit jacket and yanked off his tie.

"Couldn't stand the monkey suit any longer?" Sabrina chuckled as he rolled up his shirtsleeves.

"Hey, we're here to eat, drink and be merry. Ten bucks says my brothers aren't wearing theirs, either."

"I'm not taking that sucker bet."

Inside, the gleaming wood and glass interior opened onto a deck overlooking the Willamette River. Hand in hand, they meandered through the crowd until they reached the huge oval table reserved for family.

Sabrina giggled. "You win."

Con was sans tie and jacket, and his redheaded angel was perched in his lap. Brianna Rose babbled to Murphy and fed the dog soggy pieces of breadstick while Bailey attempted to refasten a bib around her perpetual-motion daughter.

Kate was next to her, snapping photos. Liam's shirt had a fresh drool spot on the shoulder from their teething seven-month-old daughter, Colleen. The raven-haired, emerald-eyed cherub bounced on his knee, gnawing on his discarded tie.

Aidan's tie was gone, but he made it to the table wearing his jacket. However, he quickly slipped it off and hung it over his chair before helping Zoe into her seat. Her red dress strained at the belly with the weight of their soon-to-be-born son. In the current name debate, Finn was the front-runner.

Letty, the O'Rourkes' honorary grandma, was seated next to Sabrina. Bailey's mother was across the table, and Zoe's mom was there in her wheelchair, with her nurse.

Maureen and Wade shared the head of the table…holding hands. Their twenty-five-year friendship had blossomed into romance, and Grady couldn't be happier. His mom had been alone too long.

The servers poured champagne. Maureen tapped her glass, and conversation ebbed. His mother rose. "Cherished friends. My glorious family." Her gaze traveled the table, greeting each person.

Her glance rested on Grady, and she smiled and picked up her flute. "May your past be a wonderful memory. May your future be filled with delight." She lifted her glass. "And may your now fill you with contentment. *Sláinte mhath!*"

"*Sláinte mhath!*" rang out as everyone drank to good health.

Champagne flowed and food kept coming. Music and laughter swelled. Grady ate until he couldn't hold any more, and he and Sabrina danced until they were breathless.

Grady returned from the bar carrying filled glasses to see Sabrina waltzing Colleen on her hip so Liam and Kate could share a quiet dance. A pang stabbed his chest, and he set the flutes down. They'd been hoping for a child for sixteen months.

Craving air, he stepped onto the deck, and the party noise faded. White lights draped railings, twinkled from potted greenery. Grady leaned on the banister, watching silvered waves drift in the moonlight. He and Sabrina had each other. They were healthy and deliriously happy. His wife was glowing with happiness.

"Grady?" Sabrina's hand on his shoulder startled him, and he pivoted. "Are you all right?"

"Needed air. It's getting crazy in there."

"Since when did crazy ever bother you?" She took his hand. "Missing your dad tonight?"

"I'll always miss him. But no, I'm not mourning him anymore."

"You're down, though."

She always could read him too easily. "I'm fine, honey." He squeezed her fingers. "Let's get back to the party."

"Wait. I want to show you something."

He grinned. "Always glad to look."

"You are so bad." Smiling, she withdrew folded papers from her purse. "These were faxed to my office right before my speech."

He scanned the forms while his heart tried to pound out of his chest. "Sabrina? Are these…"

"Yes! The two-year-old twin boys we met three months ago when their grandmother had to put them into foster care. The grandmother decided in favor of adoption." Sabrina's eyes were liquid amber. "She chose us! She just signed the adoption release."

"And it's official? The little imps are *ours?*"

"I was going to wait until we got home so we could celebrate in private, but…yes! We're going to be parents!"

He staggered. *"Twins!"*

She grinned. "We've never done anything halfway, Dimples."

Grady wrapped his arms around her. "I love you, Sabrina." She was his past. His present. All his tomorrows.

He scooped her up, twirled her in a giddy circle. *"Yee haw!"* Laughing, Grady tossed back his head. *"Two* babies!"

And damned if the brightest star in the sky didn't wink at him.

* * * * *

nocturne™

THE FINAL INSTALLMENT OF
THE BLOODRUNNERS TRILOGY

Last Wolf Watching

Runner Brody Carter has found his match in
Michaela Doucet, a human with unusual psychic powers.
When Michaela's brother is threatened, Brody becomes
her protector, and suddenly not only has to protect her
from her enemies but also from himself....

LOOK FOR

LAST WOLF WATCHING
BY
RHYANNON
BYRD

Available May 2008 wherever you buy books.

Dramatic and Sensual Tales of Paranormal Romance

www.eHarlequin.com   SN61786

Silhouette®
Romantic
SUSPENSE

COMING NEXT MONTH

#1511 SECRET AGENT AFFAIR—Marie Ferrarella
The Doctors Pulaski
CIA agent Kane Donnelly thinks posing as an orderly to
monitor rumors of terrorist activity will be easy. Then he runs into
Dr. Marja Pulaski, the woman who saved his life only days prior. As
the investigation progresses he finds himself entangled with the feisty
resident, risking his heart—and possibly his mission.

#1512 THE GUARDIAN—Linda Winstead Jones
Last Chance Heroes
When Dante Mangino goes to investigate a panty theft, he doesn't expect
to wind up protecting his old flame, Mayor Sara Vance, from a stalker.
Dante refuses to get involved again. But as the danger to Sara escalates,
so does their simmering attraction. Now he must come to terms with old
feelings—and the one woman who captured his soul.

#1513 THE BLACK SHEEP P.I.—Karen Whiddon
The Cordasic Legacy
Accused of her husband's murder, Rachel Adair knows she must turn to
the one man who can help her...the same man she betrayed years ago.
Dominic Cordasic is stunned when his ex-fiancée walks through his door
seeking his help. He promised himself he'd cut this woman from his life
completely, yet he can't say no to her plea. Worse yet, he may still love
her.

#1514 HEART OF A THIEF—Gail Barrett
The Crusaders
When the legendary necklace security expert Luke Moreno agreed to
safeguard goes missing, he has a hunch it has something to do with his
former lover, amber expert Sofia Mikhelson. Framed for a crime she
didn't commit, Sofia doesn't know who she can trust, but must team up
with Luke if she wants to survive. But how can she stay so close to the
only man she's ever loved, the same man who believes she's set him
up—again?

SRSCNM0408